# CURVY GIRLS CAN'T DATE BAD BOYS

---

## KELSIE STELTING

Copyright © 2020 by Kelsie Stelting

All rights reserved.

No part of this book may be reproduced in any form or by any electronic or mechanical means, including information storage and retrieval systems, without written permission from the author, except for the use of brief quotations in a book review.

This is a work of fiction. Names, characters, businesses, places, events, locales, and incidents are either the products of the author's imagination or used in a fictitious manner. Any resemblance to actual persons, living or dead, or actual events is purely coincidental.

For questions, address kelsie@kelsiestelting.com.

Structural Edit by Sally Henson

Copy Edited by Tricia Harden

Cover design by AngstyG

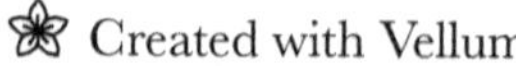 Created with Vellum

*For Grandma Norma, thank you for choosing us as family.*
*Your love for others is something I aspire to always.*

ONE

I PREFERRED WATCHING Ryde Alexander on the big screen as opposed to sitting across from him. But here we were at Halfway Café, drinking expensive lattes and eating smoked salmon bagels that were only half as good as the muffins at Seaton Bakery but cost five times as much. Good thing money was no object for him, because otherwise I might feel a little guilty for leaving my food mostly uneaten.

"So, Friday? Are you free?" He flipped his hair out of his sea-green eyes

With a slight shake of my head to clear my thoughts, I asked, "What?"

An annoyed look flicked across his face but was quickly gone. Ryde didn't leave his acting for the set. Every second I spent with him, he was putting on one act or another. "I was telling you my friend's movie is premiering Friday. Are you free?"

"Which friend?" There were a few premieres coming up that Dad was keeping his eyes on.

"Ambrose. I've only been talking about this movie for the last ten minutes."

I knew—I'd checked out after minute one. I flashed him a guilty smile, doing a little acting of my own. "Sorry, babe. I'm a little distracted."

Seeming a bit relieved, he reached across the table and took my hands. "If this arranged marriage is going to work, we have to get to know each other. We have to try."

A heavy dose of unexpected guilt swept through me. I wasn't the only one being pressured to marry someone not of my choosing. Ryde was just as implicated in this Indian tradition-turned-business arrangement as I was.

"I know." I sighed. "Tell me, how's filming going?"

His eyes lit up. He loved talking about himself—especially his work. "We're doing a stunt today. Sixteen-story jump into the crash pad."

My eyes widened. "Sixteen stories?" Just the

thought of being that high made my stomach turn, not to mention jumping off.

"Of course my double's doing it, but it should be fun to watch. Something good for my Insta account, anyway. Speaking of..."

He lifted his phone from where it lay face-up on the table and snapped a selfie of the two of us. I barely had a second to flash a smile before he pulled it back and frowned. "Can you lift your chin a little more?"

My eyebrows drew together. "Lift my chin?"

"Yeah, your neck kind of disappeared in that one." He showed me the photo on the screen, then demonstrated stretching his neck out.

"You know," I said, "I'd rather not. That picture is just fine."

His lips formed a thin line for a moment, then he flashed his movie-star smile at the phone. "I'll just do one by myself then. My fans deserve better than 'fine.'"

I sipped from my latte—if only to keep my mouth busy with something other than a scathing retort—as his thumbs flew over the screen. The selfie he edited and posted would easily garner hundreds of thousands of likes. None of which mattered to me. I hardly got on social media, as to not affect Bhatta Productions' carefully curated brand.

Across from me, Ryde rose to standing and shoved his phone into his pocket. With an openly frustrated look, he said, "You know, I thought when I got into a relationship, it would be with a girl who actually liked me." He dropped a hundred-dollar bill on the table. "See you Friday. I'll pick you up at six. Be red carpet ready."

I lifted my eyebrows to show him I heard and rested my chin on my hand. What a great start to the week—getting up an hour early so I could make a breakfast appearance with my arranged boyfriend.

Dad required us to have at least one date in public each week—which he said was doing wonders for his movie set to premiere this summer. For my self-esteem? Not so much.

I'd always liked my body, the curves, the shapes, the colors, but Ryde picked apart everything without saying anything I could repeat as rude. I was tired of it, and with my high school graduation, and therefore my wedding date, getting nearer, time was running out. I needed to find a way out of this arranged marriage with Ryde before it was too late.

I glanced up and caught sight of a strong,

tattooed arm with a leather jacket draped over it. Most people who came into Halfway Café didn't have tattoos like that. No, just Chinese symbols they didn't really understand or Roman numerals and the like. The tattoo sleeve covering this arm was like nothing I'd seen before.

I followed the muscular arm up to the face, and my mouth fell open. I'd seen him once before. He'd delivered food for movie night at my friend's house. The delivery boy with the motorcycle and the intense gaze.

I followed said gaze past the counter. The barista gave him a disgusted look and turned away to whisper with her coworker. My gut gave a visceral reaction to the slight. What right did they have to judge him?

I stood and took the receipt and money to the counter. I could have easily left the bill on the table, but I wanted a chance to see the barista's overly done face.

Keeping my eyes straight ahead—and off of the delivery boy—I set the receipt and money on the counter a little harder than I needed to.

The barista who had been so rude to him set down a canister of beans and smiled pleasantly at me. "Let me get you checked out."

Each courteous word and action she extended my way just irked me more. So she could only be polite to people with money?

She took the receipt and rang up our meals. "Would you like the change?"

All seventy dollars of it? "No." Her eyes lit up for a moment until I said, "Pay off the next few tickets with it." No way was I giving her a tip and rewarding her profiling.

With a disappointed look, she began tapping on the screen. I watched, making sure she didn't just pocket it for herself. When all the money had gone in the cash drawer, I lowered my voice so the tattooed guy couldn't hear and said, "And next time, why don't you save your judgement for yourself."

"Excuse me?" she said.

I turned my gaze toward him, then back to her, then walked outside.

Brisk spring air greeted me, and I already felt better away from the rich stuffiness of the shop. I breathed in the breeze before continuing to my car.

"You know," a voice said from behind me, "I can fight my own battles."

I jumped, not having heard the shop door open. Turning to the sound of the voice revealed an amused expression on the guy from the café. He wore all black, and his dark hair fell over his forehead. Each muscle on his wiry arms rippled as he shrugged on his leather jacket and folded his arms across his chest. His brown eyes had a glint in them that confused and intrigued me all at the same time.

"I don't know what you're talking about," I said, finding my voice.

His full, pink lips curled into a smile. "I'll see you around, Zara."

How he knew or remembered my name, I had no idea. All I knew as I watched him race away on his motorcycle was that I wanted to hear him say it again.

TWO

I GOT in my car and drove to school. I was actually ready to be back and see my friends again after spring break. High school was never something I thought I'd cling to, but knowing my freedom was gone as of graduation day made me see things from a new perspective. I might not have been the homecoming queen or the valedictorian or outstanding at anything, but I still deserved to enjoy high school. Who said you had to be perfect to have a good time? To be free?

An image came to mind of the delivery guy driving away on his motorcycle, open leather jacket billowing around his waist. Where was he going? He looked to be my age—did he have school? Had he dropped out? Was he in college? Was delivery work his only job? What did the tattoos up and down his arms mean? Or were they just another form of the rebellion I saw in his eyes?

I tried to clear my thoughts of him as I pulled into my parking spot near the school entrance. Dad had paid for the second-best spot. The only person to outbid him had been Kai Rush's father, an actual billionaire.

I picked up my Gucci backpack—the only part of my attire that wasn't restricted to Emerson Academy's bland uniform—and started inside.

A pair of freshmen crossed in front of me, holding hands. When had freshmen started looking so young? And since when was I jealous of them?

Jealousy wasn't an emotion I liked, and the overwhelming sense of it flooding my body just frayed my nerves. I had to get a grip on myself. My emotions were the one thing I had control over, and I didn't want to lose that too.

I squared my shoulders and walked into school. A few people greeted me on the way in, and I smiled and nodded at them. I'd always gotten my fair share of attention for being a movie producer's daughter, but my relationship with Ryde had ensured I never walked inside without several positive—and sometimes negative—greetings.

"Zara, you look tired," Merritt said, surrounded by her cronies, Tinsley and Poppy, as usual. They wore their cheerleading uniforms today, even though there weren't any games. Maybe a competition?

I flashed her a wide smile, if only because I knew it would annoy her. "Stayed up late 'talking' to my boyfriend last night."

Her face flashed disgust before rearranging into another perfect smile. "So my brother stopped mourning the fact that he could do a million times better?"

I didn't miss the possessive way she said *my brother*. She didn't know I'd happily return him, given the choice. The coercion of the arrangement was being kept private to help protect our image, even from Merritt. Still, I answered with a smile. "We had an *amazing* breakfast this morning."

Tinsley frowned. "Why'd he take a selfie if you were with him?"

Of course she'd already seen his Instagram post.

"Because he's embarrassed of her," Merritt said. "Obviously."

A flood of anger rushed through me at just how close to the truth she was, but I composed myself and winked. "Or maybe he just wants to keep me all to himself." With a little wave, I left their stunned expressions behind me and continued toward my locker farther down the hall.

Ray and Ginger were already there. Ginger leaned back against the locker, looking up at him as he rested his forearm on the navy metal over her head, saying something to her with his lips in a loving smile.

"Ugh," I said with a teasing grin. "Can you two take your cuteness somewhere else?"

Ginger's cheeks flushed red, and Ray smiled. "One of us better make it to video class on time," he teased, extending his hand for her books.

Ginger rolled her eyes before handing them over.

"See you soon," he said.

"Not soon enough." She smiled after him as he started toward the first-hour class they took together.

I turned the combination to my locker. "What's it feel like to be *that* in love?"

Ginger opened her mouth, but my friend Rory answered as she approached us. "Amazing, wonderful, fantastic—"

"I get it," I laughed, pulling my books from my locker.

Jordan and Callie walked up to us next, and finally our group was complete. I'd missed the Curvy Girl Club so much, even if we'd only been apart a week. "How are you guys doing?" I asked. "How was spring break?"

Callie grinned and stuck out her arm. "I got a tan in Cancun. Can you see?"

I stared at her white skin. "Um...yeah?" I turned to Jordan. "And the business trip in Brazil?"

A dreamy look crossed her face. "Amazing. I never thought I'd get out of California, much less the United States."

"That's awesome," I said. She deserved to see the world. "How'd it go with the production company?"

"They want to dub my mom's videos in Portuguese and play them on a local station!" Her grin couldn't have been wider. Turning to Ginger, she said, "Thanks for helping get her YouTube channel off the ground. It's changed our lives."

Ginger's cheeks warmed. "It's no problem. Really. What about you, Zara?" she asked. "How was break?"

I was about to tell them how horrible my beach

day had been with Ryde and his friend Ambrose—
and the obnoxious sunscreen tattoo he'd given
Ambrose after he fell asleep tanning—but the bell
rang.

"Catch us up at lunch," Callie said with a wave.

Ginger and Jordan started toward video.

Rory smiled at me. "You can tell me."

We started toward current events class, and I
launched into the story. By the time we walked into
class, Rory had tears of laughter streaming down
her cheeks, and I felt a little lighter too. Just because
my relationship with Ryde was a complete dumpster fire waiting to happen didn't mean I couldn't
make every other part of my life as good as it could
possibly be.

## THREE

DAD and I sat at opposite ends of our long table, eating the meal our chef service had prepared. Tonight was chicken cordon bleu with a wedge salad and sparkling mint lemon water.

He sampled a bite in his mouth. "A little dry."

I took a sip of my water and set it on the table. What was there to say? He hardly cared when I spoke anyway.

"How was school?"

"Good," I said.

"Are we at this again?" he asked. "I hear five words from you all day and half of them are 'good'?"

"Technically, that would be one-fifth."

He eyed me across the table and let out the

world's heaviest sigh. He thought *I* was being diffi-cult? How about him?

"Until we can revisit my arrangement with Ryde, I don't see anything to talk about." I stared at my plate and the food that suddenly looked unap-petizing.

Dad put his silverware down and folded his fingers. "Enlighten me. What is so wrong with this multi-million-dollar movie star who thousands of girls would kill to marry?"

"Nothing." I stabbed at my chicken.

"Zara," he pleaded. "I miss talking to you. Since your mother's been gone, it's always been the two of us—"

"And the nanny," I muttered.

"—I miss having you as my partner in crime."

I looked up at him, the hope in his eyes nearly tearing me apart. "I used to be your partner in crime, but lately I'm nothing but a pawn in your business. You want me to marry the most vapid, shallow, judgmental, self-obsessed—"

"I tried to pair you with our head of PR! He's helped allocate hundreds of thousands of dollars to charity!"

"He's thirty years old!" I cried. "That's gross!"

Dad frowned. "And what about the director's

assistant? A young twenty-five, and on his way to—"

"A bald head and a bad attitude?" I finished. "And don't even start with the parade of 'suitable' Indian men who just want me to be a sari-wearing housewife."

He stood with his plate. "I try. I go outside our culture to find you a match, I listen to you in ways my parents *never* would have considered listening to me, and this is the repayment I get? An ungrateful attitude and constant argument." He shook his head with all the disappointment he could muster. Which was a lot. "Ryde is a perfectly fine young man. He shows up to work on time. He doesn't throw a prima donna attitude like most of the other actors, and he's good at what he does. With a career that's shaping up like his is, you will be well taken care of and have plenty of opportunities to pursue what it is you want."

The resolution behind his words shattered me, and it took all my strength to lift my chin and say, "But what if what I want is to find true love?"

"Then you will be always disappointed." He sighed. "Love isn't something you find. It's something you create."

"That's not—"

He shook his head. "I'm eating dinner in my office."

Without Dad here, the dining room felt too large. I clung to the feeling of isolation, though, because soon I wouldn't have that option. I'd be married—to Ryde if my dad had his way—and I'd never get a chance to see who I was by myself ever again.

I knew girls even younger than me were getting married all the time in my parents' home country of India, but hadn't he come to the United States to start a new life for himself? And he'd created a good one. Who would have thought the son of an engineer and a homemaker would eventually create his own movie production company? One of the fastest growing and most successful in Hollywood at that.

Not feeling hungry anymore, I took my plate to the kitchen and set it in the sink before going upstairs to my room. For a while, my homework was enough to distract me, but there were only so many references you could site on an English composition research paper about fifth-century literature.

When I finished and uploaded the document, it was nearly time for me to go to sleep. To relax, I lay back on my bed and flicked through channels on the TV. I hadn't expected to hear my name.

"Zara Bhatta and Ryde Alexander are the latest 'it' couple on the Hollywood scene. Spotted this morning at a café in his hometown, they seem to be getting quite cozy. I suppose it pays to have connections. Bhatta is the daughter of Viraj Bhatta, owner of Bhatta Productions..."

I almost flipped it off, until a video of Ryde and his friend Ambrose flashed across the screen. Reporters were shoving mics in their faces, trying to get the best question in.

"Ambrose, how do you feel about your best friend coming off the market?"

His friend sent a sultry smirk at the camera. "More girls for me."

I rolled my eyes. These were everyone's heroes? Their crushes? Sure, Hollywood, acting, fame seemed so alluring from a distance. When you'd gotten up close and personal like I had, you realized that the sparkle was all a trick of the light. In reality, it was ruthless deals, contrived connections, and secrets seconds from becoming scandal.

I couldn't help but long for something real, but I knew that possibility was just as out of reach as a future without an arranged marriage.

# FOUR

MY ALARM WENT off at five in the morning. With bleary eyes, I padded downstairs and got a glass of water before throwing on a pair of tennis shoes and stepping on the treadmill. Our home gym wasn't anywhere near as elaborate as the one I saw in Kai's house, but it worked. I especially loved the big screen TV in front of the treadmill. It was supposed to give you the chance to pretend like you were walking outside, but I used it to watch TV.

Most people thought because of my size I wasn't healthy, but that didn't bother me. They weren't in the doctor's office with me seeing my excellent blood pressure and glucose levels or in the gym with me at five in the morning catching up on soaps. Because of my connection to the industry, I knew most of the plus-size actresses had personal trainers and top-tier dieticians. They just didn't care to change their size to make other people happy.

I loved seeing people like Jordan Sparks, Amy Schumer, or Rebel Wilson on the screen, crushing their careers regardless of what people said about them. They could laugh their way to the bank.

Beth, our house manager and my personal lifeline, peeked her head in the room. "Breakfast is out on the table."

I thanked her and then asked, "Are you eating with me?"

With a regretful look, she shook her head. "I've got to run some errands for your father. Rain check?"

Forcing a smile, I nodded, "Of course."

Beth had been my nanny before I was old enough not to need one, but she was such a big part of our lives, Dad kept her on full-time to help manage the household. Of course, that meant he had even more opportunities to be gone.

I slowed down the treadmill until it came to a stop, tossed a white towel around my neck, and made my way to the breakfast nook. As I sat down to eat the omelet and toast prepared for me, my dad walked in wearing one of his better suits.

"Where are you going?" I asked.

"I have to make a last-minute trip to New York. We're trying to sign a book adaptation deal, and the author's being a little flighty."

I nodded. "How long will you be gone?"

"A few days should do it, I think. Do you want me to ask Beth to stay overnight with you?"

I wanted to say yes, but I shook my head instead. Showing weakness wasn't something I wanted to do in front of my father right now.

He walked closer to me and placed a kiss atop my head. "You know I love you, right, Zara?"

Closing my eyes against the stinging sensation his words created, I nodded.

When I blinked them open, a conflicted expression was on his face. "I'll see you in a few days."

"See you in a few days," I repeated.

The house was now quiet, as Beth had left and the cleaning service wouldn't be in until I was already at school. The silence weighed on me, and I turned on my music app to drown out the quiet.

With the music playing, I went back upstairs and began getting ready for the day. I'd always worn makeup and done my hair for school—being a Bhatta, reputation mattered. Whether I'd chosen it or not, I was a part of the Bhatta Productions brand, and we had to represent well.

I dressed in my school uniform, curled my hair and pinned it away from my face before going through my makeup routine. I finished just in time to get in my car and head to Emerson Academy.

As I drove down the road, my Bluetooth speakers began ringing. A call from Ryde. I hit the answer button on my steering wheel and tried to hide the annoyance I felt just at the sight of his name. "Hello?"

"Hi, Zara, how are you?"

"Good, you?" Why was he asking about me? Ryde never looked farther than his own mirror to show concern for others.

"Great, I'm doing fine." He laughed heartily.

"Okay? Did you need something?"

"Nah, I have *everything* I need right here." His laugher echoed around me, and then he started coughing.

My eyebrows came together. "Are you high?" I glanced at the time. "It's not even eight o'clock yet."

"Nooo." He burst out laughing.

"Ryde," I admonished.

"Yes. 'Brose and I decided to make a night of it."

In the background, I heard Ambrose laugh and say, "Hey, 'Brose before hoes, right?"

My eyes were physically unable to roll around my head as much as I wanted them to. "Ryde, take a shower, drink some coffee, and get your act together," I said and hung up. It was way too early to be dealing with this.

I dialed my dad's number next and said, "Hey, guess what your number one boy is doing."

I wasn't above tattletaling, especially when my future rode on proving to my dad that Ryde was not the guy for me.

I didn't know what I'd been expecting from my father, but it wasn't the chuckle coming through my car speakers.

"You're laughing?" I demanded. "Your star actor and soon-to-be son-in-law is wake-and-baking and you're laughing?"

"Honey, he's a kid still. Let him get it out of his system before the big day, then we can do something about it. But as long as he's showing up to work on time and doing a good job, I'm not worried about it. It could be medicinal for all I know. I don't know his medical history."

My gut dropped at hearing my dad reference the wedding. Even though I was only a few minutes from the school, I pulled over to the side of the road and tried to compose myself. In all the fantasies I'd had about the man my parents would pair me with, none of them had looked like this.

My parents had been in love—and not the kind of love Dad said you "created." The kind of love that kept him at Mom's bedside every waking hour when she was sick. The kind of love that made her eyes spark every time she saw him walk into a room.

With my marriage coming up and a host of failed dates behind me, that kind of love was looking far more impossible than ever before.

"Zara," Dad said.

I jumped, realizing he was still on the phone. "Yeah?"

"The plane's about to take off. I'll talk to you later."

FIVE

"GUESS what my soon-to-be husband is doing right now," I said to my friends, leaning against the wall of navy lockers.

Jordan smirked. "Confessing his undying love for Ambrose?" At my deadpan look, she said, "Come on, you have to admit they're close."

I rolled my eyes. "A regular bromance, waking up and getting high together before eight in the morning."

Callie's mouth fell open. "They're doing *what*?"

Ginger snorted. "Who said they woke up to do it? Maybe it was an all-nighter? I saw them talk about you on channel six last night. Looked like they were going out to party."

"Ugh." I groaned. "I cannot wait for this new

relationship thing to blow over. I just want to worry about graduating high school."

Callie patted my arm. "Hang in there."

I was, but by a thread. "Thanks." I readjusted my bag. "I better get going. I have a meeting with Birdie."

Rory kissed her fingers and held them up like in *The Hunger Games*.

With a laugh and a shake of my head, I did the same. "I'll see you guys later."

"Say hi to Ralphie for me," Jordan called.

"I will," I promised over my shoulder.

We'd only shared a few minutes together, but my friends had already made my day better. I dreaded the day when graduation would come and I'd be on my own again. I'd never been a girlfriend person. Girls seemed to be jealous of the money my dad had or out to get something from me, and it was always easier to focus on school or my life at home than stepping on land mines and waiting for one to blow up.

The bell rang, and the halls immediately began thinning. Tardies weren't accepted at the Academy —five in a semester and you were expelled.

Our guidance counselor's door was already open, but I knocked on it anyway.

"Come in," she yelled at the same time her bird squawked.

She shook her head, her carrot earrings swinging. "I swear he talks, sometimes."

I wanted to tell her she should have that checked out, but I kept my mouth shut.

"How are you doing, Zara?" she said, sitting down and indicating that I should do the same.

"I'm fine." That was a lie, but the last thing I needed was a woman wearing vegetable earrings psychoanalyzing me. I slid into one of her wooden chairs and crossed my legs, trying to get comfortable on the hard seat.

"Good, I wanted to talk to you about your college plans...or lack thereof."

I nodded. "What about it?"

She folded her hands on her desk and leaned forward. "Students at the Academy often go to top-tier schools and perform in the top of their classes. They go on to be doctors, lawyers, changemakers. Yet you've submitted no applications, and you're dangerously close to missing deadlines."

"I'm not going to college," I answered simply.

If someone had walked in and judged the situation based on her expression alone, they would have thought I'd singlehandedly shut down every college in the country.

"Is that what you want?" she asked, still composing herself.

Did she know my father? It didn't matter what I wanted. But I pressed ahead. "My father doesn't believe in college. He says it trains people to fit inside boxes when all the success you could ever want can be found outside of them. He said unless I want to work in a field that requires a certification, I can learn all I need to in the real world, without wasting my time attending classes that won't apply to my future career."

Birdie gaped at me like I had Ralphie's blood on my fingers.

"Those are my dad's words, not mine."

She seemed to relax a little, but her back was still stiff. "And assuming you don't want to train for a career, what do you plan to work toward?"

"I'll intern with the production company until I find the position I like best. Once I do, I'll learn what I need to then. College isn't the only place where learning can happen after graduation."

"But the scholarships..."

"It's not like money's an issue," I said. "And I know there are a thousand people who would kill to be in my position," I said, quoting the refrain I'd heard so often lately, "but I'm not one of them."

She frowned, then leaned forward, her carrot earrings leaning in like they wanted to hear what she had to say. "Look, Zara. I'm going to be honest with you. You're a bright girl. You get along with your peers. You have confidence that could take you far. I hate to see you waste that gift, that *potential*."

Even though her words brought out an aching in my chest, I looked at her steadily and said, "I'm not."

Her mouth opened and closed for a moment. "It sounds like you have your mind made up."

Or had it made up for me. "I do."

She shooed her fingers toward the door. "Get to class then. I don't want you to miss out on any learning."

The weight of her disappointment swept through me, but I nodded. "See you, Bird."

"Bye, Zara," Mrs. Bardot said.

As the door closed behind me, I muttered, "I was talking to Ralphie."

SIX

EACH OF MY friends seemed to have hobbies, passions. Rory was an amazing artist, Ginger excelled at videography, Jordan was busy saving the world now that her mom didn't need her to work all the time, and Callie always volunteered with animals. All I wanted to do when I got home was veg out in front of the TV.

I didn't want to admit it, but my conversation with the guidance counselor got to me. Mrs. Bardot acted like I was throwing away my future, and maybe I was. But she didn't understand my culture, either. There was no way my dad would let me make nothing of my life as his only child. He had too much pride for that, too much drive.

I went to the refrigerator and looked at the

stacks of prepared meals. I took one labeled pasta primavera and followed the heating instructions. The door to the garage opened, and I looked over expecting to see Beth but finding my dad instead.

"You're home early," I said.

He dropped his bag and coat by the door and scrubbed a hand over his face. "Unfortunately." He went to the liquor cabinet and poured himself a tumbler of bourbon.

I'd only ever seen him drink outside of a party three times. Once after Mom's funeral, again when a major actor pulled out of a deal at the last second, and now.

The microwave dinged. Carefully setting my food on the table, I slid onto a stool. "Tell me about it."

He swallowed and clenched his jaw. "Said I don't have a feel for the 'younger generation.'"

"And?" I asked. "That's what the writers are for. What book is it?"

"We signed an NDA, but it's a young adult novel."

I smiled, thinking of some of my favorite YA novel to movie adaptations—*Everything, Everything, To all the Boys I've Loved Before,* and *The Kissing Booth* to name a few. Taking an author's idea and bringing it to the big screen could help them reach an audience with their message that never would have been possible before.

"Did you tell them you have a teenage daughter?" I asked.

He tossed back a gulp and cringed. "They said that doesn't mean I get teenagers."

I looked away because I couldn't meet his eyes and think the thoughts going through my head. My dad *didn't* get me. He thought I was just another moveable cog in the machine of his business and life. Whether it was because he married young into an arranged marriage and lost his childhood or because he was a middle-aged man, I had no idea. Ever since Mom died, it was like we existed on opposite planes, never quite crossing and definitely not meeting in the middle.

It didn't take a genius to see he was devastated, and even though we didn't see eye to eye, I still loved him. I didn't want to see him this distraught. "There are always more books out there, right?"

"This one is going to be huge." His eyes gleamed with the light of possibility that kept him working long hours, even on the weekends and holidays. "Getting this deal could help Bhatta Productions reach a whole new demographic."

I put my hand in my chin, not sure what to say. "Sorry, Dad."

He nodded toward my food. "Your dinner's getting cold."

"That's what microwaves are for, right?"

With a smile, he came to my side of the island and kissed my cheek. "I'm going to get some food and head to bed."

"Sounds good." As I went to the microwave to reheat my food, he walked to the fridge to see what prepared meals we had.

While the microwaved hummed, I said, "You know, Dad, you could always watch vlogs done by teenagers. Watch the movies, see what makes them tick."

"I've done some, but I could do more," he agreed. "I'm just not sure it would be enough."

"True." There was more to teens than what they showed in most movies or the best versions of themselves people posted on social media. We didn't just wear fancy clothes to school and hope for boys to like us. Some of us had real goals and talents—like Ginger with her video skills or Jordan and her dream of becoming a doctor.

He set another prepped dinner on the counter. "Hey," he said. "You know who could teach me about teenagers?" Dad looked at me like I was an untapped oil well, ready to begin spouting black liquid gold.

"Whoa, whoa, whoa," I said. "The last thing you want is to be learning about teenagers from me."

"Why is that?" he asked.

"For one, I'm getting married after my high school graduation. And if you haven't noticed, the average age for someone to get married is well into their twenties, not to mention having children."

His smile just grew wider. "No one said anything about you having children. And no one said that it had to be perfect. You are a teenager. You can show me how you think, let me get into your head."

Was he delusional? We'd spent the last seven years barely existing in the same place, and now he wanted to 'get into my head'? Why now? And why me? Clearly, I was the last person whose opinion mattered to him. A bitter, metallic taste filled my mouth, and I realized I'd been biting my cheek too hard.

"Zara," he said. "It will help the business."

Always for the business. Not for me or for the sake of our relationship. I wanted to argue, but I could tell he was determined, and nothing could stop a Bhatta when they really wanted something.

"Okay," I said. "I'll do it, but on my terms."

He lifted his hands. "Whatever works for you. I don't want to distract from your schoolwork or your relationship with Ryde."

"Oh, you can distract me from that relationship." I got the food from the microwave and turned away.

"Did you guys work everything out this morning?" The hope in his voice made me get even more angry.

"If by working everything out you mean I ignored him for the rest of the day, then yes, we're doing swell."

He sighed and shook his head. "Goodnight, Zara. Let me know tomorrow what works for you."

I went to my room, carrying my food that was cold again, but deciding another round in the microwave probably wouldn't help matters. As I sat on my bed and began picking through the pasta primavera, I thought about my dad and the teen lessons. Although my first inclination was to be enraged, I tried to find the bright side, like my mom always told me to do.

Maybe this wouldn't be such a bad thing after

all. Maybe if Dad got to know me, really know me, as a person and not as his daughter or the next in the line of Bhattas, he would know that this marriage by arrangement wasn't right for me.

I finished my show and went to sleep feeling hopeful about the lessons, and that somehow, I could make my dad see the real me.

SEVEN

"YOUR DAD WANTS you to do what?" Jordan asked, punctuating her question with a slam of her locker door.

"He wants me to tell him about being a *teenager*," I said to her and our small group of friends hanging around the lockers. "I guess there could be worse things to do on a Thursday night."

Ginger laughed, making her green eyes crinkle at the corners. "Watch him show up with a notebook and start taking notes on you."

I grinned, as that was exactly something my dad would do. I just hoped it would work. "The first lesson's tonight, so I'll text you guys and let you know how it goes."

Rory hugged me, her long hair tickling my

cheek. "I have to go catch up with Beckett for dinner, but you've got this. You're the most articulate person I know."

"Exactly." Callie patted my shoulder comfortingly. "*Please* text us what happens so we can laugh about it later."

I rolled my eyes. "We're going to have plenty of material."

We went our separate ways for the day, and I couldn't help but wish I were a "normal" teen like them. While they could go home to their families and worry about schoolwork or hang out with their boyfriends without pressure for the future, I had a reputation to uphold. Dad was always dragging me along to a mixer for work or a dinner with actors he wanted to schmooze or making up for the kind of life we lived by taking me to cultural events at Brentwood U.

As I walked to the parking lot, I thought about what it would be like to be them. To see the guys around me and think of the possibilities. But all the guys around me seemed so...lackluster. Not that there was anything wrong with my friends' boyfriends. They were perfect for each other. But all the available guys at the Academy? I couldn't even fathom being interested in them, feeling a spark like I had with that delivery driver I hardly knew. And really, maybe that was a good thing. You couldn't miss what you never had, right?

I got in my car and drove across town, playing music so loud I couldn't think. A valet took my car at Halfway Café, since it was nearing dinner time, and I approached my dad's table. But someone else was sitting with him. Ryde.

I reached them and pasted an unconvincing smile on my face. "What are you doing here?"

Ryde gave his best smile in return, putting on a show for my dad. "Hi, honey." Gag. "Your dad told me about lessons, and he thought it would be great if I joined so he could get the male perspective too."

"There certainly isn't enough of that in the world." I took the seat at the table as far from both of them as possible.

Dad shook his head at me while Ryde just smirked. The last thing I wanted to be was his entertainment. Scratch that. The last thing I wanted to be was his wife, but entertainment was high on the list.

Undeterred, Dad held his pen poised over the yellow legal pad tucked into an expensive-looking portfolio. "What are the main things I need to know?"

Ryde shrugged and looked to me. I let out a massive sigh. "I'm going to need something to drink for this."

Dad chuckled. "So jokes about alcohol are in."

Shaking my head, I got up and went to the ordering counter. I got myself a big caffeinated drink, knowing I would need the energy to deal with all of the events that were sure to ensue. I also grabbed the most edible looking thing on the menu that didn't include seaweed. I wished I could be at Waldo's Diner, drinking milkshakes with the girls, but no. I was here with my dad and an actor talking about what it meant to be a teenager.

Hot take, maybe if you want to know about an average teenager, don't ask a twenty-year-old with a million-dollar net worth and a seventeen-year-old months away from getting married.

I went and sat back at the table, where Dad and Ryde were already deep into a conversation about the family business. Yet another reason why Ryde wasn't the best person for teenage lessons, but I wasn't going to bring this up to Dad. Apparently, Ryde had earned his place as the golden boy, and trying to debunk that would just make me the enemy. Which would be counterproductive, considering my whole goal for the lessons was to get Dad to understand me enough to let me out of a relationship with Ryde.

I took a long sip from my double shot latte, watching what was practically a bromance unfold before me. Ryde complimented Dad on the work they'd done on the movie Ryde starred in. Dad told Ryde he "got" his work. Ryde's nose got even browner, and Dad's chest puffed even bigger.

Could Dad not see what was happening? Ryde was outsmarting him in his own game. It made me dislike Ryde that much more.

With a chuckle, Dad said, "We probably should save the shop talk for the set. Let's continue on the lessons. Let me have it."

I opened my mouth to speak, but of course Ryde cut in first. "What you need to understand, Mr. Bhatta, is hormones. Teens are loaded with them, and they're like a constant little nudge in your ear saying, have sex, have sex, have sex."

Dad seemed disturbed. "Is that how you feel, Zara?"

"Absolutely not," I sputtered. I'd never thought of sex much, but I was curious what it would feel like to become that close to someone. To fall in love and lose track of time and space.

Ryde lifted his eyebrows and raised his hands in defense. "I'm just the messenger."

I rolled my eyes. "Not all teens are pigs."

"Tell me, Zara. What are they?" Dad pressed, as if desperate to hear about anything other than hormones. That made two of us.

Taking a deep breath, I sighed. "I feel like the main thing you need to know is that teenagers are just regular people, but the difference is we feel like we're given the freedom of a child and the responsibilities of an adult. We're constantly asked to choose our future, our major, our career path, when we can't even choose our own curfew."

"You always come and go as you please," Dad said. "Surely you're not feeling imposed upon."

Frustrated, I rolled my eyes toward the exposed ceiling rafters. "Dad, this isn't going to work if you're constantly second-guessing what I'm saying. You just have to take it as it is and think about it."

With a sigh, he folded his arms and rested them on the table. He lifted a hand and twirled it through the air as if saying, *go on.*

Feeling hopeless, I looked down at the table. None of this was getting through to my dad, but maybe it was just good to get it off my chest. "The thing that the movies get wrong is that we're not just kids going to school. We have things that we want to do, goals. We haven't given up on our dreams yet."

I choked over that last sentence, because my dreams seemed farther away than ever before during a time that should have been all about possibilities. I had always wanted to have a loving relationship like my parents had before Mom passed, but at what cost? Would it take years of suffering and trial and acceptance before I could love Ryde? Would it be worth it?

Ryde reached across the low table and put his hand on my knee. "Zara is so right. When I was in high school, I was just trying to pass trig and get some girls to notice me. I wasn't thinking about much else."

"Oh, they noticed you," I said, rolling my eyes.

"What?" Ryde said.

I rolled my eyes again. "You know half of the senior class and most of the juniors were interested in you. Remember after you got your first role your senior year that one girl offered to pay a thousand dollars to switch lockers so she could be next to yours?"

Ryde smiled in a self-satisfied way. "Oh yeah, I remember that."

"And what did that feel like?" Dad asked.

"Like everything I'd worked so hard for was finally coming true," Ryde said. "And now I have my dream job and a beautiful girl to spend my future with."

Dad grinned between the two of us, clearly pleased with his matchmaking ability.

Ryde's acting skills were truly unfortunate. In this very same restaurant, he'd told me he thought he would be marrying someone who actually liked him, and that definitely wasn't me. But now he had my dad completely convinced he was falling for me, making me look petulant because the "feelings" weren't reciprocated.

I mean, he was cute—in the early Matt Damon kind of way—with his six-pack abs and blond hair and blue eyes, but I was looking for something more. Something *real*. I never wanted to date an actor again. You never knew who they really were— only who they wanted you to know.

Nothing about Ryde, or the family he came from, seemed honest. It was all a game to them, each action signifying a political act that would get them closer to the top of the food chain and everyone else closer to the bottom.

Our relationship was just another step in that direction, and I hated to be part of it. But what choice did I have? Dad was the only family I knew. And even though he was strong-willed and staring at me like a test subject in a zoo, he was my dad.

"Next question," Dad said. "How do teens feel about money?"

Ryde smirked. "Great, if you can get some."

Dad scribbled notes, hanging on to Ryde's every word.

I took another drink of my latte and checked out. If I was going to convince my father against an arranged marriage, I'd have to find another way.

## EIGHT

WHEN I GOT home that night and lay down in bed to relax, a message was waiting for me on *Sermo*, the chat app everyone at school used to talk with each other. Having a password protected messaging app was way better than using your phone's messages, which could show up on your screen and be easily read by parents or other nosy people.

Jordan: How was the lesson?

Zara: Ryde hijacked it.

Callie: Seriously?

Ginger: How did he even know about it?

Zara: My dad invited him.

Rory: Ugh.

Zara: Yep.

Callie: :( Anything we can do?

Zara: Unless you want to put out a hit on a certain obnoxious actor…

Jordan: There's always chocolate…that solves everything.

Rory: True. We can totally get you a chocolate muffin from Seaton's.

I grinned, thinking of the delicious food available at Seaton Bakery. Just the thought made my mouth water.

Zara: Please?

Jordan: I can get it. But it'll cost you your first-born child.

Zara: If it's Ryde's, you can have it.

Rory: LOL

Callie: You have to admit you two would have GORGEOUS babies.

Ginger: Right? Could you imagine the complexions?

Zara: Ew, ew, ew. I'm sorry I brought it up. No baby talk.

Ginger: Wahhhhhh

Zara: LOL

Callie: What if you just…talked to him? Didn't argue, didn't fight, just told your dad how you feel?

My heart constricted. Talking with my dad? He

would have to learn how to listen first. And I would have to keep from getting frustrated at that fact. It always felt like my mom *understood* me, and Dad loved her so much that he got me by proxy. Because the fact was I had. I'd told him. Each time he brought a guy home, it was wrong—all wrong, and each time I told him so, he grew more frustrated.

I wished more than anything that my mom was here. That she would sweep my hair back and say something like, "Men are like Assam tea. It takes a moment for the message to sink in."

Maybe I just needed to brew him a fresh batch, pour the purest water and talk with him—not as his daughter, but as *me*.

Mom used to always make tea when things were hard—even when she was sick, she'd sit with me while I brewed tea just the way she liked it. Ever since she died, I drank coffee, not wanting to relive the memories of her thin, shaking hands so weak she couldn't lift the cup to her mouth. But I'd do anything to feel her closer now.

I went downstairs and found a tea kettle, then filled it with water and set it on the stove. Near the coffee maker, I found jars of fresh teas and set to work. Even though it had been seven years since I'd made tea, the steps came easily. Like my muscles had remembered them even when my mind begged to forget.

Soft footsteps sounded in the threshold, then froze. I turned to see Dad wearing his silk pajamas and house shoes. Even in his nightwear, he looked polished, like he could step into a board room and take command. To be fair, the buttons and lapels helped.

"Darjeeling?" he asked, gesturing toward the mugs.

I nodded.

"It was your mother's—"

"Favorite," I finished with a sad smile. "I know." I nudged a cup his way.

He picked it up and sat at the bar. With his eyes closed, he took a tentative sip, and his lips formed a soft smile. Would the taste make me feel that same way?

I took a seat near him. "Is it okay if we talk?" I asked.

Slowly lowering his cup, he nodded. "What's going on?"

I wrapped my hand around my mug, feeling the warmth transfer from the ceramic to my skin. It was almost too hot, but I held on anyway. As I took a deep breath, hints of citrus and more savory notes filled my nose. It took me back to being an eleven-year-old girl, lifting the cup to my mother's lips.

A tear rolled down my cheek, and I wiped it away. "Daddy, I don't want to get married to Ryde."

His eyebrows furrowed together, and his shoulders straightened as he opened his mouth to argue.

"Please, Daddy, let me get it out."

Seemingly frustrated, he obliged all the same.

"For eleven years, I watched you and Mom together. The perfect team. You reached for the stars, and she kept your feet on the ground. You showed her how precious she was, and she adored you. When you weren't around, I'd watch her iron your clothes, even though we could have hired it out a million times over. She'd say, 'Why would I let someone else do it when my husband can wear my love every day?'"

He closed his eyes against the memory, but I kept going.

"Daddy, I deserve the chance to have *that* kind of love. I deserve to have someone who loves me like the moon loves the stars, always shining for each other."

"You don't understand," he said simply. "Marriage isn't about choosing someone. It's about choosing love."

Hope began slipping from my chest, and I was flailing, desperate to hold on to it before my dad shut everything down. "How can you choose it when you don't exist?"

"You might not understand now, but I hope you will eventually."

"When?" I asked, tears flowing freeing now. "When will I understand? When I'm fifty and in a loveless marriage? When Ryde is cheating on set because his culture doesn't teach him to 'choose love'?"

"That's enough," he said, his voice forceful.

My fingers squeezed so tightly around the cup, it slipped from my fingers and slid across the island, sending the liquid everywhere and the mug crashing to the ground.

For a long moment, my father looked at the mess, then he turned to me. The problem? His expression didn't change. To him, I was a mess. Something that needed to be cleaned up.

Even worse? Maybe he was right.

"Wipe up the tea," he said. "The housekeepers can get the pieces." He stood from the counter, leaving his cup of tea half drank.

With him out of sight, I collapsed, just like the

cup, onto the floor, surrounded by shards of ceramic and my hope.

Today had been long, hard, and not what I had hoped for. I hadn't even realized how much hope I had been holding on to until it was snatched away. I sobbed into my hands, crying for my future, for my mother, for all I had lost, and all I would never have the chance to gain.

NINE

INSTEAD OF WORKING out like I usually did in the morning, I dressed for school. Dad and I had our second teen lesson scheduled bright and early with Ryde. I couldn't tell which was worse—seeing my dad after our conversation last night or facing Ryde knowing he was my future.

I walked downstairs to head to the garage and found Beth in the kitchen. My heart sank a little that Dad didn't want to talk or even attempt to repair the damage that had been done last night. All the broken pieces had been swept up, but nothing had been fixed.

At the sound of my footsteps, she looked up and smiled at me. "Good morning, sweetie. How'd you sleep?"

"Not long enough," I said, patting underneath my eyes.

Smiling, she shook her head. "Oh, to be seventeen again."

"Trade you?" I said.

She chuckled and batted her hand through the air. "Want me to make you some coffee?"

I readjusted my backpack on my shoulder and said, "Nah, I'll let Dad spend ten dollars on a cup at Halfway."

A knowing smile formed on her lips. "Rough night?"

"When isn't it a rough night?" I asked.

Her eyes filled with compassion. "It's been extra hard for you two this year, hasn't it?" It wasn't a question, just a statement, but tears filled my eyes, and I nodded all the same.

"Oh, honey." Her arms wrapped around me, and I leaned into her hug. Beth was the closest thing I'd had to a mom since I was eleven. Even though she was nothing like my mom, I felt the love all the same.

Feeling too close to completely breaking down, I pulled back and wiped at the corners of my eyes, careful not to mess up my makeup. "I better get going."

She rubbed my shoulder and said, "Just remember, your dad loves you. You're his world."

That was the problem, I thought, as I waved goodbye and went to my car. I didn't want to be his world, something he could control. I wanted to be his daughter, someone he could simply love.

When I reached the café, I could see him through the front window, dressed in a perfectly crisp designer suit. When Mom stopped taking care of his clothes, he had a personal stylist take over. I wished that had been the only thing to change.

I went inside and ordered at the counter before going to sit with Dad. He looked up at me from his phone, then back down at the messages.

"Good morning, girlfriend," Ryde said close to my ear.

I recoiled from his voice and looked him up and down. He looked like a little boy in rolled pants and a tight shirt. Why was my first reaction to him always disgust? Behind him, I could see the barista checking him out like he'd descended from heaven for the sole purpose of kissing her silly.

Dad caught sight of us and waved us over. "Daylight's burning!"

Ryde chuckled. "So true, Dad."

Dad puffed up his chest. "Dad? I like it."

Ryde fist-bumped him across the table, and it took all I had not to vomit.

Dad rubbed his hands together and looked right at Ryde. "Let's get started. I feel like I need to get a better understanding of what motivates teenagers."

"Motivation?" Ryde laughed. "What's that?"

Dad shook his head. "Clearly you're motivated or else you wouldn't be one of the top actors of your age."

Ryde acted like he was embarrassed to be caught, but I could tell he was pleased. "I feel like when I was wanting to become an actor, I had so many pressures crashing down on me. I needed to graduate, I needed to please my parents, and I needed to figure out what to do for the rest of my life even though I'd hardly lived yet. I wanted to have the opportunity to be anything, to be everything, and acting sounded like the perfect way to do that and have an adventure. My parents couldn't be prouder. And now the pressure I have is created by a career that I love."

Part of me was jealous of his passion for his career, but another part was frustrated. Why did he get the freedom to choose how he lived his life when I was being forced in every aspect?

"What about you, Zara?" Ryde asked.

I stayed silent, rolling the words over on my tongue. How could I tell Dad the truth, that I was motivated by his pressure, but in the opposite direction? The more he pushed me one way, the more I wanted to prove that I could make a life on my own.

"You can say it," Dad said. "You're not going to hurt my feelings."

I raised an eyebrow. At least he knew me a little bit. "Why would I be motivated when I don't have a say in my own life?" The more words I spoke, the tighter my throat got, as I realized how little control I actually did have. "Excuse me," I said. I stood from the table without waiting for their permission and went to the restroom.

I needed to get myself together. I stood in front of the mirror, wiping my eyes and carefully dabbing at my makeup to be sure it didn't run down my face before school. Who was this girl who fell apart in public and cried in front of her father and movie stars? I wanted to be the real Zara, the one who was poised, confident and knew how to react in each moment. But that girl seemed farther and farther away with each day that passed.

I didn't know how, but I wanted to get her back. I finished wiping my eyes and took a few deep breaths of the purified air.

Shaking my head, I left the bathroom and joined Dad and Ryde, who were busy in a conversation about a new movie and what genres they expected to be popular in the coming years. Ryde was banking for a continuation of the trend toward remakes, with while my dad expected high concept films like *Avatar* would make a resurgence.

"Sorry," I said, "had something in my eye."

Ryde examined me for a moment, but my dad simply nodded. "So, you're motivated by adversity." He smiled like he was proud. "You are a Bhatta for sure."

Whatever being a Bhatta meant. I wasn't so sure anymore. I took a drink from my latte, which had cooled considerably since we came into the café. The flavor was so comforting, and I drank deeply.

"And what about romantically?" Dad asked.

I nearly choked over my latte while Ryde asked calmly, "What do you mean?"

"Well, it seems like a lot of teens' lives are dominated by relationships with the opposite sex, even though they don't want to get married. What is the intrigue there? Why is it so important?"

Both Ryde and I were silent, but for different reasons. Wasn't Dad just asking what I'd tried so hard to communicate to him the day before? But here he was with a notepad, ready to write down whatever Ryde said.

Before he could speak, I cut in. "Almost all of my friends have boyfriends. They are funny, they enjoy time together, they share secrets that no one else knows or understands. It's almost like an exclusive club of two, that no one can get into, and once you're in, you're in. You want to explore and discover and learn and enjoy as much as you possibly can, because everyone's always reminding you how ephemeral it is, even though it feels like it will last forever."

Dad scribbled onto his legal pad, writing quickly. He was so clearly unfazed, it cut me to the core. This was all an assignment to him. All about signing the next big deal, making more money for the bank account.

"In the male perspective?" Dad looked up at Ryde with an analytical eye, but I also saw something else in his expression. The same face he made when he was testing someone. Was he evaluating Ryde for me? The thought soothed the jagged edges of my heart. Maybe Dad wasn't only invested in furthering his business like I had thought, because the way he looked at Ryde made me think he cared about his answer for more than the business.

Was Dad doing these lessons to help me get to know Ryde? In a weird way, it was kind of sweet, even if it was misguided.

Ryde cleared his throat, and I did my best to listen. "When you first become a teenager, it's about all the feelings you have in your body. They're all new, and they're pushing you to do things you've never done before. But soon you realize that physicality isn't enough. You want the closeness to go with it. You want to *know* the other person in a way no one else does." He reached out to hold my hand, and I found myself not pulling away as I usually would.

Dad's lips formed a smile as he continued drafting on his legal pad. From the surface of the coffee table between us, his phone went off. Lifting it, he said, "That's our time. Zara needs to leave for school, and we need to get to the shoot."

Ryde nodded. "I'll see you there."

Dad stood, taking a final drink from his chai latte. "Have a great day at school, Zara."

"I will," I promised.

Dad exited the coffee shop, leaving me and Ryde standing awkwardly together.

Turning toward me, Ryde looked at me openly

with wide green eyes. "It was nice to see you this morning. I always love seeing you first thing."

One of the dormant butterflies in my stomach lifted a tired wing.

"I'll see you tomorrow night?" Ryde confirmed. "It's red carpet."

"I'll be at my house, ready to go."

He left first, and I waited until his Lamborghini had pulled away to exit myself. As I stepped into the fresh spring air, I heard the rumbling of a motorcycle, and my eyes found the source. A black bike pulled up to the café. He got off and lifted his hood. I lifted my gaze to him, and his honey-brown eyes collided with mine.

I shuddered as I got into my car, because I could feel something.

*Butterflies.*

And I didn't even know his name.

# TEN

I CLASPED a pearl necklace around my neck that used to be my mother's and examined myself in the mirror. The full-length black dress clung to my curves and flared out at the ground, making my figure look even better than an hourglass. The pearls added a hint of dignity, as did my updo with curls falling around my face. Red-carpet ready? Ryde would get more than that.

I threw some lipstick, mascara, tissues, money, and my phone into my clutch and went downstairs. Ryde was usually on time, and I didn't want him to be waiting on me, watching me make my entrance. Dad and Beth looked at me from the dining room table as I came down the final steps.

Beth folded her hands over her heart. "Zara, you look beautiful."

"Thank you, Beth." I glanced at Dad, waiting for his reaction. Mom always dressed more colorfully for the red carpet. I remembered watching them leave, always thinking my mom could have been a queen with all her ornate jewelry and jewel-encrusted gowns.

Dad nodded approvingly. "Smart choice on the black. That'll photograph well and match whatever Ryde wears."

I couldn't help the pride that rose within me. I wanted to make my dad proud of me, even though I disagreed with him ninety-nine percent of the time.

"When should he be here?" Dad asked.

"In a minute," I answered.

As if on cue, the doorbell rang, and Beth let him in.

He stepped inside, clearly confident in his fitted suit pants with a slick leather jacket and a white shirt. Photos of him in this outfit would be all over the news tomorrow.

"You look smart," Dad said.

I had to agree, even if begrudgingly. It was the perfect mix of polished and edgy, going perfectly with his character in the action film he and Dad were working on. Especially with his hair effortlessly gelled in all sorts of messy directions.

Ryde tugged his jacket. "Thanks, Dad."

Beth made a face that made me smile.

Ryde took that for happiness at seeing him and said, "Let's get out of here?" He extended his arm for me.

"Sure," I said and looped my arm through his.

Grinning from ear to ear, my dad said, "Have a great time, and if you get photographs taken of you, be sure it's doing something good."

"Image is everything, right?" I said. It wasn't like happiness or fulfillment mattered.

"Exactly," Ryde said wholeheartedly. He didn't even catch the dejection in my voice.

We walked outside, where a limo was waiting in the driveway. The driver leaned against the car with his hands folded over his waist, but when he saw us, he popped up. "Good evening, Miss Bhatta." He opened the door for me, and I slid in, sitting on the opposite side as Ryde.

He got his phone out and said, "We need a selfie."

The driver closed the door behind him, and Ryde slid over to my side of the limo, pressing his side against mine and holding out his phone. The pose he had us in was way more suggestive than reality, but sex sells. Even if it's at the outrage of a million tweenage girls.

After clicking the picture, he moved to the other side and began tapping at the screen. I looked down at the empty bench seats, wishing we were at the Valentine's dance again, surrounded by friends. At least then I felt more comfortable, like I could breathe. Here, in this tight dress, with this guy who cared more about his follower count than my feelings, I felt claustrophobic. Like I was suffocating.

"How far is it to the premiere?" I asked, desperate for fresh air—any air that didn't have to be shared with this vanilla movie star.

"About an hour and a half," Ryde said.

I sighed. An hour and a half. So, I did what any girl would do on a date with a movie star. I got my phone out and began scrolling through social media. I was immediately greeted by Rory and Beckett's smiling faces. My friend and her boyfriend were on a date at a paintball place, and they were absolutely covered in blues, greens, yellows, and every other color of the rainbow. Their happiness shined from within and translated even through a simple, unfiltered picture. No amount of editing

Ryde did on a photo would ever come close to looking like that.

I closed my screen, because I just didn't want to cry right now. I needed time to accept that Rory's story wasn't mine. I wouldn't have that type of romance, no matter how much I may have wanted it.

Wrappers crinkled from across the limo, and I looked to see Ryde snacking on something that almost resembled food. "Hungry?" he asked.

I was—getting ready after school hadn't left me much time to eat. "What else do you have?"

He went to the mini fridge near the front and said, "We have some diet soda and some rice cakes."

I frowned. "That's all? Any protein?"

"Sorry," he said, not sounding apologetic at all. "I didn't have them stock that."

"You just had a hankering for rice cakes?" I teased.

He shrugged. "I figured you were trying to watch your weight, and I was trying to be supportive."

My head jerked back. "What? Why would you think that?"

He rubbed his hands over his knees and looked

me straight on. "Look, you've gotten some nasty comments on social media and in the press, and I know that those are hard to handle. Shedding a few pounds could probably help change that for you. Heck, you could probably get some positive PR with a good before and after photo."

Was I correctly hearing the words coming out of his mouth? Because if I was, he was in for a world of hurt. "No one, not you or the media or your social media followers have any say over how I look. *No one.* My appearance is for me, my health is for me, and none of the things or people you mentioned have any say in what I eat or how I exercise or feel about myself. They're not in my doctor's appointments with me, they don't fall asleep in my bed at night, and they don't have to look in the mirror every day. They have absolutely no room for input in my life, and neither do you." When I finished, my chest was heaving with the force of how I said those words, and my head still had that dizzy, hot feeling from being so angry.

Ryde simply raised his hands and said, "You don't have to be such a rip about it."

"Excuse me?"

"You heard me. I was just giving you some helpful advice, and you bit my head off because, for whatever reason, you think you're better than me."

This conversation was getting more ridiculous by the second. "You have no idea what's going on in my mind, mostly because you're too selfish to look outside of yourself."

"Oh really?" He leaned forward, his elbows on his knees. "We went to high school together, if you don't remember. I saw you walking the halls, thinking you were better than everyone else. You never went to any of the theater parties, you never tried out for any sports, and you never had any real friends because your nose was too far in the air to see anyone else."

His words hit my chest like blow after blow. Maybe I didn't want to get close to anyone because I'd *lost the one person who had always been my best friend.* Maybe I didn't have time for "theater parties" because my dad was too busy dragging me to industry events. But none of that bothered me as much as the hypocrisy in his words.

"Have you looked in a mirror lately? You're an Alexander, and being an Alexander means you think you're better than literally everyone else. Merritt 'walks the halls' like she owns them, even though I know for a fact that the Rushes donate *way* more money to the school. And all *you* care about is how many likes you get. It's vapid, and it won't last. Especially with that receding hairline."

Okay, the last part was a low blow, I had to admit, but I was absolutely fuming from the words he said. I knew what other people thought about me; I just didn't think that the man my father had chosen for me to marry should agree with them.

Ryde lifted his hands like he wanted to touch his hair, but let them fall into his lap. "You're just bitter because any success you'll have is going to be because of your father."

"And any lasting success you have will be because of *me*."

Ryde folded his arms over his chest, refusing to say another word.

That was absolutely fine by me. If I never heard another word out of his stupid mouth, it would be too soon.

ELEVEN

AS WE PULLED up to the movie premiere, I could see the crowd of paparazzi held back by a flimsy red rope and various stars in the process of being photographed as they moved toward the building.

"Look," Ryde said, drawing my attention away from the window and all the glamor outside. "I know things are awkward, but can you at least act normal for the premiere?"

I narrowed my eyes at him. "Act normal?"

"Like we're in love."

"That *would* be an act."

"Every major outlet's there," he said desperately. "We need to look good."

I raised my eyebrows and widened my eyes in

mock surprise. "Oh, it's possible to look good with me? What if I don't stretch my neck far enough?"

He gave me a sardonic look.

"Yes," I finally said. "I'm not going to make a scene." Bhattas didn't back down on their promises, and they certainly didn't make headlines for anything other than positive remarks.

The limo pulled to a stop, and the driver got out.

Ryde took a deep breath. "Ready, camera..." The door opened. "Action."

He stepped out of the limo and extended his hand to me with an adoring smile on his face. Man, he was a good actor. I slipped my hand into his, trying not to be completely repulsed by him and everything he stood for.

It was a challenge, but I wasn't a bad actor myself. Poise and control were practically in my DNA. I could manage this for an evening, but not a second longer.

Cameras flashed in all directions, and I kept my eyes smoldering on Ryde, on the photographers, on the interviewers.

Someone from *Pop!* Television stopped us. "Ryde, tell us about this beauty you have here."

"She's the love of my life." He pulled me closer

to him. "Couldn't be happier to celebrate my friend's success with her by my side."

The microphone came toward me. "And how does it feel to be here with a movie star? This must be every high school girl's dream."

I flashed an adoring smile at Ryde, feeling disgusted with myself all the while. "Amazing."

"We better get inside," Ryde said apologetically. "We'll see you afterward with our positive review!"

After stopping for a few poses at the end of the carpet, we walked inside. Everyone thought premiers were this glamorous ordeal, but honestly, it was kind of a pain. You still had to wait in line. The popcorn still gave you gas. The soda was still flat. And the chairs you sat in were just as covered in farts as any other theater seat.

This time, though, I had Ryde with me, which made it ten times worse. The second we got through the doors, Ryde was interrupted by fans wanting autographs of various items. As I stood to the side while he signed and schmoozed, I couldn't help wishing that I was at movie night with my friends in Kai's home theater. The spacious leather couches with room to spread out would have been much more comfortable than this, and I wouldn't have to stand next to someone who thought rice cakes were an ideal snack.

My stomach growled, so I excused myself and made my way to the concessions. If only to spite Ryde, I got a large non-diet soda, popcorn with a double dose of butter, and a box of Milk Duds just because I couldn't watch a movie without them.

When I reached Ryde again, he was standing with Ambrose. They had a real bromance going on, always touching each other's shoulders and making inside jokes. Of the two, Ryde was more attractive, but Ambrose was a close second with his smoldering gray eyes, hollowed cheeks and a jawline that could cut glass.

Noticing me, Ambrose grinned at me from under his dark, shaggy hair. "Hi, Zara."

"Hi," I answered. "Congratulations on your premiere. How exciting." I took a long sip from my soda and caught Ryde's disappointed look.

"Thanks, I can't stay long, but I wanted to make sure and say hi to you two. You have a spot reserved next to me. Right in the middle."

"Great," I answered.

Ryde tucked Ambrose under his arm and scruffed up his hair. "Go get 'em, tiger."

Ambrose punched his way out of the grip and held up a pointed finger. "I'm watching you, bro."

"See you inside, man," Ryde said, then he turned to me, disappointment dripping from his features. "You showed me."

"Whatever do you mean?" I asked innocently and extended the Milk Duds to him. "Thought you might be hungry after all those rice cakes."

He rolled his eyes and started toward the escalators leading up to the theaters. I followed a step behind him, more than ready for this night to be over. An usher took our tickets and led us to seats near the middle of the theater.

Before I sat down, I picked up the gift bag atop the seat, thankful that it would give me something to do other than talk to Ryde. Besides, he was socializing with everyone around us, putting on a good smile like a politician greeting each parent and kissing every baby that he could. Every person he crossed was a well of potential money or power to him. It felt sleazy to me.

Inside my bag, I found an action figure of the superhero character Ambrose played, along with a copy of the book upon which the movie was based. Ambrose stared back at me from the cover, intense and brooding.

Ryde reached over me, dipping his hand in my popcorn bag, and I pulled it away. "Isn't this too high calorie for you?"

He looked around to check if anyone was listening— they weren't— and then said low, "I thought you said you were going to act normal."

I barely contained my eye-roll. "This is normal, didn't you know?"

He turned away from me and continued his conversation with someone else, anyone who would listen to him. The minutes passed on like molasses, and I couldn't wait for this thing to be over so I could go home, put on pajamas, let my hair down, and forget all about Ryde Alexander.

Ambrose and his fellow cast members walked onto the stage in front of the big movie screen, and over the sound system, we could hear them introducing their characters in the film.

Everyone around us seemed excited, and it sucked that this felt like just another day. I was here with a movie star, watching a film before anyone else, and I was still unhappy. What was wrong with me? A pit of dread grew in my stomach. What would it take for me to feel satisfied? To feel like my life wasn't slipping through my fingers before I'd even had a chance to live?

Eventually, Ambrose came and sat next to us, and we watched as the movie began. It wasn't a bad film, honestly. Being the daughter of a major producer helped me know what was good, aside from just having my own opinions. Ambrose was a talented actor, and if he kept his reputation in check, he would have a long career ahead of him.

As the end credits rolled over the screen, we clapped especially loudly for Ambrose. When the final line rolled off the screen, Ambrose leaned over and asked, "Are you guys up for a little after-party?"

Ryde didn't even bother to consult me. "Of course we are."

We followed Ambrose out of the theater, albeit slowly for autographs to be signed. Then we parted ways with him and got into the limo and drove across town to the outskirts of LA. Closer to the manufacturing district in Seaton, which confused me.

"What are we doing here? I asked.

"We usually have parties out here because they're less likely to be caught by paparazzi," he explained.

I didn't respond, just got out of the car when we reached an old warehouse building. A security guard let us in, and we walked into a full-blown party with loud music, a bar in the corner, and seating spread throughout. I wasn't sure how, but Ryde immediately found Ambrose, and they began talking. It was like they had magnets for each other or something.

I found myself quickly bored, leaning against the bar, hoping a bartender would get me a drink. An older man, probably around thirty, came over to me and put his arm around me. "How are you doing, baby girl?"

I shrugged out from under his shoulder. "Just fine *by myself*, thank you."

He grumbled something with a few derogative words and walked off before another guy came over. This one was younger and much more attractive. He smiled down at me, his blue eyes shining. "You doing okay?"

I saw him check my hand—he thought I was old enough for a ring. I wasn't, but that didn't stop my dad from planning my marriage. "Honestly?"

He nodded.

"My feet are killing me, and I'm so ready to be out of this dress."

His eyes twinkled at that last bit. "Well, I couldn't blame you. Can I get you a drink?"

"Yeah," I said, "that would be nice. If the

bartender would actually come this way," I said loudly.

He patted the bar top. "I'll be right back."

As he departed, my eyes scanned the room. I caught Ryde with Ambrose, having a funny moment judging by how much they were laughing. He seemed completely oblivious to the fact that I was there.

Meanwhile, Mr. Blue Eyes was returning with a martini glass that had an orange peel curled around the rim.

"That was fast," I commented.

He handed it to me. "I hope you like it."

I took the drink and carefully sipped. It was strong, but sweet. I made a point to hold it without drinking more. I wasn't exactly in the mood for a hangover on top of everything else.

"So, what brings you here?" he asked.

"I'm here with a friend," I answered. "Loose definition of the word friend. What about you?"

"I worked on set. Remember the control team about halfway through?" His words were free of ego, but I realized I recognized him now.

"You were one of the guys who helped detonate the bomb!" I accused. "You were a bad guy."

His grin glinted. "If it weren't for Ambrose, we would have gotten away with it."

I laughed, shaking my head. This was what a date should have been like—easy conversation and no mention of what I should or should not be eating.

An arm slipped around me, and I looked up to see Ryde. He had a threatening smile on his lips aimed at the guy. "Hi, Dayton."

"It's Dalton," the guy said.

"Close enough," Ryde said with a shrug. "So I see you've met my girlfriend."

Dalton looked between us, confused. "Girlfriend? Sorry, man."

The slightly betrayed look on Dalton's face made me angrier than Ryde butting in. I wasn't Ryde's girlfriend—I was his mail-ordered child bride, if anything. And I should be able to talk to anyone I wanted to without Ryde acting like he owned me.

Dalton left almost immediately, and Ryde gave me a frustrated look. "I thought you agreed to act normal. Why are you hitting on some other guy?"

"I wasn't hitting on him; we are having a conversation. And maybe I wouldn't have had to if my date wouldn't have been off having some bromance instead of hanging out with me."

"Ambrose is my friend. You want me to just ignore him? This is his big night."

"Well, allegedly, I'm your girlfriend."

"Unfortunately."

I narrowed my eyes and walked away. I was done with this. I just needed to get away from Ryde and from the expectations he seemed to have of me. If he didn't remember, he was the one with a choice here. He *chose* to be with me, not the other way around.

"Fine, go!" he yelled behind me.

He didn't need to tell me twice.

I left the building and stepped onto the street. It was spring, so at least it wasn't miserably chilly. I could order a cab and be home before two.

I checked my phone, but the app said they didn't service this area. With all the abandoned buildings, it made sense, but that didn't make my situation any easier. Somehow, all the limos had disappeared, and the street was fairly empty aside from the vehicles of people who lived in the few factories that had been converted to apartment buildings.

An uneasy feeling settled over me. This wasn't

the best part of town, but I held my head high and started walking closer to a service area. I could take care of myself.

From across the street, I heard someone say, "Come here often?"

I looked up and saw the same guy from Halfway Café leaning against his motorcycle, arms folded across his chest.

# TWELVE

I TOOK HIM IN, from the tattoos on his muscular arms to the way his ankles casually crossed over the other.

I glanced down at my dress and shrugged. "Typical Saturday night."

"You're with the celebs?"

"Not anymore."

He glanced around, taking in the empty street around us. "Need a ride?"

I looked down at my dress again and then at his motorcycle. "I'm not exactly dressed for it."

The truth was, my heart was racing just thinking about it. Motorcycles were dangerous—I knew that at least—and what about this guy? I only knew that he delivered delicious Thai food and overly priced coffee. And that he had the most intense brown eyes I've ever seen in my life. Besides that? I had no idea. Why was he out this late? Why was he in this part of town?

What was his name?

"Oh, I get it," he said, shadows crossing his angular face. "You're afraid."

My chin immediately jutted out, like my body knew I was not to be challenged. "Of course not."

"Then you think you're too good for me." His expression was unreadable.

"What does that mean?"

"You saw the way those girls talked about me. They think I'm beneath someone like you. Do you agree?"

He was looking directly at me, challenging me in a way I'd usually only done to myself. And then a new thought hit: he remembered me from the café.

From behind me, I heard Ryde yell, "Zara, what are you doing out here?"

"I'm going home."

My eyes stayed on the guy across the narrow street from me, wishing the one behind me would stay in my past. But he walked right up to us and jerked his thumb at the guy leaning against the motorcycle like he saw movie stars every day. "Who's this?"

I opened my mouth to answer, but remembered I didn't even know his name.

"I'm her ride," the guy said, his voice firm, sure of himself.

Ryde took in the motorcycle, then looked back at me. "You have to be kidding. Your father would never approve of that. Come back inside."

The way Ryde said the words, like he was in charge of me, irked me worse than anything he'd said all evening.

"Give me the helmet," I said to the guy as I stepped onto the asphalt.

A pleased smile crossed his face, and he reached into the back of his bike to pass me a black helmet.

"Zara," Ryde said from the sidewalk in disbelief. "Come on. This is crazy."

I reached the motorcycle and took the helmet. Knowing it wouldn't go over my up-do, I pulled the pins from my hair and shook out the curls. The guy watched me, his eyes burning every exposed inch of my skin, until I had the helmet clipped under my chin.

"You're really going with him?" Ryde asked.

"No, I'm getting away from you."

I had to pull my dress up so I could part my legs enough to get onto the motorcycle. But once I was on, I bunched it up around me so it would stay away from the ground.

The guy said, "Put your arms around my waist."

For a moment, I hesitated. What was I doing?

I should have just gotten off the bike, make up some excuse to Ryde, and went along with my life.

"Zara," Ryde said.

Motorcycle guy must have heard my thoughts, because he turned his head back to me and said low, "Take a risk for once in your life."

Even this stranger knew the type of life I led. It was obvious from the car I drove to the people I spent my time with. I knew, if I was going to take a risk like he was asking, now was the time. I wrapped my arms around his firm middle and held on.

His muscles rippled under my arms as he lifted his leg to kicked the bike to life. I jerked back as he accelerated and took off down the street, then held on even tighter. My stomach bottomed out as he sped into a turn, and the wind blew my hair behind me.

This was like nothing I'd ever done before, but I'd never felt more *alive*.

He didn't ask where I needed to go, just drove. The air became charged somehow, and I recognized the hint of saltwater hitting my nose. Were we driving to the beach?

The big expanse of ocean opening up in front of us confirmed my guess. It looked black this late at night, only punctuated by the white caps of waves. The view became even better as he parked in Seaton Pier's parking lot. He turned off the bike, and I got off. As he slowly lifted his helmet from his head and shook out wavy brown hair, a rush of nerves came over me. What was I doing? I didn't know him at all.

"Come on," he said, turning toward the boardwalk.

Whatever spell he held over me grew stronger as I unclasped my heels and followed him across the boards and onto the sand. About halfway down the beach, he sat down and patted a spot next to him. "Unless you're afraid to get your dress a little dirty," he said, one eyebrow raised.

I was, but I wasn't going to tell him that. I sat beside him and listened to the waves crash over the shore. The sound was cathartic and therapeutic at the same time. How he knew this was exactly what I needed, I had no idea, but I was thankful he was the one I found outside the party.

"What's your name?" I asked. "I'm assuming you don't go by Delivery Boy."

He smiled sardonically toward the ocean. "Ronan."

His hair curled around his ears, contrasting the porcelain of his skin. I took in his arms. One was tattooed more than the other, but it looked like there were more in progress. As I traced the lines with my eyes, I wanted to know more. To know everything.

"Go to high school?" I asked.

"No."

"College?"

He shook his head but left it at that. I wondered what was hiding behind the dark sea of his eyes, mirroring the one before us.

"I go to Emerson Academy," I said, needing to fill the silence.

"I know."

"How?"

"Your uniform." He glanced over his shoulder at me again. His eyes flicked lazily over my bare shoulders. "That morning in the café."

Heat stirred the butterflies in my stomach. Ronan had noticed me. *Remembered* me.

"So, you and the movie star?" He almost said it with a hint of humor. Like my involvement with Ryde amused him somehow. But there was nothing funny about it to me.

"It's over," I said. "Beyond over."

"Why were you with him in the first place? You don't strike me as the kind of girl who likes pretty boys."

I shook my head with a heavy sigh. "I'm not. I'm just a girl with a dad who wants me to date the upwardly-mobile."

"Oh." He drove a finger through the sand, drawing small circles.

Our conversation felt like a dance, between his questions of why I was here and my questions of why he had brought me.

"If you could do anything," he asked, "what would it be?"

"It's not a question of doing anything," I answered. "The question is of *being* something."

"And what would that be?"

"Free."

He smiled at me. "I think we can arrange that, at least for a little while."

# THIRTEEN

HE STOOD from his spot in the sand and extended his hands to me.

"Where are we going?" I asked as he easily pulled me up.

"Walking. Don't you ever get tired of just being still?"

"No," I answered honestly. Sometimes, I wished time would just stop. It seemed like my life was hurtling toward a destination I had no control over and my crash landing was just moments away.

He began walking along the packed part of the sand, his sneakers leaving small indents behind. The moon reflected the shallow impressions. He waited as I caught up, my heels hooked between my fingers and my dress lifted with the other hand.

The damp sand felt cool and refreshing under my bare feet, and with each step I took, I already felt freer. Ronan's aura of mystery still hung over me, though.

"Can I ask you something?" I asked.

He nodded, slowly continuing his path down the shore.

"Why were you outside the club?"

"Just got off work."

I nodded. But something still didn't make sense. "Why did you give me a ride?"

His shoulders lifted in a shrug. "Why did you accept?"

I shrugged too. My stomach growled, standing out even with the crash of waves against the sand.

A small smile lifted his lips. "Hungry?"

"Starving."

"Let's go." He turned course, and we walked together toward the boardwalk.

This time, getting on his motorcycle seemed more natural, and I easily slipped my arms around his waist. I realized Ronan felt solid, more so than anything I'd been holding on to lately.

He took off down side streets and alleys, easily taking each turn like he'd done it a hundred times before until he pulled into the lot of a Thai restaurant. He stopped the bike and helped me off.

"Where are we?" I asked.

"Best place in town," he said. "Hands down."

We walked up sloping cement steps, and he pushed open the back door. Inside the kitchen, several staff worked over sizzling grills. One took notice of him and said, "Hey, Ro."

Ronan lifted his chin. "Can you get us something?"

He nodded and cracked his spatulas over the grill, easily pushing around the food he was preparing.

I fiddled with the clasp on my clutch, wondering how many times Ronan had taken a girl back here.

I was immediately appalled at the thought running through my mind. What claim did I have on him? What right did I have to be disappointed? The only time he'd even touched me was when he said I could put my arms around him on the motorcycle, and even then it was technically me doing the touching. If anything, he was a knight helping me find my way.

Dalton from the club had been far more suggestive in much less time.

The cook shoveled a combination of rice and

meat into a couple takeout boxes and handed them to Ronan along with some plastic silverware.

"Thanks, man," Ronan said.

"Any time."

Ronan walked out the back door and held it open for me. His legs easily took the couple of steps down, and he sat on the bottom step, opening a container.

I sat beside him, deciding I didn't care anymore what happened to my dress. What was it compared to all the other gowns in my closet?

He stuck a spoon into one of the boxes and handed it to me.

"Thanks," I said.

He opened his own box and held it out. "Cheers."

With a smile and a slight shake of my head, I tapped my box to his. "Cheers."

Whether it was the late hour or the company, I had no idea, but it was the most delicious food I'd ever tasted. It melted in my mouth, flavor bursting with each bite. "Oh my gosh, this is so good."

"Told you," he said with a grin.

I turned the box and made a mental note of the restaurant's name. "I'm never ordering food from anywhere else ever again."

He laughed, and the sound warmed me from the inside out. Maybe because it seemed so at odds with his dark exterior or maybe because it seemed so pure. Either way, I had butterflies tickling the edges of my stomach and an easy smile on my lips.

My eyes caught sight of a tattoo surrounding his elbow as he lifted a bite to his mouth. I brushed my fingertips over his skin. "What does this one mean?"

He lifted his arm, examining the black lines and stars surrounding it. "It's a compass."

"I don't see any directions."

For a moment, he looked me over, dark eyes taking me in, and I felt like I had to be utterly still, waiting until he made his decision to tell me or not. "Everyone's so focused on doing what they should, but they don't realize they don't know what they actually want until every other marker is gone."

The meaning behind it caught me off guard. Maybe I hadn't expected something so deep, but now he had me thinking. Did I only want to get away from my father's plan because I didn't like it or because it was my only option?

Ronan took another bite, and I did the same, using eating as an excuse to think some more.

"What about your other tattoos?" I asked. "Why did you start getting them?"

He paused, not moving.

"Sorry," I said, averting my gaze. "I didn't mean to pry."

With quick, jerky movements, he shook his head. "It's just...personal."

That answer only made me want to know more, but we'd reached a line he wouldn't cross and that had me thinking maybe I should draw one of my own.

Despite my curiosity, I simply nodded and busied myself with eating the rest of my food. It really was good.

Over the horizon of dingy shops and closed down storefronts, I could see the sky glowing with the lightening blue hue of twilight. Soon, the rest of the world, including my father, would know about my early exit from the party. I hadn't seen any paparazzi, but there was always someone on the inside looking for dirt to paint the cover of the next day's tabloid.

"I should get home," I said. Before someone else has a chance to hit my dad with the news.

Ronan nodded. "Where do you live?"

I hesitated for a moment, wondering if I should give him my real address or just grab a cab. Something told me I could trust him, though. He'd had hours to do something wrong, and he'd hardly even touched me.

"In Brentwood," I answered. "Near Rolling Green."

He nodded, but I didn't miss the realization that flashed across his face at my mention of the neighborhood. I didn't feel ashamed, though. My family was rich—I hadn't chosen it any more than I'd chosen my skin color or the size of my feet.

He dropped his box in the dumpster, then reached out for mine so he could do the same with it. I handed it to him and walked to his motorcycle, getting the helmet from the back.

Ronan easily swung his leg over the bike and waited for me to get on behind. As he kicked the engine to life and I wrapped my arms around his waist, I couldn't help the overwhelming sense of sadness that this evening was coming to an end.

He took me across town, only asking a few questions at intersections where I could be heard over the roar of his bike.

Eventually, the security guard on the cameras took me in, barely concealing his surprise. Still, the gate slid open, and Ronan continued up the drive.

At the front driveway, he turned off his bike,

and I got off. I held the helmet to my middle, not willing to let go of the night yet.

"Will I see you again?" I asked.

"Only if you want to." A flicker of hope flashed across his eyes.

I nodded and got a pen from my clutch. I wrote my number on the inside of his palm, and when I finished, he held my hand in his.

"I'll call you," he promised, his voice rough.

As I nodded and walked inside, I could only hope he would.

## FOURTEEN

WHEN I WOKE TANGLED in my blankets, every part of me hurt. My feet ached from wearing heels the night before. Soreness permeated my muscles from all the walking and moving. And my eyes burned with exhaustion. Even though what looked like afternoon sun streamed through the window, I was still beyond tired.

Something landed on the bed beside me, and I jerked upright.

My father was in the room, fully dressed for the day in slacks and a dress shirt with his arms folded across his chest. "What is this?"

The rag of a magazine he'd thrown at me had a photo of Ryde and me on the cover with a jagged line through the middle. The title read *YOUNG*

*LOVE GOES WRONG* with a call out saying *How Will Hollywood's Hottie Deal with Heartbreak?*

I shoved the magazine off the bed and groaned. "Couldn't they have thought of a better headline?"

"You think this is funny?" Dad asked, his voice dangerously low.

Rubbing my face, I said, "I'd have to be a little more awake to think anything, much less be amused."

He shook his head in disgust. "I want you showered, dressed, and downstairs in half an hour. Ryde is on his way."

Just the sound of Ryde's name sent a wave of anxiety rolling through me. The night before had been crazy, but I didn't regret any of it. I'd rather spend a night on the beach with a complete stranger over an evening with an image-obsessed celebrity any day of the week, even if it meant facing what was sure to be a nasty article written about me in a magazine.

I got up and made my way toward the bathroom. When Dad heard about how Ryde had treated me the night before—the way he'd spoken about my size—surely he would see this was not a good match. Even the Adam Sandler wannabe with an axe-throwing setup in a bar Dad had set me up with would be better than Ryde. At least I'd get some laughs out of the deal, if only at his expense.

That was it, I thought, as I washed the night before from my skin. I would tell Dad he could choose someone—anyone—else and hope that would be enough to keep him at bay.

After showering, I didn't bother putting on any makeup, and I only dressed in sweats. Ryde was shallow enough that might be enough to get him to call off this whole ordeal. I smiled at the thought. That was my ticket out. My father might still be able to control me, but Ryde was his own superficial, conceited, vain person. He could get out of this if he wanted to.

I lifted my comforter to find my phone, and it tumbled out, bouncing on the mattress and falling on the floor.

A message from a number I didn't know waited for me, and I hurried to open it.

Ronan: *Acribus initiis, incurioso fine.*

I thought back to my ninth-grade Latin lessons and the phrases we had to remember. It brought a smile to my lips.

*Excited for the beginning, careless how it ends.*

FIFTEEN

I SMILED and held the phone to my chest, a giddy excitement working its way through my body. Ronan was like no one I knew. Dark, secretive, brooding, but full of life. Everyone at the Academy or Dad's work was so done up—carefully curated for the external world. My friends had let me in and shown me their real selves, but they weren't full of the danger I saw in Ronan's eyes. My curiosity demanded my attention, drawing my thoughts toward him.

As I pondered his message, I began my trek downstairs. There were several messages from my friends asking about the premiere, and even one with a link to an article about my early exit. I didn't have time to answer their questions yet, so I tucked my phone in my bra and continued to the dining room where I could hear Dad and Ryde's low voices.

I couldn't distinguish them, their words. Not without revealing myself. The moment I entered the room, they stopped talking and turned toward me, looking uncomfortable. What had they been discussing?

I waited for them to speak, wanting a chance to read the mood in the room. Ryde wouldn't meet my eyes. Was he contrite for how he'd acted or still upset with me for leaving?

"Take a seat," Dad said, all business. He got like this sometimes when I'd gone too far off track in his opinion. I could still remember the conversation we'd had after I'd bleached and then dyed my hair lavender my freshman year. It was back to black in no short order.

I sat as far away from him and Ryde as I could get and waited. If Dad felt like he was in charge, he'd let his guard down so I could tell him the truth.

He stood from his chair and paced in front of us. "Last night should have been fun for both of you. Together." He eyed me, and my cheeks heated just thinking of Ronan. "Instead," he pointed at Ryde, "you let the media dictate your actions, which if you expect to have a successful marriage and a long career as an actor, you need to learn better." He turned toward me. "Zara, you let your hot head get in the way of what could have been a great night for you and your future husband."

I opened my mouth, ready to argue, but Dad cut me off with a slice of his hand through the air.

"I don't want to hear it. You're acting like a spoiled child, but soon you will be an adult with real responsibilities and a husband. You need to start acting like it. Not like some wild harlot hanging on to a vagrant from the back of the motorcycle."

"How did you—"

"You think I don't speak with security? Nothing happens in my house without me knowing about it."

Anger welled within me and threatened to spill through my eyes. I hated when I got so angry I cried. I wanted to be calm and not show him how much his words affected me, but my voice shook as I said, "I am not marrying Ryde."

"You are," he said, his voice a delicate balance of power and fury.

Desperate, I looked at Ryde. "You can't want this."

His jaw was set as he stared straight ahead. "I do."

"It's settled," Dad said, resting his hands on the table. "We will continue your dating."

"So what Ryde wants matters more than what I want?" I asked, my jaw trembling.

"You're a child," Dad said. "You don't know what you want... Now, Ryde, go home. Sleep off your hangover and get your act together. Zara, go to your room."

"Happily," I growled and shoved away from the table.

By the time I reached the top of the stairs, the tears had fully built and were streaming down my cheeks. Angrily, I wiped them away and paced my room. I couldn't keep it all in, so I sent a video call to each of my friends. I hoped talking to them would cure this panic rising within me and help me think more clearly.

One by one, their faces appeared on the screen.

"What happened?" Jordan asked the second she saw my expression.

The girls listened while I explained the horrors —and pleasures—of the night before.

Callie's eyes were wide. "I can't believe you rode on a motorcycle!"

"With a complete stranger!" Rory added.

Ginger smiled dreamily. "It sounds like something out of a movie."

"I can't decide whether it's a horror or a satire," I retorted, settling on my bed, the covers still a mess.

"Definitely a romance," Ginger said.

Rory looked hopeful. "Did he get your number?"

My cheeks felt warm, and I couldn't hold back my smile from the memory of his text and the message behind it.

"He did!" Jordan cried. "What did he say?"

I repeated the words, and Jordan looked confused, but the others' eyes lit up.

"He said that?" Callie asked dreamily.

"What does it mean?" Jordan asked.

Rory grinned and repeated what it meant, then added, "The Academy has a freshman Latin requirement."

"Ah," Jordan said. "But he doesn't seem like an Academy guy. How does he know what it means?"

I shrugged. "Unlike Ryde, I have a feeling there's more to Ronan that meets the eye." My heart sank. "Guys, what am I going to do? Dad is going to make me marry him."

Jordan's eyebrows furrowed together. "He can't *make* you, can he?"

I lifted my gaze toward the ceiling, her question one that I'd wondered myself many times. "It's different in Indian culture. Family is everything, and he's all I have."

Callie frowned. "So, it's either marry Ryde and have the family you've always known or don't and be alone. Completely."

Sadly, I nodded. She put the dilemma into words I didn't even have for myself. The totality of the situation struck me harder than ever.

Rory's look was full of emotion. "You know you always have us, right?"

Tears threatened to return as I nodded. I knew I had my friends, but could that replace what I would lose? I wasn't so sure.

SIXTEEN

THERE WAS a note on my door when I woke up the next morning.

*I had to go on a business trip, and I expect you to behave while I'm gone. I get back Friday and will meet you at the house at 6 p.m. to ride together to dinner with the Alexander family. – Dad*

I let out a sigh and crumpled the note before throwing it in the trash. I didn't need to keep the reminder about dinner with the Alexanders. I'd be dreading it all week. Not only would I have to suffer through a meal with Ryde, but I'd get to see Merritt on her home turf, along with her cheerleading coach mother and double-dealing father.

The whole family was a shark pit, and Dad was asking me to walk the plank and become a part of it. I was practically chum to them, and I didn't feel like being ripped to pieces.

I brought my phone to the bathroom and started a song playing while I got ready for the day. Through the Bluetooth speaker, I could make the music loud enough to drown out my own thoughts. Something I desperately needed right now.

The music paused for a moment and then came back at full force. I jumped for my phone, hoping it was a text from Ronan. I'd responded the night before, and my heart had been strung tight waiting for his response.

Ronan: When can I see you?

Zara: Tonight.

I paused the music, waiting for his response, which quickly came.

Ronan: Where?

Zara: Seaton Bakery. 6?

Ronan: I'll be there.

Those three words brought an anticipatory smile to my face. I couldn't wait to see him tonight and learn more about the guy on the motorcycle who made my heart beat faster than ever before. The date had me actually looking forward to the future instead of dreading it.

I finished getting ready with the music playing

and then went to school. I couldn't wait to get to my friends at the lockers and tell them who I was going to see that night, but Merritt blocked my way only a few steps down the hallway.

"Hi, Zara."

"Merritt," I said and kept walking to go around her.

She stepped in front of me again, followed by Tinsley and Poppy. Were they training to move in formation now?

I rolled my eyes and said, "Get on with it."

A muscle in Merritt's neck ticked before a placid smile replaced her look of frustration. "I heard about what happened this weekend, and I just want to let you know, if you break my brother's heart, you will pay." Her eyes narrowed, and her full, glossy lips formed what she probably meant to be an intimidating look.

Honestly, I couldn't help but laugh. She thought I was afraid of what she'd think? She had nothing on my father.

"I mean it," Merritt threatened.

"I'm shaking. Can't you tell?" I took advantage of her stunned silence to continue on to my friends.

Merritt might have been queen of the high

school, but that was nothing compared to the world that was waiting for me after graduation. She wanted to throw cupcakes at me? Have fun getting suspended right before graduation. Wanted to make everyone hate me? Go for it. I probably wouldn't see half of them after we crossed the stage.

I half-expected her to yell "you'll be sorry for this" as I walked away, but she didn't, and I was glad. Unfortunately, she had blocked me from actually telling any of my friends about the date. I grabbed my books from my locker and sent a quick message to the group chat.

Zara: RONAN AND I ARE GOING TO SEATON BAKERY TONIGHT!

Jordan: AHHH!!!

Ginger: Eek! That's awesome!

Callie: Does that mean Jordan can go check him out and tell us how hot he is?

Rory: I'm sure Zara could tell us that. ;)

I smiled as I slid into my seat for class.

Zara: He's hot enough that I'm nervous... Video chat me after school to pick out an outfit?

Ginger: We've got you. <3

My first-hour class began, and I did my best to focus even though I was more excited about this than I had been about anything for a long, long time. Unfortunately, Academy academics waited for no one. With the end of the year looming closer and closer, our teachers were beginning to pack on all the assignments to make sure they covered everything they wanted to during the year.

I focused harder than I ever had before in each class so I could do as much homework during the day as possible. Then, I drove straight home and got to work on the rest of it. I wanted this night to be for Ronan and me, and I wouldn't have my studies distracting me from what could be my last adventure.

After changing out of my school uniform and into a robe, I refreshed my makeup, and then I called my friends. Each of their faces came up on the video screen, along with a couple of extras. Carson was in the screen with Callie, and Kai was sitting beside Jordan.

Callie nodded toward Carson. "Is it okay that we brought them?"

"Yeah," I said, "a guy's perspective could be good." My voice sounded breathy—foreign. When had it gone from strong to insecure? Because of a boy?

I could see Carson's cheeks getting red on the

screen. "I'm not sure that I'm the greatest guy for the job."

True, I thought. He was sitting right next to Callie and still hadn't made a move. "Kai, what about you?" I asked.

He grinned smoothly. "Always up for a challenge."

Shaking my head, I went to my closet. I wasn't sure what the evening would entail, but I thought a ride on his motorcycle was pretty likely. That meant no short skirts and nothing that would be too tight to lift my leg up. That eliminated about a quarter of my wardrobe, so I moved to my dresser and pulled out a pair of leggings, then held out two shirts from my closet.

One was a brightly colored hoodie that was more laid-back, and another a flowy T-shirt in red.

"What do you think?" I asked the others, holding out the two options.

"Red, definitely," Rory said.

Kai nodded.

"It will look so good on your skin," Callie said.

"Agreed," Jordan said.

With a frown, Ginger added, "You're so lucky you can wear red."

I laughed. "Thanks, guys. I'll text you and let you know how it goes."

"Can't wait," Jordan said.

"Good luck," Rory added.

I hung up the phone and took a deep breath. This was it.

SEVENTEEN

I GOT into my car and started across town. By now, I knew the directions to the bakery without typing into my GPS. My friends and I all loved their sweets, and it had become somewhat of a tradition to treat the person you loved with a drink or dessert from Seaton's.

Rory had fallen in love with Beckett in one of the booths, Jordan ate breakfast there nearly every day, and Ginger told me she'd gotten her boyfriend, Ray, his first soy latte there.

What firsts might happen for me at Seaton Bakery?

I didn't play music in my car, because I wanted to think. Like the last bite from a bowl of ice cream, I wanted to savor the flavors of this day and roll them over my tongue. I wanted to remember every-thing about this night, in case it was one I'd be thinking about after all of my hopes had come to an end.

I thought of Ronan and the jagged edges of his jawline, the hard lines of his shoulders and down to his muscled waist. My mind's eye landed on his lips, perfectly curved and arched. Not too full, but not too narrow either. I wondered what they would feel like against mine, if I would ever get to feel them. Just the thought of kissing him sent a jolt through my system. Something about him was like electric-ity… charged, dangerous, and exciting. The fact that he wanted to see me again made me hope that he felt the same way about me.

I reached Seaton and caught sight of his motorcycle farther down the gravel parking lot, held up by its kickstand. It brought back so many memo-ries, despite being just one night. How had it only been a few days ago that I'd done one of the craziest things ever and rode on a motorcycle with a complete stranger? It felt like a lifetime and like seconds ago all at the same time.

I parked my car a few car widths away and walked inside. His forearms rested against the counter as he spoke easily with the guy there. He hadn't realized I'd entered yet, so I watched him for a little bit. Ronan was different here, and in the Thai food shop, than he had been in Halfway Café. Here, he seemed at ease, more like himself. I wondered if he would ever be that comfortable with me. Ever feel safe enough to let down the wall he kept around his secrets.

Like he'd felt me watching, his eyes looked up and caught mine. They were warm, melting, burning like fire.

I didn't mind the heat.

He walked slowly toward me, like he had all the time in the world to make it across the shop, and I waited, my heart pounding and my joints suddenly frozen.

"Zara." My name rolled off his tongue, sending goosebumps rising over my flesh.

"Ronan," I replied.

He nodded toward the counter. "I'm assuming you wanted to eat?"

How could he behave so normally when just his voice had my stomach in knots? I nodded—a safer bet than trusting my voice.

How people ordered when they went out together said a lot about a relationship. About the person. Who spoke first, what would they order, how kind they were with the people behind the counter...there was so much information to be gained.

"I ordered already," Ronan said softly. "What would you like?"

The man behind the register grinned at me. "Jordan's friend, right?"

"Yes," I said. "You're Chris, right? Gayle's husband?"

He chuckled easily. "That's usually how people know me. 'Gayle's husband.' The second-best half."

I couldn't help but laugh along with him. "That means you married up, right?"

"I sure did," he agreed. "What can I get you, honey?"

I got my usual—a pumpkin cream muffin and a latte. Ronan pulled out his wallet to pay, even though I knew my finances had to be far more flexible than his. I didn't bring it up though. If he wanted to pay, that was his decision.

We went down an aisle formed from separated tables, and Ronan sat in a booth in the back corner, his back against the wall. As I sat across from him, I realized how strange it felt to see him in the bakery, sitting across from me. He belonged on an unlit back road gunning his motorcycle engine or backstage at a hole-in-the-wall concert venue. But I didn't mind having him across from me, getting a full view of the way his dark hair curled around his ears or the rise and fall of his muscles as he rested his elbows on the table.

"It's nice to see you face to face," I said.

His lips lifted in an effortless smirk. "I didn't mind having your arms around me either."

My cheeks heated, along with other dormant parts of me. What was going on with me? I'd been on date after date and none of the men, none of them, had ever come close to making me feel this way.

I looked toward the table, trying to hide how much he affected me. "What did you want to do tonight?"

"I don't know," he answered honestly. He splayed his fingers on the table and then curled them under. "When I saw you the first time, I knew I had to know you."

I looked at him, my eyes wide because I'd been feeling the exact same thing. Was it enough that we had this strange connection that I couldn't quite explain? Should I cling to it? Or did that mean I should run as far away as possible?

I chose to stay.

"What do you want to know?" I finally breathed.

"Everything."

I could have told him I was a senior, that my dad was a producer, but that all seemed too bland for Ronan. He deserved the real stuff. Something *more*.

After I told him about my mother, he asked me questions about her, only curiosity in his eyes. I told him about when she got sick, how hard it had been to watch her go through chemo and how devastating it had been to hear they'd done all they could. I shared how *angry* I'd been—how mad I still was—that my dad hadn't let me sit with her in the last days, because he didn't want my memory of her to be at her worst, but that hadn't mattered, because my mom had been my best friend. I didn't care how I remembered her or if I saw the hard parts, because I knew that her last memories of me were that I was absent.

A tear fell down my cheek and I hurried to wipe it, but Ronan put his hands on mine, stalling them in their path. "Your mom knew you loved her."

I glanced up. "How do you know?"

"Because I can see it in your eyes, and if I can, I know she could."

My heart warmed, lightened, as I let go of something that had haunted me for years. How had someone I hardly knew seen through me so quickly? How had he healed my cracks? It unnerved me, unsettled me.

But I couldn't stay away.

## EIGHTEEN

WE FINISHED OUR FOOD, and then Ronan offered to take me for a ride on his motorcycle.

My father would have been livid that I disobeyed him so quickly after our last blowup. But he wasn't here. He wouldn't know. And he didn't care to understand.

We went out to the parking lot, and I slipped what I was beginning to think of as "my helmet" over my head. This time, it was easy to slide my arms around his waist, to hold on tight. I felt the familiar tingle of excitement as he kicked the motorcycle to life and started down the road.

I watched again as the town of Seaton passed around us. There were factories, run-down apartments, and even some people hanging out on the street, holding cardboard signs. I wondered if Ronan was taking me to the pier again, but we passed by that too. There was a scenic road that ran along the coast of California, and often drew tourists from all over just to take in the sights.

Ronan turned onto the road and started north. He drove like he had nowhere to go, but he wanted to get there fast. Sunlight bounced off the rippling ocean, hitting my eyes in rays of magnificent colors. I couldn't tell what was better, the view or the feel of the guy in front of me. His worn-in shirt rippled around his muscled arms, and I trailed the designs on his skin down to his fingers. While everyone else worried about their appearance or got tattoos they could hide, Ronan obviously wasn't concerned about who could see them or whether he could cover them up.

Pink hues had begun to tint the sky when he slowed down at a scenic overlook. We were high up on a set of curves, but there was plenty of space for us on the turn-off as we approached the rocky edge.

My mouth fell open at the scene unfolding in front of us. We could see for miles, not just the ocean, but the rocky walls leading up to a long ribbon of highway with fuzzy city shapes in the background.

"It's beautiful," I breathed and took in some of the fresh ocean air.

"I hoped you would think so." He reached under the seat of his bike and retrieved a woven blanket. I watched him walk, powerfully but meandering, then turned my gaze back toward the ocean. He spread the blanket on one of the bigger boulders, then easily sat and crossed his legs. "You coming?"

My movements were slower, but eventually I came to sit beside him. One thing I noticed about Ronan was that he was still. He didn't force things or pressure something into existence. He let the moment be. And for a little while, so did I.

Sounds of the wind slowly blowing past and the distant echo of waves against the shore formed our world. Only seldomly did a car pass by and break the silence.

"You know," Ronan said, "Emily Dickinson used to talk about the sunset as an 'amber revelation,' but I think she was wrong."

I lifted my eyebrows. "You're questioning Dickinson?"

He smiled. "Only saying that she couldn't see into the future."

"And why is that?"

Ronan studied me much too closely. "When you look into the sun like that, your eyes go from brown to amber." He lifted his hand and brushed back a stray piece of hair that had crossed my face in the breeze. "They're the most beautiful color."

I wasn't used to people who could throw me off guard, but Ronan had. I took him in, his own eyes a shade of brown all their own. My skin was sensitive where he'd touched my cheek, and my mind was just as frazzled. I searched for the first thing I could say and asked, "How do you know Dickinson?"

"You want to know where I met her?" He chuckled softly. Shook his head. "I used to go to Brentwood Academy."

"What?" I couldn't believe the words that had come out of his mouth. Ronan looked like the furthest thing from an Academy kid, but he was quoting Dickinson and texting me in Latin. The pieces of the puzzle clashed and collided, not quite fitting together.

He looked forward, then down at his hands hanging limply in his lap. "You want to know why I look like this."

I felt bad for judging him, but it was the truth. He didn't need my answer to know; he just continued. "My stepfather was the ultimate Academy guy. Ever heard of Roy Taylor?"

My eyebrows came together. "The owner of the Brentwood Badgers?" The guy was stupid rich, and Dad was always trying to work out deals to get his players acting on screen or promoting a movie.

"That's the one," he said with a sigh, seeming disappointed in the fact.

"So why…" I didn't finish my question, just let it hang there, but Ronan finished it for me.

"Why do I look like this? Why do I drive an old motorcycle and deliver takeout?" His words were bitter but resigned. "Because I didn't want anything to do with him, or his money, after I graduated."

I could understand the draw of choosing freedom over comfort, but what had Roy Taylor done that was so bad? "What was he like?"

Ronan shook his head, like he was considering whether or not he wanted to go down this path with me, but finally he said, "Powerful. Demanding. And when he can't get what he wants by pure intimidation alone, he uses force."

The guy sitting beside me was strong, no doubt, but hearing him talk about his stepfather made him look like he was five years younger and much less capable. Had Roy hurt him? The thought of someone laying so much as a finger on Ronan made my stomach sick.

He ran his hands over his tattoos. "You wanted to know why I got these."

It wasn't a question, but I nodded.

His thumb circled a star near the lines of his compass, and upon further examination, I noticed a circular scar underneath the black ink. The closer I looked at his arm, the more of the scars I saw.

"What are those?" I asked. I couldn't imagine anything that would cause such a unique, circular mark.

"Cigarette burns."

As my mind pieced together the round tip of a cigarette and the circular formation of his bruises, I really did feel sick. "Your stepfather did that to you?"

His jaw was tight as he nodded.

So much rage and disgust built in my body, it was hard to keep from shaking. Roy Taylor didn't present as the kind of guy who did despicable things like that to their children and spouses, but here he was, one of the wealthiest and most well-liked people in Brentwood, and he used his power to abuse his stepson. I didn't miss the fact that all the burns were where they would be covered by an Academy's long-sleeve uniform.

I swore to myself that I would never attend another one of the Brentwood Badgers' sporting events again, not as long as Roy Taylor owned the team.

I covered the mark with my hand and said, "I'm so sorry that happened to you."

Ronan's jaw trembled for a fraction of a second, but he simply covered my hand with his and looked straight ahead. It might have been the dim lighting, but as he held me tighter, I swore I saw a tear in his eye.

NINETEEN

WE DIDN'T TALK much after Ronan's confession. I had the feeling that opening up like that wasn't easy for him and that he didn't do it often. Honestly, I wondered if anyone knew about what his stepfather had done. If they had, it would have been in the public eye in seconds.

Had Ronan kept the secret from the public for his stepfather's benefit? I didn't know how I would feel about it if he had. Part of me wanted to tell the police about Ronan's stepfather, but I knew that would just scare him away, and right now, some part of me needed to be near him. Near the realness of him.

When the sun sank behind the horizon, he put his arm around me, and I didn't know if there was a better feeling in the world. He held me to his side like if the sun wasn't going to come up in the morning, at least we would have this night. When the sky faded from dark blue to black, he stood.

The message was clear. We needed to go home. To reality.

He put the blanket away and helped me onto his motorcycle, and then we made the drive back home.

As we pulled into Seaton Bakery, it struck me that we had yet to kiss. He'd only touched me a handful of times, but each contact felt more intense, more passionate than anything I'd had with another guy. No amount of goodnight kisses after dates set up by my father compared to one simple stroke of Ronan's finger over my cheek.

He stepped off his bike with me and twisted his fingers through mine as we walked toward my car. I desperately wanted him to kiss me, to feel his lips, the charge of his skin on mine, but he simply looked at me. His eyes searched me, and I wondered if he was finding what he was looking for. I was beginning to think I had.

"Thanks for tonight," I said.

His thumb traced a slow circle over the back of

my hand, sending shivers down my spine. I kept my gaze on his, looking up into his dark black eyes.

"I want to see you again." He said it like it was an admission, not a wish.

"I want to see you again too," I breathed.

"When?" he asked, throwing the ball back into my court.

"Do you work tomorrow night?"

"Yes. But the day after I'm free."

My mind did the math. I had three days before Dad would be back—in control again. I beat back the fear and focused on the man in front of me. "I'll see you then. Emerson Trails?"

He nodded. "Meet me at the north trailhead."

"I will."

Before I knew what was happening, he bent and kissed my cheek, and then he walked away.

My skin sizzled, imprinted from his touch. As I got into my car, I held my hand to my cheek, wanting to savor the feeling forever. Knowing what his lips felt like on my skin made me want his kiss that much more, but I knew I had to wait. I would be waiting and wishing until the time we spoke again.

I woke exhausted from my late night with Ronan and the hours I lay in bed afterward examining it.

In the last two days, I'd heard nothing from Ryde—no texts, no dates, no gifts in my locker like my friends often got from their boyfriends. And my father expected me to spend a lifetime with him? Could I be brave enough to live a life on my own like Ronan, one of poverty perhaps, if it meant the freedom to choose? I didn't know.

When I got to school, there was hardly enough time to say hi to my friends, but I promised to tell them more about the date over lunch. We sat together in the cafeteria now because the AV room was too small for our growing group. When we first started spending time together at the beginning of the school year, it was the five of us girls and some-times Carson. Now, everyone had a plus one. Everyone except me.

We sat around the round table, pushing too many chairs together so we all fit. Ray and Ginger sat down, immediately swapping out items from their meals. Since she was on the health-food meal plan, he always got extra of the good stuff and gave it to her. Rory and Beckett sat side by side, and the way their arms pressed together, I could tell they were holding hands under the table. What would it feel like to be that in love? Where you could see each other every day and still wanted to hold their hand when you got the chance?

I glanced away from them and caught sight of Jordan and Kai approaching the table. At least they weren't holding hands. But they probably would soon enough.

"Hey, girl," Jordan said, taking the seat next to mine. "I can't wait to hear about this date."

"We have to wait on Callie," I said, craning my neck to find her.

She and Carson walked side by side. Carson had his straw in one hand and shot the wrapper at her. It bounced off her head, and she elbowed him, laughing the whole time.

I groaned and turned back toward the table. "Can't they just admit they love each other already?"

Callie set her tray on the table next to Kai. "What?"

"Nothing," I mumbled.

"Okay," Jordan said, "everyone's here. *Spill.*"

I glanced around to make sure Merritt didn't have ears on our conversation. When I spotted her in her usual seat across the cafeteria with all the football guys, I leaned in and told them all about the night I'd had with Ronan. I didn't tell them about the cigarette burns, because that felt private even to me, but I did tell them about the sunset and the way his kiss on my cheek lit my body on fire.

Ginger had her head rested on her folded hands. "You watched the sunset together? That is so romantic."

"It was," I said, unable to quall the giddy smile on my face. I never thought I'd be the kind of girl who would be watching the sunset at the beach or sitting on the back of a motorcycle, but I liked it.

Jordan frowned. "What are you going to do about your dad? Is he still stuck on Ryde?"

There went my smile. Just a mention of my "boyfriend" had my mood souring. No matter how much I liked Ronan or how much possibility I felt in his touch, when Dad said the word, I'd have to say goodbye.

Callie frowned. "Can you just talk to your dad?"

"I've tried," I said. "I've yelled, cried, begged, pleaded—nothing. He's been planning this since I was a little girl, even telling me about princes and princesses who've had arranged marriages with people fit for them from other kingdoms. He's never even stopped to consider what I want. That I might not want to continue the 'tradition.'" The more I talked, the louder my voice got, and Callie raised her hands in defense.

"I'm sorry," she said quietly. "I know this is hard for you."

"It is," I admitted, feeling heat behind my eyes. "But it's not your problem to solve. Not that there is any solution."

Ronan wasn't what my father wanted for me, not even close, so why did I want him so much for myself?

# TWENTY

THE NEXT DAY, Ryde texted me around five and asked if I wanted to hang out.

I stared at the screen, wondering who had put him up to this. I mean, my father, obviously, but why? Why would Ryde text me of his own volition when he couldn't get bonus points from my dad for trying to be around me?

Out of plain curiosity, I agreed that he could come to my house and hang out. At least that way I wouldn't have to get dressed up again or go out. I had plenty of homework to work on anyway. Maybe I could even catch up and get ahead for my date with Ronan the next day.

Ryde came over about an hour later, carrying two takeout bags. I groaned, already thinking he probably bought me a salad. Catching my expression, he said, "Wait, wait, wait." He put the bags down on the kitchen island and opened a lid on the closest box, revealing an assortment of desserts. Was this his way of apologizing?

He looked down toward the floor and rubbed his arm. "I feel bad about what I said in the limo. You are absolutely right, and I had no business saying those things to you or acting like your body was anyone else's business."

I stared at him, my eyebrows drawn together. "Why the change in heart?"

He shrugged. "I guess I want to make this work, and if I do, that means treating you the way you deserve to be treated."

I raised my eyebrows, still not buying it.

Seeming a little frustrated, Ryde said, "Look, I'm trying. Can you at least do the same?"

With a tired sigh, I nodded and reached for a cannoli covered in mini chocolate chips. It looked delicious. "Where did you get these?"

"La Bella, by the mall."

I nodded. They were one of the better Italian restaurants in the area.

"Maybe someday soon we can go together," he suggested.

I finished the cannoli and wiped the crumbs off my hands. "Maybe after we survive this dinner with your family."

"I think it will be okay," he said, as if his family wouldn't try ripping me to shreds, even with my father around.

Maybe it was because he was used to Merritt. Even though I wasn't afraid of her, I was tired of her. She was constantly trying to see how she could make life miserable for other people, and I hoped for her sake—and others around her—that she would grow out of it.

"What do you want to do?" he asked, leaning over the counter. I didn't miss that he hadn't partaken in any of the desserts.

With a shrug of my shoulders, I said, "Maybe we can go sit outside?"

"Sure," he said. We walked up the stairs to the patio. The hot tub water steamed into the air , and I thought after Ryde left I should come for a soak. It was so relaxing to be in the water and feel the heat warm my muscles. Unlike now. My shoulders were tense just being around Ryde.

Being with him wasn't like being with Ronan. It was a game, a chess match, and I had to make each move carefully, even though I didn't quite know what I was playing for. Up until now, I hadn't been as meticulous with my movements as I should have been, but I needed to get it together and fast.

"How's your dad doing?" Ryde asked.

"On a business trip." I folded my feet underneath me on the chair and opened the takeout box I'd brought out with me. There was a square of fudge that looked especially appealing.

"Who's he pitching this time?"

I took a bite and shrugged. Usually Dad didn't tell me too much about the deals he was attempting until they were already done so he could let me know what he learned, what worked, what didn't, and how he managed to seal the deal. This YA book adaptation was a huge leap from the norm.

Looking disappointed, Ryde nodded.

"How was filming today?" I asked.

Now it was his turn to shrug. "It was fine. We're getting toward the end, and I'm ready to be done with it."

That, I understood. Most people thought the life of an actor was glamorous, but I'd been close enough to the industry for long enough that I knew it wasn't. It was hard work, long hours, and plenty of networking so you can know the right people to get the job. If Ryde didn't get something lined up soon, he could be looking at months or years of auditioning for the next big role.

"How's Ambrose doing post-launch?" I asked.

"Offers for other roles are coming in," he said, a small hint of jealousy in his voice. "Brose could take his pick of pretty much anything. What do you think of the teen lessons?"

The change in subject didn't surprise me. Ryde and I had a hard time actually talking about anything, much less staying on the same subject for long enough to dig beneath the surface. "Honestly, I think the lessons are kind of pointless. What's the point of learning about teens if you don't want to really understand them?"

Leaning back against the patio couch and lacing his hands behind his head, he said, "I wish my parents would try to understand me."

"What do you mean?" I asked, when what I really wanted to know was what there was to understand. That boy was about as deep as a raindrop.

He shook his head. "You wouldn't get it."

"Don't play the poor-misunderstood-me card," I said. "It doesn't look good on a million-dollar movie star."

With an exasperated expression, he leaned

forward and put his hands on his knees. "Okay, I'll play."

"And that means?"

He seemed intrigued, like my dismissal of him got him off somehow. But something else also showed on his face. Disappointment? "When's the last time your parents used your bank account to make a house payment?"

I struggled to keep my expression normal. The Alexander family was struggling with finances? Their father was a leading financial banker on the West Coast, and with her mother as the cheer coach, Merritt got free tuition to the Academy. Why would they have trouble with their finances?

Ryde's expression sobered. "I shouldn't have said anything." He stood up. "Forget I came over."

I wasn't able to get out another word before he walked inside and left me alone on the patio.

## TWENTY-ONE

"YOU SEEM OFF," Rory said in current events after Mr. Sullivan asked us to partner up on covering a local event from that day. "Everything okay?"

"I guess." I took the copy of the *Everyday Emerson* lying on my desk and began flipping through the sections, even though the biggest news I'd heard lately wouldn't be found within the pages.

In the past few days, I'd heard about how despicable Roy Taylor truly was, as well as the Alexander family's financial hardships. I still hadn't told my friends—it didn't feel right to share gossip, especially when I didn't know if the latter was actually true.

"We should cover this," Rory said, pointing at a

headline in the sports section. "*Badgers Owner Donates Millions to Children's Hospital.*"

"What?" I lifted the paper to my face, reading the article.

"Beckett told me about it," Rory said, her head in her hand. "They're building a new wing for the burn unit because of it."

"The burn unit?" I breathed, feeling like the ground was shifting beneath me. I scanned the words, including a sickening quote about Roy Taylor and how much he cared for children and their well-being.

"Are you sure you're okay?" Rory asked.

Swiftly, I nodded and said, "I've already heard of this. Let's pick a different one."

She shrugged and pointed out something else, an editorial about a local, elusive group called *Dulce Periculum*. The headline read *Cops Double Down Efforts to Catch Local Vagrants.*

Still, as much as the capture of DP would affect the town, I could hardly focus on the article through the thoughts rushing in my mind. I thought of Ronan as a child, the irony of his stepfather donating to a burn unit when he himself had scarred his own child. It made me want to punch his worthless face and gently hug Ronan, all at the same time.

"It would stink if DP got caught," Rory said while we waited our turn to present.

"True," I agreed. *Dulce Periculum* was as much a part of this town as the Academy or Seaton Bakery. The club had been doing stunts and pulling pranks for as long as history had been recorded. The best prank of all time was when they disassembled a police car and then reassembled it on top of the Emerson courthouse. They never damaged anything—more like inconvenienced those with power or wealth.

"They kind of brought Beckett and me together," Rory said. "It would be like the end of an era."

I forced a smile and nodded. I knew I was being a bummer, but I didn't know how to pick myself up right now. The only thing I had to look forward to, really, was my date with Ronan. And even though his text said he wasn't worried about how we ended, I couldn't help but feel like graduation was a ticking clock toward the end of life as I knew it.

Rory took the lead during our presentation, and I chimed in where I could, but my mind was already on tonight and what I would say when I saw Ronan. He had been a bright spot in every day since I met him, and I wanted to be the same for him.

After school let out, I went to the mall to buy something for our date tonight, but I realized I had no idea what to get him. I didn't know what he liked to eat or what his home needed or if he would like a particular piece of clothing. Ronan was so raw, existing on his own outside of a need for anything else.

I left the mall without buying anything, thinking that getting the wrong thing would be worse than coming with nothing at all. I got in my car and drove across town to Emerson Trails. The main trail had had plenty of cars parked in the lot, but Ronan had asked me to go to the north trailhead.

I drove around Emerson Trails for several miles until a dirt lot came into view. There was only room for a couple of vehicles there, and his motorcycle had taken one of the spots. I parked behind him, taking in the sight of his lean body propped against his bike. He had a paperback book folded over and was reading it, but at the sight of my vehicle slowing, he closed it and put it under the motorcycle seat.

"What are you reading?" I asked as he walked toward me.

"*The Outsiders*," he answered, coming closer and taking my hand.

My fingers easily slipped between his, and I asked, "Have you read it before?"

"I read it about once a year," he said.

I wondered if he felt like one of the boys in the book, cast away from society, or if there was something else that kept him coming back to the story.

Leaving it at that, he began walking toward the small trail opening. This was one of the offshoots of the main trail, so it was narrower and less kept up than the others, but that meant it was less crowded, even on beautiful spring days like this.

We heard the occasional sounds of cars passing by, but as we walked, it was soon replaced by the audible quiet of the forest, only punctuated by birdsong and the occasional movement of a small animal.

Ronan kept his hand in mine, just walking down the dirt path. It was nice. Ryde and I had only ever been on dates in the public eye or at my house. Everything felt forced, difficult, but with Ronan it was easy because I only needed to be myself.

"I've been thinking about you," he said softly.

I glanced at him and saw a small smile on his lips. "Yeah? What were you thinking about?"

He slowed so he could take my other hand in his, and we came to a complete stop, standing only inches apart from each other.

"I've been thinking about this." He leaned in and carefully placed his lips along my jaw.

Shivers went down my spine, and he hadn't even kissed me on the lips yet. I could feel his breath on my skin, and it was pure magic.

"And this," he added, kissing the exposed skin of my neck.

I was putty in his hands, and all I wanted to do was reach up and run my fingers through his hair, but he held my hands firmly in his. Slowly, he leaned back, and I lifted my heavy eyelids, trying to clear through the fog of want that was building in me and clouding my judgment.

"I've been thinking about you too," I breathed.

He smiled like my response made him happy, and then continued walking. I didn't know how he was moving, but my legs took action on their own, and I continued walking with him. How he could just move on after transforming the spark of need inside me into a blazing bonfire, I didn't know. I simply followed, silently begging for answers. For *more*.

"How was your day?" he asked.

It seemed like such a mundane question for Ronan, but I answered anyway. "I got to pair with one of my friends to cover something in current events." I waited to see if that sparked any recognition, but his face was an unreadable mask.

"What did you learn about?"

I struggled with whether or not to mention the new hospital wing. I couldn't ruin this moment. Ruin the easy way he walked with me and the gentle way he held my hand. Maybe that made me selfish, but was keeping someone from pain ever the wrong answer? "The police are cracking down on *Dulce Periculum*."

He seemed amused by that. "What are they doing?"

I shrugged. "Something about adding extra security around town and questioning of subjects brought in for vandalism."

"But DP doesn't vandalize anything," he said.

"How are we supposed to know that for sure, though? They're about as obscure as it comes."

He shook his head. "Ever since the group started a hundred years ago, people have been speculating about them and making up rumors just because they don't know the truth. People are afraid of what they don't know."

"You seem to know a lot about them. Are you sure you're not one of them?" I teased.

He shook his head. "I did a project on them while I was in school. There's years and years of speculation, but hardly any real evidence."

I simply shrugged. I definitely didn't know as much about them as he did. "One of my friends thinks that they helped her and her boyfriend come together. I guess they saw them on the trails, actually, and it kind of gave her the courage she needed to make a move."

"Sometimes we just need a little push." Ronan smiled, seeming genuinely happy at the story. Was he a closet romantic?

Not much with Ronan was straightforward. I felt like I got little clues every now and then and had to put them together like a detective. Each book he read, author he referenced, micro reaction—they told me more and more about him.

"So why the trail?" I asked finally.

"I figured you didn't want to hang out in a one-bedroom apartment with three other guys."

I lifted my eyebrows. Another clue. He lived in an apartment with roommates. I couldn't imagine fitting four people in a one bedroom, though.

At my expression, he said, "It isn't so bad. I'm hardly around anyway."

"What do you do when you're not working or whisking women away on motorcycle rides?" I asked, a teasing hint in my voice to cover just how much I wanted to know.

"I work out or write at the library." I was barely wrapping my mind around that when he added, "And for the record, you're the only woman who's ever been 'whisked away' on the back of my motorcycle."

## TWENTY-TWO

I LAY DOWN on my bed that night, looking forward to the next morning when Ronan was going to meet me at Seaton Bakery for breakfast. It was the first breakfast date I'd ever been excited for.

When my alarm went off in the morning, there was already a message on my phone from Ronan.

Ronan: Good morning, beautiful.

Three words that completely melted me from the inside out. I found myself smiling giddily, in a way I had never done before. Was this what falling in love felt like? Was this what I would be missing out on if I couldn't change my father's mind about the arranged marriage?

I never wanted to lose the sense of excitement and wonder and happiness that I had in this moment. So I clung to it as I got in my car and drove to the bakery.

I looked around on the road, wondering if I would somehow see Ronan driving to meet me, catch a glimpse of whether or not he was as excited as I was. I hoped he was. When I arrived at the bakery, he was waiting outside, and he came toward me, holding a book.

"For you," he said.

I smiled and took it. It was a book of love poems from the eighteenth century.

"Open it," he said.

I flipped it open, and the book automatically turned to a central page where a light purple flower was pressed inside. It was stunning, better than a massive bouquet that cost hundreds of dollars, because I could tell it had come from Ronan's heart.

"Thank you," I breathed.

His smile was genuine. "You're welcome."

We walked inside together, my fingers slipped through his, and this time, I said, "Let me order. I have a few favorites here."

With a smile, he said, "Okay, I'll go get a cup of coffee."

After I ordered, I glanced over and saw him

pressing drip coffee into a cup and carefully stirring the contents. His body was long and lean, and now I understood why he wanted to write. It was like every part of him was in control—had the strength to be in control. It hurt my heart thinking about the reason why he might need to be so strong, both physically and mentally.

Gayle grinned at me from behind the counter and said, "Hi, Zara!" She lowered her voice. "Are you here with him?"

My cheeks flushed as I nodded.

"He looks like a bad boy." She waggled her eyebrows, then her expression turned serious. "Is he good to you?"

I glanced back at Ronan, who was walking back to our corner booth. Since his back was to me, I lifted the weathered book of poems. "He gave me poetry and a flower." I couldn't believe how happy the simple gesture made me.

She smiled even wider. "Chris still writes me love notes. Sometimes when he flours the counter for baking, he'll leave messages for me so I see them when I go to make the dough."

I'd thought my heart couldn't be any fuller, but it expanded painfully. "My dad used to leave messages for my mom in the shower steam on the mirror. It would disappear when he was done, but when she finished her shower, she could see it there."

Gayle covered her chest with her hands. "That's so precious."

My eyes stung as I nodded. "It was."

A concerned look crossed Gayle's face, but I couldn't indulge my emotions, not with Ronan waiting on me. I wanted this to be a happy day. I ordered muffins for both of us and a latte for me.

When I reached into my purse for money, Gayle said, "This one's on the house."

"Are you sure?" I asked, holding up the bills I planned to pay with.

"Your money's no good here." She lifted her chin toward Ronan. "Have a good date with the bad boy."

With a smile, I nodded and met Ronan, sliding into the booth. Suddenly, it struck me why he always wanted to sit here. He wanted to see every-thing going on in the bakery—who came, who left, who might cause us harm.

I'd never had to worry about that.

Shaking the sadness that gripped me, I pushed a pumpkin cream muffin his way. Ronan wouldn't want my pity, and I needed to honor that, even if he couldn't hear my thoughts.

"This is good," he said appreciatively after taking a bite.

"The best," I said. I took a sip from my latte. Perfection.

He took a swallow from his drink. "I feel like you know everything about me."

I snorted. "Hardly." Ronan was the most elusive person I knew.

"What? You know I live in a one bedroom with four roommates. You know about my stepdad. You know I'm going to be a writer when I 'grow up.' I want to hear about you."

The fact that he wanted to know more about me made me happy in a way I didn't entirely understand. Even my dad, who claimed to want to know me, wasn't as invested in understanding me as I was, only as he wanted me to be. But if I told Ronan how much his question meant to me, I'd become a complete basket case, so I kept it light. "Well, I was born on..."

He laughed, the sound as pure and precious as gold. "The real stuff."

With a shake of my head, I turned my gaze

toward the ceiling. "Of course you would want to know."

His elbows were on the table now as he leaned in. "Tell me."

My eyes followed the movements of his lips, and I swallowed, turning my gaze back to his eyes. "My dad's a producer, which is not as cool as it sounds. I go to school, I do homework, and I tag along to parties where I'm hardly allowed to speak a word. I don't feel that special ninety-nine percent of the time."

"Zara Bhatta." He reached out and tipped my chin up, and the combination of the way he looked at me and the full use of my name had me spinning. "Your value doesn't come from the people around you. Don't let anyone convince you that you don't have a magic all your own. Acknowledge it. Embrace it."

His words formed a lump in my throat. I'd been telling my friends all this time that they were incredible and not fully believing it about myself.

I nodded, owning it. "I'm strong."

The sentence seemed strange coming from my lips, but the second the words hit the air, I knew they were true. I'd dealt with the crushing pressure of my father's business, the devastation of my mother's loss, and now the weight of a future I hadn't chosen. And I was still standing.

Ronan's eyes shined. "And what do you want? More than anything else?"

"To choose my destiny."

An eyebrow quirked as he leaned back. "That's it. The real Zara."

My cheeks felt warm after being so vulnerable with Ronan, even though I'd only spoken a few words. It was like he could see through me, into the core of who I was, but wanted me to see it for myself as well.

He chewed over his muffin, a million thoughts hidden behind his eyes.

The alarm on my watch went off, and I groaned. "I need to leave for school."

"Skip it," he said.

I looked at him, stunned. "What?"

"You said you wanted freedom, right? Spend the day with me."

Nothing sounded better, so I did something I never thought I would: I said okay.

# TWENTY-THREE

ONCE WE FINISHED OUR BREAKFAST, I slung my backpack over my shoulders and got on the back of Ronan's motorcycle.

"Where are we going?" I asked, even though we could have gone anywhere.

"I need to grab something from my place, and then I thought maybe kayaking?"

I raised my eyebrows and dipped to the side so he could see me as he looked over his shoulders.

"What?"

"Does it look like I'm dressed for kayaking?"

He shrugged. "I know a guy." And then he kicked on the engine. "Hold on!"

I wrapped my arms around his waist, reveling in being this close to him with the wind flying through my hair. He sailed through the city, easily taking corners and accelerating into turns. Soon, we were near the part of Seaton where I'd left Ryde at the party.

So much had changed since that night—changed for the better. Ronan helped me see through things in a way I hadn't been able to before. Being with him was like adjusting a camera lens into focus and seeing a clear picture for the first time.

He slowed and parked in almost the exact same spot as that night. "Want to wait here?" he asked.

"And miss out on a chance to see your place?" I got off the motorcycle and shucked my helmet. "Not a chance."

The way he looked at me made me think he was searching for a way to argue, but he apparently gave up, turning and walking toward the old factory building. I hadn't been in any Seaton apartments, aside from Jordan's one time, so I took everything in with a curious eye.

I knew I was privileged just to be living where I did, but I couldn't believe people actually lived in this building with the dingy hallways, dim emergency lighting and old green paint. It didn't seem safe, much less sanitary. The floors were covered in dirt and dog hair like no one was around to manage the building, and a smell hung in the air like a mix of cigarette smoke and body odor. But I tried desperately to keep my expression even. If I had to work with only a high school education to pay my rent, I'd probably be in the exact same place.

Holding his back straight and his chin up, he reached to put his key in the lock, but the door sprang open.

A guy who had to be a year or two younger than me yanked at the handle. "I'm gonna kill him."

"What's going on?" Ronan demanded, stepping quickly into the room. I followed quietly behind him, worried about being left in the hallway, about what might find me.

Another voice from inside called, "He thinks I ate his cereal."

"He did!" the first one growled as he shut the door behind Ronan.

Ronan's head swung around the living room and landed on two guys playing in front of a game console. "Drex, what happened?"

A guy who looked about my age with shaggy blond hair answered, playing the game the whole time. "Brock ate Cruz's cereal."

"Thank you!" the first guy cried.

"But," Drex continued, "to be fair, Cruz finished off the last of the pizza last night."

"See?" Brock said.

The other guy in front of the TV seemed to notice me and did a double take. "Wait, you brought a girl?"

They all seemed to notice at the same time that I was there, their eyes turning to me all at once like I was an alien creature.

I gave them a small wave, suddenly feeling uncomfortable.

"This is Zara," Ronan said. He reached out with a muscled arm and pointed from left to right. "Nico, Drexel, Brock, and—"he put his hand on the shoulder of the outraged one—"Cruz."

"Nice to meet you," I said. They were still staring.

"So," Ronan said, turning back to the guys, "you're telling me I need to make another grocery run."

Brock perked up, his blue eyes looking hopeful. "If you give me the cash, I can do it. You know, save you some time?"

Ronan pretended to laugh. "And have you buy a bunch of junk again? No thanks." He held my gaze a second longer than he needed to, and I reveled in it. "I'll be right back."

With a final glance, he turned and crossed the small living room and began digging through a dresser in the corner. After grabbing a couple of items, he went into a room I assumed was the bathroom.

"So," Drex said, still gaming. "Who are you?"

The direct way he spoke caught me off guard. I instantly liked him. "Zara."

"We know your name," he said.

"Yeah," Brock added with a teasing smile, sitting on the couch with a takeout box. "What are your intentions with our Ronan?"

Cruz folded his arms over his chest and eyed me suspiciously, waiting for my answer.

I opened my mouth to speak when I heard Ronan yell from the bathroom, "Don't answer that, Zara!"

The guys each gave varying looks of frustration and disappointment, and Ronan came back into the room wearing shorts and a T-shirt. I liked the way he looked in his narrow-cut jeans, but damn did seeing the musculature of his legs do something to me.

"Ready?" he asked, running his hands through his curls.

I nodded.

He laced his fingers through mine, which caused wolf whistles and catcalls to erupt in the room.

"Oh, shut it," Ronan said, shaking his head.

With the door closed behind us and noise still erupting from inside, Ronan said, "Children."

I laughed. "How old are they?" They had to be older if they were living on their own, but some of them looked even younger than me.

Ronan looked over his shoulder like he was worried one of them might overhear, then spoke softly. "Brock's sixteen, the others are seventeen and eighteen."

My mouth fell open. "But why..."

"Why are they living in this trash heap?" He grit his teeth. "Their parents are just as worthless as mine, and they needed a place to go."

My mouth went slack, fully understanding the situation. Ronan was caring for four other guys who had been through the same thing as him. And it made me like him that much more.

# TWENTY-FOUR

HE DROVE CLOSER and closer to the shore until he reached the Brentwood Marina. I wondered what we were doing here, since he'd mentioned kayaking earlier, but then we reached the Walden Island Ferry. He parked in a nearby lot and took my hand. "Have you ever been to the island?"

I shook my head. It had never topped my dad's list. Why go to Walden Island when you could go to a private beach in Barbados? "I haven't, but my friend's been there a couple of times. She and her boyfriend carved their names in the cave there."

He lifted his eyebrows. "That's supposed to be off limits now. How did they do it without getting caught?"

I smiled and shook my head. "They went when the island was closed."

"Ah." He reached into his pocket and gave a few dollars to the ticket taker. They gave us a couple of stubs, and we walked over the metal bridge to the boat. It rattled under my feet, and I couldn't help feeling self-conscious. Most of the time I felt good about myself, but next to Ronan's light steps...I questioned myself. Did he notice? Did it bother him?

If it did, he didn't give it away. He kept a hold of my hand and led me up the stairs to the top level. There was hardly anyone here, since it was a weekday, and we got one of the tables closest to the railing. We had an amazing view of the dark blue ocean and miles of shoreline. In the distance, I could make out the fuzzy shape of the island we'd be going to.

"How long does the ferry take?" I asked.

He shrugged. "Half an hour? Give or take."

I nodded, but I could hardly focus on his answer. He'd yet to let go of my hand, and even though we had all this beautiful scenery around us, I couldn't stop taking in every single detail of his hands.

They were rough, clearly not moisturized or

manicured like Ryde's regularly were. I felt callouses along his palms where he gripped his motorcycle handles, and his knuckles protruded, large and stable. The nails were short and broad, utilitarian. These hands were capable, in the best possible ways. His skin was olive toned, but not quite as dark as mine. I liked that both of our skin got darker at the knuckles, lighter around the pads of our fingers.

He swept his thumb over the back of my hand. "Have you ever skipped school before?"

I shook my head. "Did you?"

He scoffed. "Does the last year count?"

"You didn't graduate?"

"No." His eyes were dark, even with the sunlight trying to lighten them. "I packed up my bags one night and left. Figured the streets would be better than where I was. Shade, this guy who lived in the apartment before me, took me in, kind of like the other guys. On the condition I got my GED."

"Where is he now?" I asked.

"Married, kid on the way, working in construction and living the life." His features eased at the topic of Shade. I could feel how much he respected him—looked up to him.

I had to know more, to feel more of this levity

that had come over him. "What would 'the life' look like to you?"

His lips curved softly, and he met my eyes. "Married, a kid on the way, working as a writer and living the life."

The thought of Ronan as a father warmed my heart in a way I didn't understand. He practically fathered the other guys in his apartment this morning. How would he be with a smaller version of himself?

"Have you ever thought of getting your BFA?" I asked, "Studying creative writing?"

"No way," he said, casting his gaze over the ocean. "Everyone acts like writing is a formula you can follow. It's not something you know. It's something you *feel*."

I could have listened to Ronan talk about writing for hours. "What do you want to write?" I asked, if only to keep him on the subject.

"Something that makes people see there's more beneath the surface."

"What do you mean?"

He gestured at the scant other people on the deck with us. "What do you think they see when they look at me?"

I tried to picture Ronan from their eyes,

imagine him as how I'd first seen him, but I couldn't imagine him as a stranger anymore.

"They see me as a tattooed thug. They never think there might be something behind the tattoos, that I might have more to offer."

The thought made me sad, especially since I already knew how incredible Ronan was. "So you're speaking for yourself?"

"And everyone else who's ever felt like they didn't have a voice."

I took in his words, felt them. What if we'd been doing this whole storytelling thing wrong in Bhatta Productions? Sure, the company entertained millions. But what was there beyond a quick thrill here and there? Was that what the YA author my dad had met with thought was missing? That level of feeling? Of understanding?

I couldn't wait to tell Dad about this, to see if I could help him find ways to inject more emotion into the stories to help people like Ronan feel more understood. Less alone.

Ronan stood, and I realized the ferry had stopped moving. We were here.

"Come on." He helped me up and put his arm around my waist. "Today will be fun. Have you been kayaking before?"

"Once," I answered. Beth had taken me on a kayaking tour when we'd tagged along on one of Dad's business trips to the Virgin Islands. But that wasn't exactly the same as going with an Italian eyepiece like Ronan. "Are we just wearing our regular clothes?" I asked. I may not have gone to the beach much, but I at least knew the Pacific was a regular ice bath in April.

"Don't worry," he said. "I know a guy."

"Of course you do," I said. He seemed to be just as well connected as my father, but instead of movie financiers and acting talent, Ronan seemed to know all the important people. Like the owner of the rental shop we were approaching.

The middle-aged man with stringy, thinning hair slapped Ronan's hand and patted his back. "What do you need, man?"

"Can you hook us up with a kayak and a couple suits?" Ronan asked easily, like he was letting his friend in on a secret.

"Sure thing." The wrinkles around his friend's eyes deepened as he grinned at me. "You must be a special girl to steal this one's heart."

I didn't miss the blush on Ronan's cheeks. No one had planned to steal anyone's heart, but I found mine becoming Ronan's with each day that passed, with each fact I learned about him.

The guy handed me a suit and led me to the small lean-to covered with a curtain where I could change. I easily took off my uniform and squeezed into the suit. It sucked tightly to each part of my body, and I couldn't help but hope Ronan would take notice of my curves in this. I knew they looked good, especially with all the work I'd been putting in to stay healthy. Would seeing me up close like this help him make the move to kiss me on the lips? I ached to feel his mouth on mine, to discover what it would feel like to have his arms around me, exploring my body.

"Ready?" Ronan called.

I plucked at the suit and readjusted a spot around my waist. "Ready."

The curtain whipped to the side, revealing Ronan in his wetsuit. It wasn't completely on, the arms wrapped around his waist, revealing his muscled chest and toned abs.

While my jaw practically rested in the sand, his eyes hungrily took me in. The power of the wetsuit. He whistled low and said, "You look good."

I chewed on my bottom lip. "You think so?"

His hands easily slid around my waist and settled somewhere on my hips. "I know so."

We were close now. Close enough for me to feel his breath on my cheek, for the heat from his hands to radiate through my body. I only had to lift my hand an inch to press my palm to the swell of his abs. His skin was warm under my fingertips, his muscles firm.

He closed his eyes like he was trying to compose himself when all I wished was that he would give in.

He linked his fingers with mine, removing them from the plane of his stomach, and led me toward the shore where I could see his friend now, situating two kayaks he had pulled off one of the stands. One was bright yellow, and another was electric blue. Ronan released my hand and easily took hold of one of the kayaks, stepping into the water like it wasn't cold.

He held it and looked back at me. "Go ahead and get in."

It was the equivalent of holding a door open, keeping my kayak steady, and I didn't hate it. Still, nerves took over my body. He was strong, but I wasn't the smallest girl. What if he couldn't steady it as I got in?

"It will be fine," he said, as if sensing my concern.

Yet again, here was Ronan helping me feel heard without ever speaking a word. Trusting him completely, I stepped in and slid into the seat with my legs extended in front of me. Ronan's friend handed me an oar while Ronan easily climbed into the blue kayak.

His friend pushed me off into the water, and Ronan paddled alongside me. Like he'd done it a hundred times before, Ronan told me how to dip my paddle in the water to send me forward, turn, and stall without splashing the icy water over me. For a while, he took it easy, letting me get used to working the kayak on my own, but then he started paddling farther away from the shore. I followed him until the waves weren't crashing against the front of my kayak, but rocking me gently.

The soft sound of the waves blended with the distant sound of gulls was music to my ears. When was the last time I'd been able to depart from the city and just be? It had taken Ronan to get me outside of myself, outside of the daily turmoil my lifestyle put me in.

"How did you learn about this place?" I asked.

He rested the oar over his lap. "I worked here for a summer once."

Ronan spoke like he'd lived a thousand lives, even though he was only a year older than me. I simply nodded, mulling over the questions in my mind about him and his life and the way he viewed the world. I'd never met someone with such a simplistic, straightforward perspective, and it was more than refreshing. It was inspiring.

"Are you cold?" Ronan asked.

I shook my head. Between the wetsuit working its magic and the sun's unimpeded rays, I felt great, but maybe Ronan had more to do with the warmth I felt radiating from the inside out.

"Good." He slipped his oar into the water and paddled, moving farther yet away from the shore. I followed him, admiring the way his shoulder muscles moved underneath the wetsuit. Soon, we were so far out that the beach behind us and his friend's rental store appeared as fuzzy lines in the distance.

"Do you see that?" Ronan asked.

"What?" My eyes scanned the water, looking for any hint of what he'd spoken about.

He pointed his oar in the water. "Orcas."

I followed the tip of his paddle and saw the

three dark shapes moving through the water. Amazement made my heart beat faster. "No way! I've never seen them in the wild like this!"

He grinned up with me. "Sometimes all it takes is a new perspective."

I had one all right, and Ronan had given it to me.

TWENTY-FIVE

WHEN THE SUN reached high overhead, we decided to head back to shore. I was thoroughly wet from a splash fight we'd had, and I felt thoroughly content for maybe the first time since my mom had died. This had been one of the best days of my life, and it had been entirely unplanned. It reminded me of the time Mom let me skip school and go see a movie with her. It was a couple of months after she'd been diagnosed with cancer, but we didn't talk about it the whole day. The entire theater had been completely empty, and she'd given me my own big bucket of popcorn. I'd felt like such a grown up, like her friend instead of her daughter. It was one of my favorite memories with her.

The thought still had me smiling when we

reached the shore and Ronan helped me out of my kayak. My feet sank into the ocean bottom as the waves lapped around my ankles. I realized I was hungry, excited to see where Ronan would take me for lunch. He seemed to know all the best places.

But first, we went to his friend's shop, and he greeted us with a big smile that I think must have been there permanently. "How was it?"

"Great," Ronan answered

"We even saw some orcas," I added excitedly. The giddiness of my response felt so foreign to me, but so *right*.

"It's a good day for that."

Ronan nodded. "We better change. I want to take her to the Crab Shack for lunch."

Crab? That sounded delicious.

We took turns changing, and then began walking down the street to the restaurant. The only vehicles on the island were emergency or working vehicles, so we didn't have to worry about traffic. It was nice, just meandering down the pavement like we had nowhere to go.

Once we reached a stand of shops and restaurants a few hundred yards away, Ronan turned off the street.

Unlike the Thai place, we didn't go in through

the back or eat on slanting cement steps. We sat in the main dining area with plates loaded with fried calamari, French fries, crab legs, and onion rings.

"This looks so good," I said.

Ronan opened his mouth, but paused.

"I'm glad to hear you think that," said a voice from behind me. An older woman with short hair smiled at us.

Ronan broke out in a grin and got up from the table to hug her tight. She smiled against his chest, squeezing him tighter.

I'd never witnessed him being so excited to see anyone before, and I watched the two with mounting curiosity. When they let go of each other, she kept one arm around him and he her.

"Zara, this is Norma. She's practically my grandma."

"Practically?" Norma said, pretending to be offended. "As far as I'm concerned, I *am* your grandma."

Ronan grinned. I was still taken aback to see him so lighthearted and at ease. This whole day, it seemed like I'd seen another side of him, a lighter side, and it made me like him even more.

"I hope you're treating my boy right," Grandma Norma said with a wink.

She had the kind of smile that made me feel like she was already my best friend. It was easy to return the expression. "Of course," I answered. "Only the best for Ronan."

Ronan cast me an appreciative smile, like I'd just aced a test I hadn't known I was taking.

She sat down at the table with us. "I hope you don't mind if I join you. It's been forever since I've seen this young man."

"One year," Ronan said.

"Forever," she clarified.

"Please, sit," I said. I reached for one of the appetizer plates and extended it to her. "Do you want to try some of my calamari? It's delicious."

She batted her hand at me. "I can always go back and make myself some if I'm hungry. I'm glad you like it, though."

Grandma Norma owned the restaurant? Of course Ronan knew her.

Then she looked at Ronan. "I like this girl.

Ronan popped a piece of popcorn shrimp in his mouth and grinned at me. "She's a pretty good one."

I loved the casual way he said it and the look in his eyes as he did. Like the words had even more meaning behind the simple statement.

For the next half hour or so, I listened as they caught up about the town and people who made a living there, commuting back and forth on the ferry every day. They even shared about the summer Ronan had stayed there between his junior and senior year.

Slowly, I was piecing together the story of his life, and I didn't mind the gradual pace like I thought I would. Instead, each hint of information felt like a precious gem, a gift to add to a priceless collection.

"I saw your stepfather donated all that money to the hospital wing," Grandma Norma said. "You must be so proud."

The entire mood changed like a dark cloud had covered the sun and sent us into shadows. A blank look crossed Ronan's face. I realized he was processing behind an emotionless mask. Finally, he said, "Yes, definitely proud."

The words weren't even bitter. They were worse. Lifeless.

"I mean, twelve million dollars to build a burn unit," Norma gushed. "That's pretty special."

Ronan slowly chewed and swallowed. I longed to grip his clenched hand, to smooth the line deepening between his eyebrows. This woman didn't know what his stepfather was like, or else she wouldn't have been asking him, wouldn't have been saying those things with such a sense of awe and admiration.

The door opened, and someone walked in. Upon catching sight of the man, Grandma Norma looked to Ronan and said, "I'm sorry I have a meeting. But I am so happy I got to see you and meet this sweet girl." She squeezed him tight, and he gave her a hug back, even though I could tell he was still struggling with the news. I had wondered whether he knew about it, but now it's obvious he had not. I couldn't imagine how he felt.

A swear word I hadn't heard from him before fell from his lips, and he said, "I need to get out of here."

"Go," I said. "I'll pay."

He stiffly stood from the table and walked outside, flinging the door open too fast. The bells clanged roughly against the glass, and I cringed, quickly reaching into my purse for some bills.

I tossed a hundred on the table and hurried after him. He was already across the road, in a sandy patch of the island. He fell to his knees and ripped at his hair, letting out a strangled, guttural cry.

This wasn't strong, capable Ronan.

It was broken, twelve-year-old Ronan, hurt by the man he should have been able to trust. In his yell, I felt his rage, but more so, his hurt. His *betrayal*.

Each yell pierced my chest. I had to grip at my heart just to keep from falling apart.

His yells broke into rough sobs. Not the kind that faded, the kind that came from deep in your core, from your deepest wound.

What did Ronan need in this moment? I didn't know. I just knew what I could do, and that was be there for him. I walked beside him and sat in the sand. Not touching him, not speaking, just being there.

He glanced at me from the side of his bright red eyes, and seeing an opening, I reached for his hand.

He squeezed it back, his jaw clenching. "I need to get you home," he said, his voice rough.

Because it was the only thing he'd asked for, I said, "Okay."

# TWENTY-SIX

WE RODE the ferry in silence, and then he drove us straight to Seaton Bakery, quiet the whole time save for the wind and the roar of the motorcycle's engine. When we got back to the parking lot, I climbed off of his motorcycle. As I took off my helmet, he looked at me, regret in his eyes. "I'm sorry for earlier."

I reached out, touched his hand on the seat of the bike. "Don't be."

He held my hand, then lifted it and pressed it to his cheek. "Meet me tonight?"

I nodded. "When? Where?"

"The north trailhead. Eight."

After he sped away, I spent the rest of my afternoon texting my friends to explain why I hadn't been in school and thinking about Ronan. Sometimes he could become such a blank slate that it was hard to know what he was thinking. I just wanted to wrap him in a hug and tell him that I was there for him. That I *believed* in him. Soon, I hoped I would have the chance.

Unfortunately, when I drove my car to the north trailhead that night, Ronan's bike was in the parking lot, but he was nowhere to be seen. I got out of my car and called for him, but nothing. I got my phone out of my pocket to text him.

Except there was already a text from him to meet him about half a mile down the trail.

Half a mile? Thank goodness I'd dressed in leggings and tennis shoes in case he just wanted to walk again, but now I wondered what he had in store. Was he planning a surprise? A picnic maybe? I wasn't hungry yet, but the thought of Ronan's lips sparked my appetite. I wanted to know what they would taste like pressed to mine.

I thought about getting my headphones out and listening to music as I walked, but decided against it. I didn't want Ronan to surprise me and me shriek so loud I'd embarrass myself. No, I wanted to be my best self when I saw him.

I passed the quarter-mile trail marker and

continued walking, each step building the anticipation within me. I found myself walking faster, wanting to get to him already.

A rustling in the trees stopped me short, and I froze. I wasn't at the half-mile mark yet, and this was one of the more neglected trails. Was someone here? I could be murdered and no one would know for hours—days maybe. My heart sped, and I reminded myself that the only vehicles in the parking lot had been mine and Ronan's. Still, who or *what* was making the bushes shake? "Hello? Ronan?"

An excited cry rang out, and soon I saw people flinging themselves from tree branches, flipping and tricking through the air. One carried a black banner that read *DP* in pearlescent white letters.

I watched in wonder as they swung past, perfectly at ease and in control, but whooping and hollering with gleeful shouts.

They all wore masks that covered their facial expressions, but I could imagine the smiles each of them had. They seemed at ease with themselves in a way I hadn't seen someone be before.

As the last of them passed, I looked at the place they had been in wonder. Had Ronan planned for me to see them? How had he known where they'd be?

At that moment, one of the guys leapt back into my view, hopping easily from tree to tree until he dropped right in front of me. I didn't need him to remove the mask to recognize the beautiful brown eyes staring back at me.

My lips parted in shock. Ronan was in *Dulce Periculum*? And he was telling me about his membership in one of the most elusive groups of all time? The weight of that hit me full force. I reached out and lifted the bottom of his mask, rolling it up until full lips, sharp cheek bones, and a crop of dark wavy hair came into view.

His dark eyes seared into mine, melting me from the inside out. My mouth opened with the intention to speak, but no words came. Maybe that was good because I didn't want to speak anymore.

I leaned forward, and he met me with his lips in a collision of everything I'd been dreaming of since I first met him, first spoke to him, first felt his lips on my skin.

Our mouths and tongues tangled in a dance of passion and longing and hunger. In that moment, I realized how much Ronan had been holding back all this time. He had wanted to kiss me just as much as I had wanted him to.

His hands slowly roamed my body, feeling my back, the swell of my curves and the sensitive skin around the hem of my shirt. I wanted him to continue exploring, continue claiming all of me as all of his. Because after this kiss, I knew there was going to be no one else. No one had ever made my skin come alive, like my nervous system was attuned to only him. And there was no way you could walk away from a fire and settle for a candle. Because that was what Ronan was. Beautiful, dangerous, and full of *heat*.

That heat spread within me, and I felt like I couldn't get close enough to him. I gasped for air, not wanting to part from him even to breathe. I needed him more.

When he finally pulled back and rested his forehead against mine, he was breathless, his short gasps for air matching my own as his exhalations caressed my skin.

The truth of what he revealed to me settled in. "You're the leader of *Dulce Periculum*," I said. And I'm never going to meet anyone like you again, I didn't say.

"Yes," he said simply. "I wanted to let you know

that I'm all in, if that's what you want. Will you have me?"

The weight of what he was saying pressed in on me. Would I agree to choose him too with my dad so resolved on my marriage to Ryde? Would I risk my family for this person standing in front from me?

But then again, would I risk my heart? I'd have to live with it every second of my life.

Slowly, I nodded and kissed him again. After all, *fortune favors the bold.*

TWENTY-SEVEN

THAT NIGHT, I texted my friends and called them for an emergency breakfast at Waldo's Diner before school the next day. I hardly slept that night, still thinking of the way Ronan had touched me. My skin was still charged from being that close to him. If I touched my lips, I could almost feel his warmth from earlier. I couldn't wait to tell my friends about the day before... and the decision I'd made.

The first person I saw when I walked into Waldo's Diner was Chester. The old man smiled up at me from his newspaper and said, "Hey, girl, how you doing?"

I knew he was probably just calling me 'girl' because he couldn't remember my name, but he sort of had a pass, being older. I smiled at him. "I'm good. How are you doing?"

He set his paper down. "Same old, same old. I heard they're getting ready to tear down the animal shelter across town."

My eyebrows came together. "Emerson Rescue?"

He nodded. "Not enough funding. It's all about money, isn't it?"

I lifted the corner of my lips. I knew that, and I was only seventeen years old.

He nodded his head toward the back of the restaurant. "Your friends are already back there. Better go meet them."

I smiled. "See you around."

As Chester said, my friends were sitting in our usual circular booth, looking at their menus.

"Hey," I said in greeting.

Menus immediately forgotten, they looked up at me, and Ginger said, "If you don't tell us the whole story right now, I'm going to lose it. The anticipation is *killing* me."

Laughing, I settled into the booth beside Callie. "Where to begin?"

Ginger gave me a look.

Rory said, "Start with skipping school! Why did you ditch? No one ditches at the Academy."

"I wasn't planning to skip yesterday, but Ronan offered me to hang out with him, and I said yes."

Callie shook her head, like the thought of breaking a rule was obscene. "That was it? He just asked you?"

"I don't know why I said yes." I looked down at my hands on the table and picked at the back side of my acrylic nails. "I guess I just thought it might be one of the last crazy things I get to do before graduation."

Callie's expression changed from shock to understanding. "You had to go," she said.

Feeling understood gave me the courage I needed to say the next words. "You know when you guys said you'd be there for me if I backed out of the marriage and my dad disowned me?"

They looked at each other and nodded.

"Is that offer still good?" I bit my lip, terrified of their response.

Their eyes widened, as if they were understanding what I was saying.

"Of course," Jordan jumped in. "Our new place has an extra bedroom. It's not anything like you're used to, but it's yours if you want it."

"I do," I said.

Ginger's mouth practically fell to the table. "You're going to tell your dad about Ronan?"

I shook my head. "It's not about Ronan, not really. He just showed me what I'd be missing out on if I committed to Ryde. I'm going to tell him that I don't want to get married after graduation. And that I want to choose the person I marry—if I ever do get married." I took a breath and continued.

"I'm tired of always having to live according to this arranged marriage nonsense, like having a husband is life's purpose. Going on dates with older men when I should be having a good time, enjoying my last year of high school. We're not in India anymore; we're in the United States, and even though I still love my culture and my Indian heritage, I don't need to keep all of it. Eventually, I'll need to choose which culture is mine."

"When are you telling your dad?" Rory asked quietly.

"After my dinner with the Alexander family tonight." A sense of purpose settled over me. I would tell my father that Ryde and I would not be getting married. That I was going to choose my own path, one that included Ronan, and I was willing to take the consequences.

If Ronan could be so brave to leave behind a life of wealth and forge his own path, I could do the same. Especially with my friends and someone like him at my side.

Ginger reached across the table and rubbed my shoulder. "Good for you."

Rory chewed her lip. "What do you think your dad will say?"

My chest tightened at the thought. "Best case scenario, he's angry with me and doesn't speak to me for weeks. Worst case scenario, I'm going to need that extra bedroom. And a job."

Beside me, Callie stayed quiet.

"What do you think?" I asked her. Of all of us, she had the biggest heart. Maybe she had picked up on something I was missing.

"It sounds like you have your mind made up," she said, not quite meeting my eyes. "What do you need? How can I help."

"That wasn't an answer," I accused.

She turned her blue eyes on the table, and then looked back at me. "Do you think it's too soon to be making major life decision based on some guy you hardly know?"

Her words sliced through me like a knife in the back. Some guy? "First of all, Ronan isn't just *some guy*. He's kind, vulnerable, honest, and brave. All qualities that I want to have in my life. For myself. And second of all, marriage is a major life decision. Don't you think I should have some kind of say in it? I've been wanting to make my own choices for a long time, long before Ronan."

"Of course I think you should have a say," she said. "That's not what I meant. I just want you to make the right choice for you."

"I will," I said, "now that I actually have a choice."

Ginger nodded. "What can we do for tonight? Do you need help getting ready or planning what you're going to say?"

I shook my head. Planning it and overthinking it would just ensure that I wouldn't follow through when I had the opportunity.

"But I did want to give you some bags to take to your place," I told Jordan. "Just in case I can't get home or to my car."

She nodded somberly, and I could see the reality hitting everyone's faces. I could be homeless before high school graduation.

After we finished our breakfast, we got the bags

transferred over and went to the Academy for another day of school.

Now, all there was to do was wait for the moment when I would see my dad after dinner and tell him the hardest words. That his dreams for me were not going to come true because I had an even bigger dream for myself.

## TWENTY-EIGHT

I DRESSED in a simple LBD for the dinner at the Alexanders'. I didn't know why Dad was pushing for us all to get together tonight, but it would be fine to deal with them all at one time. A Last Supper of sorts.

While on the drive, I sent a text to Ronan. He seemed to be like my sunshine in the dark cloud of reality.

Zara:  How was your day?

Ronan:  Good. Except for Brock eating the rest of our cereal.

Zara:  Didn't you just buy like three boxes yesterday?

Ronan: Four.

Zara: How can you eat that much cereal and

not get sick?

Ronan:  He should be studied for science.

Zara: What are you doing tonight?

Ronan:  Editing. I thought you had a family dinner thing tonight?

Zara: On my way there now. (Not driving.)

Ronan: Hey, I don't judge.

Zara: True. You do drive a motorcycle. Clearly a disregard for safety.

Ronan:  Hey, you rode on it.

Zara: Touché

Ronan:  I'm glad you texted. It was hard to think about my writing with you on my mind.

Zara:  I wish we could hang out tonight.

Ronan:  Soon.

With that promise, I sent him a goodbye text and put my phone in my purse. We were pulling down the Alexanders' elaborate winding driveway with perfect hedging and an expensive stretch of bright green lawn. I wondered whether Ryde was helping foot the landscaping bill as well. And why they needed him to.

The car came to a stop, and I heard the driver come around to the back. My door swung open, and I stepped down. My father got out of another black car at the same time.

"Zara," he said. "It's good to see you." He folded me into a hug, and I hugged him back tightly, knowing that it might be one of the last I had for a while. I tried to imprint his scent of tea spices and cologne on my memory. I would miss that if he couldn't understand.

He tried to pull back, but I still held on. Smiling down at me, he said, "My daughter actually misses me? Remind me to go on business trips more often."

I smiled up at him, a little embarrassed, and backed up. "Sorry, it's just good to see you."

He extended his elbow for me, and I put my arm through his.

"Let's go inside?" he suggested.

"Sure," I answered, squeezing his arm just a little tighter.

He pressed the doorbell, and we heard echoing chimes throughout the inside of the house. Within moments, a woman in a simple black and white uniform answered the door. "Welcome to the Alexanders'. Come inside. May I take your coats?"

Dad slipped out of his blazer and handed it to her, while I gave her my jacket. I examined the broad entryway, filled with natural light coming in from stained-glass windows, expensive-looking decorations, and ceilings that stretched at least twenty feet in the air. It might have looked like a church if not for the modern art pieces lining the hallway.

After the maid had our coats, she led us into a sitting room where the Alexander family was relaxing on plush furniture, sipping from crystal glasses.

Upon seeing us, Pam Alexander, Merritt and Ryde's mother, came to greet us. She extended her arms wide and gave my father a kiss on each cheek, and then she pulled me into a hug. Her chest was hard, and I barely kept from gasping in pain.

Merritt smiled to us from her seat. "So happy to see you both," she said, being the perfect daughter.

Both Ryde and his father were drinking amber liquid and arguing with each other about something. They hardly even noticed we were there.

Ronan only had eyes for me when we were together. Just another painful reminder of how *wrong* this match was.

"Boys," Pam said with a tight smile, "greet our guests."

If only because they didn't want to get in trouble, they stood to greet us and Ryde came to put his arm around me. As the uncomfortable touch weighed down my shoulders, I had an idea.

Maybe I didn't need to tell Dad I wasn't going along with this "relationship" anymore. All I had to do was get Ryde to back out and I'd be free—at least for a little while—and then I could explain to my dad how well I was doing without the pressure of an arranged marriage. Time was a precious resource at this point.

"What would you like to drink?" Mr. Alexander asked my dad.

Dad answered his favorite drink—a Manhattan —while I whispered in Ryde's ear, "Can I speak with you privately?"

He nodded with a smirk and said to his mom, "Excuse us for a moment."

She giggled like a schoolgirl and said, "Of course this sweet couple wants to steal a moment together."

My dad smiled approvingly. If only he knew what I'd be talking to Ryde about.

Ryde led me down a hall that eventually turned into an enormous kitchen. The staff scattered, like Ryde's mere presence was a signal to leave. Within seconds, we were alone.

"Do you do that trick at parties?" I asked

nervously.

He snorted. "It's one of my better ones." He stepped closer and bent, his lips puckered.

Sheer panic welled in me as I stepped back. "Ryde, that's not why I wanted you back here."

"Come on," he said, putting his hands on my waist and pulling me back.

I shoved at his shoulders as hard as I could. "Get off! Ryde, I wanted to talk to you."

The wound to his pride was clear on his face. Had a girl ever turned him away? "What did you have to say?" he finally asked with a scowl.

There wasn't an easy way to say this. Even though I didn't love Ryde, and most of the time I didn't even like him, we still shared history. That wasn't so easy to let go of.  I took a deep breath. "Ryde, I'm sorry, but I can't marry you."

He blinked quickly. "What?"

"Look, you're a great guy, and I know plenty of girls would be happy to be in my position, but I cannot marry you. We have nothing in common, we clearly have different values, and the fact is that I'm seventeen. I'm too young to be thinking about marriage to you or anyone else."

His jaw worked furiously.  "Are you kidding me?"

My brows were in, and I was taken aback. Why was he acting so upset? He clearly didn't care for me.

He placed both of his hands on the counter, pressing them down. "You have to marry me."

What? Was this the same person or had someone hijacked Ryde's body? "I thought you didn't like this situation either?"

"What I like isn't important," he spat, being his real, vile self for once. "It's about duty, obligation."

"Obligation?" I asked, taken off guard. "Why are you obligated to this?"

His head hung down, and then he stood and rubbed his neck like he was tense and in need of a break. When his gaze met mine again, his eyes were haunted. "This isn't just about you, Zara."

I folded my arms across my chest. "Okay, now you're starting to sound like my father."

He shook his head. "How can you be so selfish?"

"Selfish?" I felt like I had whiplash from this conversation.

"This marriage is happening," Ryde said.

"And why is that?"

"Because my acting career—and my family—depend on it."

# TWENTY-NINE

"THEY DEPEND ON IT?" I asked, still dumb-founded. "I mean, I know the exposure will be nice for you, but you're 'Hollywood's hottie.' You'll be just fine without me."

Actually, the more I thought about it, the more frustrated I became. The fact that Ryde thought he could force me into marrying him was more than enough evidence for me to know he was not the man for me. But Ryde gripped my arm, and I looked pointedly down at his hand.

"You don't understand," he said harshly, still not letting go.

My voice was venom now. "No, what I don't understand is why your hand is still on my arm."

He swore low and then stepped back and said,

"Your father has a settlement check written out to my parents and me dated for the day of our wedding, along with the promise for any role I choose in any upcoming film through Bhatta Productions. If you ruin this for me, I promise, I will *ruin* you."

My mouth fell open, and I stumbled backwards. My father had bribed him and his parents so he would marry me? Now it made sense why he'd been so invested and kept coming back after everything. But what didn't make sense was why it had been done in the first place. I felt dirty, used, like my dad had sold me instead of carefully placed me with someone I could grow to love. How could he have done such a thing?

With a final glance my way, Ryde walked out of the kitchen, and I stood there, reeling in the news Ryde had shared—and his threat.

The kitchen staff began filtering in now that Ryde had left, and the flurry of activity resumed around me as if nothing happened. But the ground felt unstable beneath me, as did the only person I'd ever really relied on since Mom had passed away. I leaned against the kitchen island, clinging to the granite countertops to stay standing.

Nausea consumed me, and I swallowed, trying

to hold back the swell of disgust and betrayal rising in my throat. I felt no guilt now for turning down Ryde, for denying my father's wishes. Slave trade wasn't a part of the Indian tradition—he'd gone outside of our culture just as much as I had.

Fueled by anger, I made my way to the living room just minutes behind Ryde.

"There's our girl," Mr. Alexander said with a steely grin. It was now that I noticed the glint of desperation in his eyes. I was his family's meal ticket.

Ryde leaned back in his seat and drained the rest of his drink. "Ain't she a beaut?"

Pam laughed like the ex-pageant queen she was. "We have two beautiful girls in here, don't we?"

"Three," Mr. Alexander chuckled.

"Oh hush." She batted her hand at him. "Should we go to supper before he has a chance for any more flattery?"

Dad nodded and began standing. "We can always accomplish that at the dinner table though." The easy way he joked made me see red.

"Actually," I spoke up with a forced smile, "Dad, can I talk to you outside?"

He furrowed his thick eyebrows at me like he

wanted to chastise me for being rude but couldn't in front of the Alexanders.

He shook his head. "We can talk after dinner."

Oh, we would be talking. A demented part of me wanted to watch and see how they acted—what would they say since they thought I was in the dark? What would take on new meaning now that Ryde had brought me in on the secret?

The Alexanders led the way to their dining room and enormous table. Ryde and I sat on one side, Dad and Merritt on the other, and then the Alexander parents at opposite ends. How they spoke to each other without a blowhorn was a mystery to me.

Everything was formal, with napkins folded in the shapes of swans and several forks and knives lined up alongside the plates. Did they normally eat like this? And if so, why? Dad and I knew proper etiquette for when we went to fancier restaurants, but at home, the rules went out the window.

Just the thought seared me. Dad and I. His betrayal cut me so deeply, I had a hard time thinking of him as anything other than a villain.

Almost mechanically, I folded the napkin over my lap. I didn't want to eat, had lost my appetite long ago, but moving through this meal would be the only way to speed up the time or at least not pay attention to every second as it passed on the clock.

One of the maids circled the table with a tray of salad plates, placing one in front of each of us. She started with me, and as she set it down, I said thank you. She went to Ryde next, and he ignored her, like she was simply expected to serve. Merritt did the same, as did their parents and my father.

Pam saw her salad and whipped her head around at the maid. "I asked for my dressing *on the side.*"

The young woman put her head down, took the plate and left the kitchen like a dog with its tail between its legs.

Pam shook her head, looking frustrated. "*Honestly*, she's worked with us for a month. You'd think she'd remember a salad order. Do you guys have a maid service you like? Ours continues sending us duds."

I wasn't saying a word. The "dud" here wasn't the woman bringing food to the table and practically spoon-feeding it to them.

Dad said, "We had a wonderful nanny we couldn't live without. Once Zara got old enough, we kept her on."

"As a house manager," I added, much to Dad's

frustration. We didn't expect her to plan our meals for us, and we certainly didn't expect her to remember our dinner orders down to the location of the salad dressing. Dad and I could get food for ourselves.

The maid came back in and meekly set the salad in front of Pam. She picked up her silverware and began cutting into the salad. "Let us know if she has any friends so we can replace these disappointments."

My heart went out to the maid. I felt bad, thinking of her as that. She had a name. A life. A history. She couldn't have been more than a couple of years older than me, and yet she was taking a verbal beating with more grace than I ever could have hoped to muster.

As she walked back to the kitchen, I said, "Excuse me, what's your name?"

She looked around, shocked that any of us had spoken to her outside of criticism. "Hannah," she answered softly, like she wasn't even sure if she was supposed to be speaking.

"Nice to meet you, *Hannah*. I'm Zara. And thank you for my salad. It looks amazing."

Everyone around the table was staring at me as if in shock. Because common human decency was definitely lacking around here, and that judgment included my father. He stared across the table at me like he didn't recognize me at all. But I recognized him. I recognized him for who he truly was.

Pam was the first one to resume eating, continuing cutting through her salad like it was a steak. Mr. Alexander made some joke about hoping for real food. Merritt complained that she didn't have enough dressing, which brought Hannah back for another round of requests. I was tired of this, and we hadn't even made it through the first course.

I couldn't wait to get out of here and confront my father. What would happen after, I had no idea. If he was so invested in my marriage as to pay an actual bribe that would satisfy the Alexanders, I didn't know what chance I had in talking him out of it. And apparently I had no chance in talking Ryde out of being with me.

Finally, we made it to the dessert course, which I couldn't even stomach. Apparently, Dad couldn't either, because he pushed his plate away from him and said, "I'd like to discuss the marriage of our children."

Merritt's face soured, but Pam and Mr. Alexander looked delighted. Ryde appeared determined, resolved. I never would have guessed that Merritt and I would be in the same boat, reacting the same way to something my father said, but here we were.

"Ryde has asked my permission to marry you, Zara, and I said yes. I propose that we set the wedding date," Dad said.

My mouth fell open. He was lying, like he hadn't paid them off, and if I hadn't known, I never would have been able to tell. The thought made me even sicker than I already felt.

Pam clapped her hands together excitedly. "I think that's a fabulous idea!" She turned to me and Ryde. "When do you think? We can make it happen right after graduation. It might be a little tough to pull some of the details together, but I think we could make it happen."

"The day after graduation sounds perfect to me," my father said, all business. He smiled between Ryde and me. "These two will have plenty to learn about marriage, but I am sure they will figure it out. They have the rest of their lives to do it."

Why did that sound like a prison sentence?

Pam grinned at her husband. "It's all practice, isn't it, honey?"

He winked at her across the table. "I've never minded practicing."

Did he just make a sex joke in front of everyone? Dad laughed, but I just felt sick. The room was spinning, and I had to take a breath just to steady it.

"What do you think, Ryde, sweetie?" Pam asked.

At this point, I knew it was all a formality meant to keep me in the dark. But since Ryde blew the secret, I could tell he was acting as he answered, "I've never met anyone like Zara, and I can't wait to spend the rest of my life with her."

Gag me with a dessert spoon.

"Then it's settled," Dad said.

No one waited for my answer; no one wanted to hear what I had to say. They continued with details, discussing event planners. Apparently, Pam knew one of the best and would handle the wedding so I wouldn't have to be distracted from my senior year.

As if an arranged engagement with a movie star weren't enough to do that.

"Wonderful," my father said, "but it must stay with the people in this room until I can get a press conference together. I'm expecting no later than Friday. That will give us enough time to hit the evening news and then gain coverage for the rest of the weekend. Your fans will be devastated, Ryde," he said with a smile that showed he wasn't at all upset.

Ryde flashed me an adoring grin. "It's all worth it for this one."

Instead of looking at him, I faced my dad. "Why did you choose Ryde?"

Dad squared his shoulders. "Ryde is a good young man with a fine career ahead of him. He will support you well, and I can see he loves you dearly."

I sneered at him. "I really am going to be sick." I stood up from the table and left, going straight for the front door.

I didn't care about my coat or what my reaction looked like to the people inside. They were all out for themselves, and someone needed to be there for *me*.

I was out of here. Out of everyone thinking that they could control my life. *I* was in control. And if it meant my only possessions were the dress on my back and the contents of my clutch, I wouldn't be a pawn in their game—not anymore. This was *my* life.

I pushed through the heavy front door and out into the warm evening air. It was getting darker outside, but there was still plenty of light for me to see. I got my phone out of my clutch and texted Ronan.

Zara: I know you're probably busy, but can you come get me?

Ronan: Of course. Where are you?

I sent him a map pin and began walking down the driveway. My feet hurt in the stiletto heels I'd worn, but the betrayal from my dad hurt even worse.

"Zara!" he called from behind me. There were already about a hundred yards between us, but it felt like miles. Dad was running toward me, gaining ground fast. I ignored him and continued walking. But he caught up to me quickly and stood in front of me, his face shaking from rage.

"I've never seen such *insolence*. What is happening?"

"What?" I asked with a disgusted look toward the mansion behind him. "Worried that your precious little settlement with the Alexanders will fall through?"

His jaw firmed, and he hesitated, only for a fraction of a second, but it was long enough to give away his lie. "What are you talking about?"

"I knew you were going to set me up for an arranged marriage and that maybe it would help with your business, but I didn't know I would be part of an outright business deal. You basically prostituted me to the Alexanders!"

He rolled his eyes. "I wouldn't expect you to understand. You're only a child."

"A child *you* want to marry off! Who's the one missing something here?" My voice rose and echoed off the pavement.

Unfazed, Dad only shook his head. "You're not even going to ask me why I would make a deal with the Alexanders?"

"You've lied to me *my entire life*, and you want me to hear your explanation?"

Dipping his chin down, he said, "Don't be dramatic."

"Dramatic?" I demanded. "I'm furious. And I have every right to be."

"You can be mad all you want, but it doesn't change the fact that you're marrying Ryde Alexander after graduation."

"You're wrong," I said flatly and continued walking.

He followed after me, right on my heels. "What does that mean?"

"I will not be marrying Ryde, or any other man you choose for me. You're a pimp, not my father."

"Then you are no daughter of mine."

His words caught me, and I froze. The one thing I'd been afraid of, losing both my parents, was here. But I realized I already had. The father I'd had when my mom was around never would have sold me to the Alexanders. Never would have lied to me like this and had me engage in a lifelong contract.

He stared me down, his black eyes hard, like he was waiting for me to give up, but I was *his* daughter, no matter how much I hated that fact. There was no quitting inside me.

"I don't know what game you're trying to win," I said, "but I'm done playing it. Mom would be ashamed of you."

I didn't wait to watch my words hit their target or the impact they had; I just kept walking. I could already hear the sound of a loud motorcycle engine in the distance. I was ready to get out of here. And fast.

I'd just walked away from the only family I had left, with no idea of how my life would look afterward. I didn't cry though. That bothered me. Why couldn't I cry? Even tears of anger would be better than the nothingness that washed over me.

Maybe I was in shock. I took several deep

breaths. I didn't want Ronan seeing all the messiness behind my day or hearing the reason why I'd just walked half a mile in stiletto heels.

I stood outside the gate, listening to the hum of Ronan's engine grow closer and closer. Eventually, he pulled alongside me.

He lifted his eye shade.

I lifted my gaze.

And he saw me. Saw the hurt. I could feel it in his stance, see it in his eyes.

He handed me the second helmet, and I put it on. And then I climbed on to the back of his bike and held on, because at this point, I didn't have much to hold on to.

THIRTY

RONAN DROVE up the coast again, but this time, he didn't stop at sunset. It was well past dark when he exited the road and took a gravel path to an isolated patch of beach. This spot was rougher, unkempt.

As I shucked my heels and walked over the rough ground, he got the blanket from underneath the seat of his bike. Next to me, he spread it out and sat down. His arms opened to me, and I fell into them, letting him hold me, and finally, I cried.

I cried as the sky changed from dark blue to pitch black, as the stars twinkled, oblivious to all the suffering happening beneath them. I cried as he held me and rubbed my arms and pressed his lips to the top of my head over and over again.

As the tears subsided, I breathed deeply and watched the moon's rippling reflection on the ocean. Everything in my life seemed so dark, but here, with Ronan, I could see clearly. Somewhere between seeing him and knowing him, I'd learned to create my own compass. I'd lost everything and felt what I wanted, and I'd never be grateful enough to him for giving me that, for showing me what it meant to live life on your own terms, even if it wasn't easy or glamorous.

His steady breaths and the rhythm of his heart sounded against my cheek. It was like he was an ocean all his own, and I paced myself to his waves. Slowly, I could feel my shoulders loosening, my breath slowing, and the pain in my heartbeats easing. The weight of what I'd walked away from settled over me, but with Ronan, I could carry it. With him, I felt like I could do anything. Be anything.

I lifted my head and looked him in the eyes, and I felt *seen*. For the first time in my life, someone saw me as I was—without my dad, without the money, without the confidence I portrayed to the world.

And the best part? I saw him too.

This strong, beautiful, broken man was here with me when he could have been anywhere else.

His compass was pointing right at me, and mine at him.

I lifted my chin and pressed my lips to his, tears forming for completely new reasons. His arms circled my waist, and he held me back, kissing me slowly. Then his thumbs wiped my tears, and he held my cheeks so gently. So preciously.

I took his bottom lip between my teeth and bit softly, and a low moan sounded from deep in his chest. The sound electrified me, ignited me, and I deepened the kiss, getting lost in Ronan and him in me.

He turned me and laid me back on the blanket, kissing my lips, the wetness on my cheeks, the corners of my jaw and the tender hollows of my neck.

His T-shirt hung from his torso, and I slipped my fingers underneath, exploring the hard muscles of his stomach, the spot where his waist met his jeans.

He paused and met my eyes, his hands on either side of my head, holding himself up. I turned my gaze on his face, on how pale his skin looked in the moonlight, and how it contrasted with the dark fringe of his eyelashes. He was a living piece of art, with dark tattoo swirls on his skin.

I trailed my fingers up the marks on his fore-arms, over his shoulders, and back to his waist. As I toyed with the waistband of his pants, his breath hitched. It excited me.

He lowered himself again, and this time, I moved on top, kissing a path from his nose to his navel. A soft moan escaped his lips, and he moved us again, a dance of passion and exploration I couldn't imagine doing with anyone else.

He rose up and took my face in his hands, and then kissed me. He took his time, thoroughly kissing my lips and then moving to my neck again, leaving a trail of kisses from my collar bone down the neck-line of my dress until my chest was heaving and all I wanted was more. His hands slid over my shoulders and down to my waist, pulling me closer to him until we were both lying pressed together, the sand underneath us molding to our moving bodies.

A strap of my dress fell over my shoulder, and Ronan capitalized on the bare skin, leaving a path of heat with his mouth and teeth before lifting it back into place.

With my eyes on him, I put it back down, along with my other strap. He watched me, his dark eyes full of intensity and longing.

I sat up and unzipped the back, the zipper

audible over the quiet between us, and bared myself to him in a way I had never done with anyone else.

Ronan had me. Heart, body, and soul.

I wanted him to know I was all in, with us, with my new life, even if he didn't know exactly what that meant.

Slowly, he peeled off his shirt and his pants, and we were both bare to each other. I could see the burns on his chest. He could see the birthmark on my shoulder.

He could see *me*.

"You're beautiful," he breathed.

He was too with the light casting shadows over the hard muscles of his stomach and the moonlight giving his skin a pale glow. He was like an Italian statue carved in front of me, a piece of art and beauty. But art wasn't meant to be simply looked at. It was to be considered, enjoyed.

I stepped closer to him, and he to me until we met in the middle, our bare skin touching and warming. He kissed my lips softly, and I knew, whatever happened between us, however it ended, I would never have any regrets.

# THIRTY-ONE

I WOKE up to dusky morning rays with my cheek against Ronan's bare chest and his jacket draped over me.

Even on Egyptian cotton sheets and expensive mattresses, I'd never slept so well as I did in Ronan's arms.

He shifted underneath me, and his lips curled into a peaceful smile. Looking at me through a dark fringe of lashes, he said, "Good morning, beautiful." He pressed a kiss on my forehead, and I swore I was in heaven.

"Good morning," I breathed, smiling wide.

"You're even more stunning in this light."

I could hardly believe he was saying that. Surely my hair was a mess from the humidity coming off the ocean, and there was no way my makeup had survived the night before. But he ran his fingers through my hair like I was the most precious thing he'd seen in his life, and I believed his actions because I knew they spoke louder than words.

"What do you have to do today?" he asked.

And then it hit me all over again. The night before, the things I'd said to my father, the sacrifices I'd made for the sake of autonomy. It had cost me everything, but what I had in front of me was priceless. I had a future of my own choosing.

I shook my head. "Nothing. But can you bring me by my house to get some clothes?"

"What?" He grinned, pushing himself up. "You don't want to wear that sexy black dress all day?"

With a small smile, I shook my head. "I don't think so."

He stood and pulled his T-shirt over his head, and I couldn't help but be a little sad, like our night together was officially over. Our actions the night before had changed me in more ways than one, and it made me sad we couldn't stay here, in this cove, forever.

I stood myself and completely zipped my dress back up, thankful for the privacy of the cove and the early morning. But the sky was growing lighter by the second. Reality was calling, and it wasn't the kind of thing you could decline or avoid.

"I'll shake out the blanket," he said.

"Meet you at the bike." I walked toward the motorcycle, where it gleamed against the eastern rays. My clutch sat on the back, and I figured it was time to see what was waiting for me. What hateful messages I'd surely received from my father. But when I went to turn it on, it was dead.

Great.

"Anyone worried about you?" Ronan asked as he approached me with the blanket folded.

It struck me that we'd shared so much, but he hardly knew about my present, about the pressure from my father or the friends who had my back or the future I hurtled toward.

I shook my head and put my phone back in my clutch. "Not anymore."

We got on his bike, and it took a couple of hours to get to my house in Brentwood—my father's house in Brentwood, I corrected myself. It wasn't my home anymore. No, this immaculate southern-style home with modern flare was the farthest thing from home.

Home was somewhere you could trust the people inside. And I didn't. Not anymore.

Ronan slowed by the keypad, and I typed in my code.

*Error* flashed across the screen. Narrowing my eyebrows, I tried again.

*Error.*

I could feel Ronan's eyes on me as I tried the code again and received yet another error message and then one to contact security. I pushed the red buzzer, and one of the regular security guys came on the screen.

Recognition crossed his face immediately, and he frowned. "I'm sorry, Zara, your father asked us to change the code."

"Can you please let me in? I'd like to change. I'll be right back out."

Even on the black and white screen, he seemed sympathetic. "Sorry, kid."

I wanted to argue, but the screen went black. Angry tears burned my eyes, and I pushed the button over and over again, with no luck. Finally, Ronan covered my hand with his and then made me look him in the eyes. "What's going on, Zara?"

I couldn't hold his gaze for long. "My dad locked me out of the house. Can I use your phone?"

He seemed like he had a million questions to

ask, but he simply reached into his pocket and handed me the phone. I typed in the only number I remembered: Beth's. After a few rings, she picked up. Her voice was a balm to the acid in my soul.

"Beth, it's me. Security won't let me in." My voice cracked, this close to breaking.

"Your father told me this morning, but when I tried to call you, your phone was dead. What happened?"

I glanced at Ronan standing beside me, not ready for him to overhear the whole story. I'd rather tell him myself than have him overhear it. "Can you do me a favor?"

She paused. "Anything, honey. What do you need?"

The moisture built up in my eyes. I had a whole room, a whole closet, and all that I owned was sitting in Jordan's car. "Nothing," I said finally. I wiped at my eyes. "But can I say goodbye?"

"Of course," she said, her voice breaking. "I'll be out in a few minutes."

## THIRTY-TWO

I HUNG up his phone and extended it to him. He looked at it like it was a foreign object, then gestured toward the house. "You had a fight with your father?"

Slowly, I nodded.

"Did he hurt you?" Ronan's eyes were clouded with rage, some of it I knew for his own stepfather and not my own.

"No." I shook my head quickly. "Not physically. It's just...my father had a whole life planned out for me, and I finally told him I didn't want it."

His chest rose and fell, and he gave a clipped nod before hugging me to his chest. "Do you need a place to stay?"

"Do you think Brock would give up his bed?" I

teased, which got a little smile from him. "No, I can stay with one of my friends. I'll be okay."

Maybe I was convincing myself more than him, but I needed to keep going right now. Stopping to think about everything that had gone wrong would only steal attention from the things going right.

He took my bare shoulders in both of his hands and held me at arm's length. "If you need anything, let me know. I'm here for you."

With a quivering smile, I nodded and whispered a thanks before I could fall apart again. I had so many people supporting me. Why wasn't my father one of them?

The hum of the garage door pulled my gaze away from Ronan. Beth's car was pulling out of the garage and coming down the long driveway.

"A friend of yours?" Ronan asked, moving his hand from my shoulders. Now he linked one of his hands with my own. A steady source of support I desperately needed right now.

"She raised me," I said simply. "But she works for my dad."

"Your nanny?"

I nodded.

"I had plenty of those." His voice was almost

nostalgic. Like maybe not all of his memories were painful.

The gate slid open, and Beth got out of her car, which was still running. She glanced toward the top of the gate, looking for what I knew was there. A camera. The fact that she was helping me would probably cost her her job. Now I felt bad for asking.

"Beth, you should go back," I said. "I'm sorry I called you out here, I just—" My voice cracked.

"Shush, honey." She took me in her arms and held me tight. "As far as I'm concerned, I work for you."

Her words were meant to be comforting, but they broke my heart even more. I missed my mom more than ever, missed having someone who saw me as a child and not as a movable piece in a high-stakes game of chess. But now we couldn't clear the board and start over. Real damage had been done.

Beth pulled back and said, "You can always call me if you need anything." At that moment, she seemed to notice Ronan, doing a double take in his general direction. "Is this the boy?"

A smile split my face, and I wiped away my tears, nodding.

He stepped forward, extending his hand. "I'm Ronan."

Beth stalled at the sight of his tattooed hand reaching out to her, but Ronan kept a gentle smile on his face. His tattoos were for him, not to please or deter anyone else.

She took his hand in hers and held it firm. "You take care of my baby girl, alright?"

"I wouldn't think of doing anything else." Once she let go, he got on the bike, and then I sat behind him.

As he pulled out of the entranceway, Beth gave us a small wave. I tried to smile, but couldn't, knowing all I was saying goodbye to.

I wasn't sure where Ronan was taking me, but he drove to the outskirts of Brentwood, into Emerson, and stopped at Waldo's Diner.

"What are we doing here?" I asked.

"Thought you could use something to eat."

Hungry was the last thing I felt, but he was probably right. I needed my energy, especially since I hadn't been able to stomach dinner the night before. We took off our helmets and left them on the bike but brought my bags inside.

Chester looked up at us from his table and said, "Hey, girl!"

I returned his greeting with a smile and said, "Hi there, Chester, this is—"

But Ronan was already extending his hand and shaking Chester's.

"How are you, Ronan?" Chester asked. "Gotten into any trouble lately?"

"Only the good kind," Ronan replied with a smirk.

Chester shook a finger at him. "To be young again. Are you taking care of my girl?"

Ronan looked me up and down, heat in his eyes. "I wouldn't dream of doing anything else."

"Atta boy."

Ronan put his arm around my shoulders. "We'll catch you later, Ches?"

He nodded. "Bye, Ronan. Bye Zara."

As we walked away, my mouth fell open. "He knows my name?" I whispered. "I thought he just called me 'girl' because he couldn't remember it!"

Ronan chuckled. "He sees more than he lets on. Don't let him fool you." As usual, Ronan walked to a corner booth and took the spot with his back to the wall and his line of sight on the entire room.

"I can't believe you know Chester though," I said. "You know everyone."

"Just the right people," he said.

A waitress came, bringing us menus, and

asked what we wanted to drink. I took coffee, and Ronan ordered water.

He excused himself to go to the bathroom, and I plugged my phone in to an outlet underneath the table. I needed to call Jordan and see if that room was still available.

While I waited for my phone to charge, I glanced around the place. There were couples and older people eating breakfast, along with a big TV in the corner playing the news. I didn't like listening to politics or hearing the latest tragedy, so I tried to tune it out.

Within a couple of minutes, my phone powered on and began vibrating endlessly. Text after text and *Sermo* chat after *Sermo* chat came into my notification screen, along with calls, voicemails, and social media notifications. My eyebrows came together as I tried to look at one notification long enough to make sense of it.

Realizing that this wasn't going to end anytime soon, I silenced my phone.

The waitress set a ceramic mug and a sweating glass of water on the table and then nodded toward the spot where Ronan had gone. "Is he eating with you?"

"Yeah," I answered.

She put her notepad in her apron pocket. "I'll come back in a little bit."

"Sounds good." Our whole interaction was so *normal* it caught me off guard. How could life ever go back to normal after what had happened?

I took a sip of the hot liquid. It was unexpectedly delicious, cleansing my soul in a way I hadn't expected.

Ronan slid into the booth across from me and took a long drink from his water. "Did you order?"

I shook my head. "Waiting for you."

He looked at the menu casually, like he already knew what he wanted.

"What are you getting?" I asked.

"Can't go wrong with a burger and fries."

"This early in the morning?"

He leveled his gaze at me over the menu. "Are you telling me a time of day makes them *not* taste good?"

With a laugh, I conceded. "True. Can you order that for me too?"

He nodded. "Where are you going?"

"Bathroom." I pulled my phone from the charger, hoping it had charged enough for me at least to make a call and see what was going on. Fear gripped my chest as I went to the single-stall bathroom. Had word gotten out that Ryde and I weren't together anymore? What rumors had the media and the Alexanders spun? I imagined all the ways his fans could come after me and cringed.

As I sat on the toilet, I pulled open my messages and went to the group chat with my friends. They would give me the news in the kindest way, I was sure.

Jordan: YOU'RE ENGAGED?

Callie: I thought you were calling it?

Rory: Did the talk with your dad not go well?

Ginger: Did you change your mind?

Callie: It's okay either way! We just want what's best for you! <3

Their messages confused me. Why were they saying I was engaged?

The low battery notification popped up on my phone. I canceled it and quickly typed in a message.

Zara: We are NOT engaged. I called it last night, and my father won't let me back in the house. Jordan, is it still okay if I stay with you and your mom?

Jordan: Of course. But you might want to see this.

Her next message was a screenshot of a news article with the headline, *Ryde Alexander Off the*

*Market. Star Announces Official Engagement to Zara Bhatta.*

What?

I nearly dropped my phone in the toilet. How did they get that out of what transpired last night? The image with the article was one of Ryde and me sitting together at the Alexanders' for supper. We didn't look too close, but we were sitting right next to each other. Looking at each other. The only people who could have caught us at that angle were my dad and Merritt and *maybe* Hannah.

I got out of the chat app and went to my internet app. Typing in my name and "engagement" gathered thousands of results. I clicked on the top one and read the story, all about how Ryde asked for my father's blessing and how happy my dad was that I was marrying such a hardworking, up-and-coming actor. There was a quote from Pam saying that I was a stunning girl, but joking that I better not break Ryde's heart. Then a lamenting quote from the leader of the Ryders, Ryde's personal fan club. It was like reading something from an alternate universe. How had this gotten out? And how had no one found out that I walked out on Ryde the night before?

When I went to my social media, I had

hundreds of thousands of new followers overnight and plenty of notifications asking me how I felt about marrying Ryde or asking to see my ring or threatening me unless I broke up with him.

I pressed the button to create a new post and set the story straight, but my phone screen went black. I tapped on it desperately, wanting to make the announcement that I was by no means marrying Ryde Alexander.

Realizing that no matter how much I hit the touchscreen, it would not come to life, I put it on the counter and washed my hands before splashing some water on my face.

Taking a deep breath, I opened the bathroom door and began walking toward the table, needing to tell Ronan about what had happened before he heard from someone else.

But he and the waitress were looking up at the news screen in the corner, and when she caught sight of me, she said, "Isn't that you?"

# THIRTY-THREE

RONAN'S EYES flicked from the screen to me, and when I caught his gaze, I could see he was comparing the picture to the person in front of him. I was still wearing the same dress as the night before. There was no denying who it was on the screen, or who I was now.

I was close enough to hear Ronan say, "Excuse me," as he stood from the booth and made a beeline to the exit. My mind wasn't working, but my feet followed him. The second he got outside, he ripped his hands through his hair, pacing quickly back and forth.

I wanted him to say something, anything, but he wasn't. And that scared me.

"Ronan?" I said.

His eyes turned on me, black fiery coals of anger and distrust. He only said one word. "Engaged?"

I shook my head. "It's not what it looks like."

His eyes narrowed, and his lips formed a line. "Tell me what it looks like then. Because I'm pretty sure the people on the news were saying that you're engaged to Mr. Oiled Abs with a Multi-Million-Dollar Trust Fund."

The anger in his voice took me aback.

"But I'm not engaged to him."

"So you're telling me that the evening news and all those reporters just shared false information with the entire country?"

"Yes!" I cried. "That's why I called you last night. I broke it off. I'm not with him."

His eyebrows furrowed even more. "So you've been with someone else this whole time? Even after he left you in the middle of the street, you stayed with him?"

I stepped closer to him, and he took a step back. That made my chest hurt even more. I still ached from what had happened between us the night before, still smelled like him, and he was departing from me like I was poison.

"Ronan, I wasn't with him in the way you think."

"You're not off to a great start, Zara." His voice was flat, which was even worse than the anger. It meant he was giving up on me. On us.

Tears stung my eyes. I'd given Ronan every part of myself except for the truth of my father's plan. "My dad arranged for me to marry Ryde. The dinner last night was to make our engagement final and set our wedding date. I ran away. I don't want to be with him."

Ronan was incredulous. "Let's say I believed that someone would arrange a marriage for a *teenager*—which I don't, by the way—that doesn't change what you did.

"What I did? I called it off!"

"But that means it was on at some point. When we were at the beach. When we watched the sunset. When we..." He shuddered. "I gave you all of me, and you never told me anything."

My throat tightened. "Ryde meant *nothing* to me. I didn't tell you because it didn't matter. *You* matter."

"Well the truth matters to me. I was always honest with you, even about DP." He scrubbed his hands over his face. "I don't even know you."

The pain in my chest was so thick I had to gasp for air. Desperation had me fighting through the ache to tell him that this mattered. "Ronan, you know me better than anyone."

"No, I don't, because keeping that secret meant you knew how this would end. The girl I fell in love with never would have led me on like that."

His words struck me one after another, and I wrapped my arms around my stomach just to hold myself together. "It doesn't have to end."

He gave me a long, cold look and shook his head before walking away. He went to his motorcycle, got on, and kicked it to life. I called his name, did something I told myself I'd never do for a man, and begged him to stay.

The last I saw of him was his rigid shoulders as he sped away.

A couple passed me, their eyes down, not saying a word. I was sure I looked a mess, with my hair tossed into a ponytail, my second-day makeup, and my dress I'd worn since the night before. But none of the external chaos compared to the feeling inside my heart.

I'd given up everything, sacrificed everything, for the chance to live life on my terms, but this wasn't my plan. I'd lost my family. My home. Now

I'd lost a piece of my heart, and I had a feeling that when Ronan loved, he loved with his whole self, but when he decided to stop, there was no turning back.

No amount of explaining or convincing could make him do what I desperately wanted him to do. To come back and tell me it would be alright.

Because right now, it wasn't. And I was afraid it would never be alright again.

I sat on the ramp leading up to the front door of the diner and put my head in my hands. Things couldn't get worse than they were now. That was, until the news cars showed up.

Someone had to have called them and told them I was here. A woman with a brunette bob shoved her mic out the window as they pulled up and said, "Zara, reports say you were here with a man who is not your fiancé. Who is he? Were you with him last night? What do you say to those who suspect you of cheating on Ryde?"

My eyes flew open wide as I stumbled to my feet. "Cheating?"

Another car pulled up beside them, the news-caster getting out much quicker than the other one. He jogged up to me. "Zara, is the man you were with your lover? Where did he go?"

Someone else got out of yet another news car

and said, "Are you wearing the same dress from last night?"

Arms gripped my shoulder, and Chester said, "You've got to get out of here, sweetie."

I'd never been so thankful for him in my life.

With strength I didn't know he possessed, he batted at the reporters with his cane and led me to his car. He opened the door to his Oldsmobile for me, helped me inside, then went to his side, yelling at the paparazzi the entire time.

Their cameras flashed wildly, but he kept cool and collected as he gunned his engine, warning them, and backed out of the parking lot.

They shouted questions at us as we drove away, but there was only one question that mattered. Chester, saying, "Where to?"

# THIRTY-FOUR

I'D ONLY BEEN to this part of Brentwood once before, when we were helping Jordan and her mom move into their new townhome. It butted up against Emerson with a main road marking the border. Following the directions I had to repeat from my GPS, he pulled up to a tidy row of townhouses painted a variety of bright colors.

We followed the parking lot up to number twelve, and he pulled into an empty spot. A concerned look drew his thick eyebrows together. "Are you sure you're going to be okay?"

I wasn't, but Chester couldn't fix that. "Thanks for dodging the reporters back there. At least I know they didn't follow us here."

He nodded. "It was the least I could do."

I put my hand on his arm. "You have no idea how much you did. Thank you."

With a smile, he said, "Anytime, Zara."

Jordan's front door opened, and she looked around until she caught sight of us and began walking toward Chester's car. "I better get inside," I said.

"See you around Waldo's, I hope."

"If I can ever show my face in public again, you'll be the first to know."

He tipped his cap at me. "Happy to hear it. Stay safe out there." He hesitated, and it was clear he wanted to say something.

Jordan waited outside the car, but I held my finger up to her. "What's up, Chester?"

He looked down at his weathered, veiny hands and said, "Ronan's a good boy. I've known him since he was little. He's had a rough life, you know."

Heat built behind my eyes, and I blinked back the moisture.

"I'm not sure what happened outside, but I hope you two can work through it. Lord knows Karen and I have had our share of spats."

"Has she ever done something unforgivable?" I asked, because I had. The more I thought about it, the more I saw it from Ronan's perspective, the guiltier I felt.

"Nothing is unforgiveable when two people are willing to fight for each other day in and day out."

I leaned over and kissed his scratchy cheek. "Thanks, Chester, for everything."

He smiled softly and lifted a hand. "Take care."

I promised him I would and then got out of the car. Jordan came toward me, eyes wide, looking between me and Chester's car backing out of the spot.

Her concern was palpable, and it nearly undid me. I wasn't this girl—the one who lost control. The one people spent time worrying about. I was strong, fierce, confident.

I was sobbing.

As Jordan came toward me, tears rolled down my cheeks. She hugged me tight, not asking anything, and said, "Let's get you inside."

I let her guide me into her home with her arm around me, and inside I found each of my friends. They were all standing in the doorway, waiting for me..

"What are you guys doing here?" I asked, stunned.

Callie immediately wrapped me in a hug, then

stepped back. "We thought you might need to be around family."

That did it. That word. I collapsed on the couch, and my friends surrounded me with their love, with their warmth. With each of them holding me together, I had the support I needed to fall apart.

I sobbed into my hands about my dad, my home, and most of all, my heart. That was the thing about crying, though. It didn't solve my problems. Didn't make my dad see eye to eye with me, didn't change the lies running on news headlines or make the man I did love forgive me.

"How bad is the news?" I asked them. I needed to know what was being said so I could have some idea of what to do. What school would be like on Monday.

My friends looked at each other like they were picking invisible straws.

Ginger finally said, "It's bad. Everyone covered your engagement, but now there's twice as much."

I braced myself. "What are they saying?"

"What aren't they saying is a better question." She winced. "Or selling."

"Selling?" I asked. My dad wouldn't auction off my stuff out of spite, would he?

Rory shook her head. "It's those stupid Ryders."

"What are they selling?" I asked, desperate now to know.

Ginger said, "They have a T-shirt of your face with the words 'THAT B*TCH' in big bold print."

I laughed. And then I kept laughing. And then I couldn't stop laughing hysterically. Was this what it felt like to go insane?

My friends chuckled awkwardly, like they didn't quite know what to make of my reaction either.

I wiped a tear of crazy laughter from my eyes. "That's the best they can do? Call me a bad name? I lost my *family*."

Jordan rolled her eyes. "I mean, that and guessing whether or not you had sex with Ronan."

"Do they know his name?" I asked. Even though he'd broken my heart and left me alone, I didn't want his name being dragged through the mud. He'd suffered enough already.

"Someone connected him to Roy Taylor," Callie said. "That's his stepdad—the owner of the—"

"Brentwood Badgers," I finished sourly. "I know."

"Roy hasn't made a statement yet, but they're calling a press conference Tuesday to talk about it."

I sagged, thinking of the vitriol that would come out of that scumbag's mouth, and almost got sick. I wasn't the only one getting hurt in all this.

"Of course," Ginger said, "Ryde's profiting from this whole mess. His movie's ranking higher than ever and #RydeStayStrong is trending." She rolled her eyes, and I had about the same reaction.

"Oh, poor Ryde won't be getting the settlement for our wedding." The disgust in my voice was palpable. "Has he said anything on the news about that?"

"Settlement?" Jordan hissed.

I told them about the news I'd heard the night before, the betrayal my dad had put me through. I couldn't believe how much had happened since I'd seen them at Chester's just a couple days ago. I launched into the story of what had happened when I'd attempted to break up with Ryde—and the truth he'd revealed.

"That's prostitution!" Ginger cried.

I nodded, sneering at the floor. "It's disgusting."

Ginger shook her head. "Ryde just posted a *devastated* selfie on social about how his heart is broken and he just needs time to heal. Now we know why he's so upset."

The more they talked about him, the sicker I

became. How could my dad have ever even considered Ryde for a husband?

Rory asked, "What did Ronan think of it all when you told him?"

The tears were back as I cried about our argument. About him leaving me in the parking lot to be attacked by paparazzi.

Jordan rubbed my back. "I'm so sorry."

I wiped at my face with the heels of my hands. "I just don't know how to fix it."

"You can't," Jordan said. "At least not right now. But some ice cream couldn't hurt."

We spent the afternoon on the couch, gorging ourselves on pints of ice cream, from cookie dough to Cherry Garcia. According to Jordan, she and her mom had been down and out for so long they splurged on some luxuries now. I savored each bite almost as much as my friends' company.

I couldn't believe their friendship was the only real thing in my life when everything else had been fabricated. Their hearts were pure gold, but they still didn't understand. They were worried about college, boyfriends, their futures supported by their parents. And me? I had no future. No boyfriend. No parents.

I'd spent so long resisting what I didn't want

that I had never thought about what I would do given the freedom to choose. I had no idea what I would study if I somehow managed to secure last-minute college acceptance along with loans or scholarships. My resume was void of work experience to apply at any kind of job, even food service positions. And I'd given a piece of myself to Ronan I couldn't get back. It was gone, given to someone who'd turned his back on me as easily as my father had.

After Rory, Callie, and Ginger left, I excused myself to their guest bedroom across the hall from Jordan's room and lay in the bed.

It was a queen, smaller than my California king at home, but I fell asleep faster than I ever had before. Deep sleep welcomed me with open arms, and I leaned into it, letting the blackness consume me.

# THIRTY-FIVE

SOMEONE GENTLY NUDGED ME AWAKE. I had no idea how long I'd been sleeping, but it was dark outside, and I felt groggy. I blinked my eyes against the dimly lit room and saw a woman who looked like the older version of Jordan. My mind slowly connected the dots and recognized her as Jordan's mom.

"Hi, Zara, honey," she said softly, sitting on the bed next to me.

I blinked slowly. "Hey. Is everything okay?"

"Don't worry. I just wanted to let you know that we got your bags from Jordan's car moved up here. I put them by the bed." She brushed my hair away from my face in a gesture so purely motherly I nearly broke down in tears.

"Thank you," I whispered.

"You don't need to thank me. I'm here for you, and you can stay here as long as you need."

"I can help clean," I said, "I don't want to be a burden."

She shushed me and brushed my hair back again. "You are not a burden, sweetie. As far as I'm concerned, you're another daughter to me. Just call me Mama Junco."

My eyes stung, and I focused on the golden necklace dangling from her neck so I wouldn't break down. I could hear the smile in her voice, but she had no idea how much that meant to me. I'd gone years without a mom, having someone hired to be my maternal replacement. In my world where social capital was the only kind that mattered, never had I had someone step up so willingly and care for me with no expectations or strings attached.

"Why are you doing this?" I asked. Because part of me felt like if I didn't have something to give, no one would have anything to give to me.

"Because everyone deserves to have a place they can be themselves without the weight of expectations. Jordan loves you, and that means I do too." She smiled gently at me. "Now, you should get some rest. I just wanted you to know you had your things."

"Thank you," I said again. It seemed like I was having trouble coming up with anything else.

"Good night, honey."

But when I closed my eyes, I couldn't sleep, so I got out of bed and went through my remaining possessions. I already knew what I packed, but somehow seeing it, having it in front of me, gave me some comfort. I unzipped my backpack, thankful it at least had all my homework and my computer. And then I opened my duffle bag.

I'd filled it to the brim with practical things like spring and summer clothes, underwear, and then I'd added my makeup off the bathroom counter, some sanitary items, and the two books that had been on my nightstand.

The one on top had come from my father. *When We Were Free* by Nattie Jones. I flipped it over and read the back-cover copy. *Loving him made her free, but the cost of being together was anything but.*

A tightness gripped my chest. I wasn't ready to read someone else's love story when mine had gone so wrong.

I turned my eyes back toward the bag and saw the worn book of poems Ronan had given me. I picked it up and held it to my chest. It was the closest thing to Ronan I would ever hold again.

My eyes flooded with tears, and they quickly spilled over. I let them pour, knowing it would be useless to try and stem the flow. Instead, I leaned into my pain and opened the book to the pressed flower. I imagined how Ronan must have seen it and plucked it. I wondered if he'd been thinking of me as he did it—what he might have thought.

He'd said he loved me.

The ache in my chest grew, making it hard to breathe.

I read the page the flower was on. Something by Percy Bysshe Shelley about love and passion and fearlessness.

Ronan had been fearless, and I'd been a coward. He'd loved so bravely, telling me about his past and inviting me into his present. I'd hardly let him in at all, except as an escape.

I've always had a hard time finding the words for my feelings, preferring to put them into action, and that had been my downfall. Bravery would have told him about Ryde, about my father, about my dreams. Cowardice had kept my secrets in the dark, where they festered until the light had revealed how terrible hiding them had really been.

I found my phone on the nightstand, and even though there were thousands of notifications, none of them were from Ronan.

I desperately wanted to hear from him, but all I had were these pages, this book. He'd given it to me for a reason.

I flipped through the pages, reading it late into the night, until morning rays came through the pale aqua curtains.

Disappointment flooded me as I came to the last page, until I saw the writing inside the back cover. The last poem had come from this century— an original by Ronan.

*Zara*
*Fleeting beauty*
*Lasting charge*
*Fading lines*
*Beating heart*
*Worth the pleasure*
*and the pain*
*Full of doubts,*
*As well as gain.*
*Fearful longing*
*Brave belonging.*
*Bare, real, here.*
*Ronan*

.   .   .

My lips parted as I read over his words, understood the meaning behind them. He'd wanted me to know that he was here for me through it all. That he understood the risk we were taking in divulging ourselves to each other.

I pictured his hand holding a pen just as surely as he'd held me the night before, the way his lips might have pressed together as he carefully crafted each word. What he must have been thinking as he handed me the book, knowing the immense gift that lay inside.

My fingers feathered over the page, feeling the indentations of his words into the page just as clearly as I felt them on my heart.

# THIRTY-SIX

MAYBE IT WAS the ache in my heart making me a glutton for punishment, but I got out my phone and looked at every message I'd gotten. Hateful ones, congratulatory ones, apologetic ones, rambling ones that didn't quite make sense, a few even tagged me in pictures of them wearing their Ryder hate shirts.

Everyone saw me a different way—a "b*tch", a cheater, a rebel, a hero.

That last one threw me off guard. I was the furthest thing from a hero. I was a coward who'd given the boy I came to love everything but the truth, and the truth was that I cared what my father thought, even with all of this going on.

I hated him, but I loved him too. He was the man who loved my mother with all his heart, the one who gave me everything the world had to offer, and the one who'd been around after my mom passed away.

But none of the messages were from him. It worried me. Now that I had nothing to offer, did that mean he had stopped loving me? And if my father could stop loving me, what did that say about the potential for anyone else to truly love me?

The door to my room cracked open, and Jordan popped her head in. Her eyes went from me to the phone screen, and her mouth fell open. "What are you doing?"

My voice fell flat. "My dad hasn't texted me. Ronan hasn't texted me."

She came closer and took the phone from my hands and set it on the nightstand, where her eyes stalled on the book. "And what is this? You're suddenly into eighteenth-century poetry?"

"Ronan gave it to me." I flipped the book open to the last page and passed it to her.

She scanned the poem, putting her hand to her heart. "He wrote this? For you?"

My lips trembled as I nodded.

She looked up from the words. "He loves you."

"Not anymore."

She shook her head and sat on the bed, closing

the book. "Guys don't just share their feelings like this, write poems for girls they don't care about. That they can just toss away."

"But I lied to him."

"You didn't lie," she said. "You kept a secret."

"That's almost worse. Because I had all the opportunities in the world to tell him, and I still didn't open my mouth."

She shook her head and set the book back down. "I still think he'll come around eventually."

"Why?" I asked, becoming frustrated at her optimism. "You don't even know him."

"But I know you," she said confidently. "And I know that you're worth it."

"Am I?" I asked, falling back into the pillows. I'd always been the confident one of our friends, lifting them up when they worried about their appearance or whether or not a guy would like them, but right now, I was feeling lower than I ever imagined I could. Why had Ronan liked me at all in the first place? "I'm just a rich girl with no original thoughts. My only goal was to get my father to change his mind, and now I don't even have Daddy's bank account to back me up."

"Zara," she said harshly, "don't *ever* talk about yourself like that. What your dad did was wrong.

He wouldn't be acting the way he is, shutting you out, if he didn't know it. You're a teenage girl, and when you should have been worrying about graduation, he was trying to force you together with an older guy you don't even like. That was wrong. And that's no reflection on you. Ever since I've known you, you've been strong and kind and supportive, and you always fight for what you want. Even if you feel a little lost right now, it doesn't mean that you're not going to find your true north eventually."

Her words made me think of the compass on Ronan's arm, how he had always found his way. If he could, I could too, even if it was going to be hard.

I gave her a hug and held her tight. "Thank you."

She held my cheek and said, "Thank yourself. I'm pretty sure I just regurgitated a bunch of the pep talks you've given me."

I laughed, feeling better.

"But you know what I don't understand?" she said.

"What?"

"I've been thinking about it all night. Who told the media? Even though it's helping his career, it has to look bad for Ryde. Like even some teenage girl wouldn't want to be with him? And it has to make your dad's company look less credible, right? That he couldn't even keep control of his daughter? Not that I think daughters should be controlled, but —well, you know where I'm going."

I shrugged. I honestly had no clue who had told. But now that I thought about it, there was one person who had it out for me. Who'd been at the right angle to get that photo. And I was going to confront her tomorrow at school.

## THIRTY-SEVEN

"ARE you sure you don't want me to give you a ride?" Jordan's mom asked us as we finished our breakfast of scrambled eggs, sausage, and toast. I couldn't remember the last time I'd eaten food not out of pre-packaged containers.

Jordan looked to me. "I'm fine driving, but it's up to you."

I shook my head. "I'm fine just riding with Jordan." Plus, I didn't want to inconvenience *Mama Junco* any more than I already had by sleeping in their guest room and now eating their food.

"As long as you're sure," Mama Junco said. "I called the school this morning, and they said that they will have an escort for you to go into the building."

She seemed sincerely worried about us, but I loved the way she respected Jordan and her wishes. "Be safe, mijas," she said.

"We will," Jordan promised. She stood and put her plate in the sink, and I did the same. Grabbing our backpacks, we made our way out to her car. The early spring morning was quiet, save for a few birds chirping in the courtyard trees. This complex really was beautiful. I couldn't imagine two people who deserved to live here more.

We went to Jordan's old car and got in. She tossed her bag in the backseat, and I kept mine by my feet. I missed my Rolls-Royce, but it was just another one of the things I would have to grieve and move on from. Thinking of how dependent I'd been on my father hurt. Now I tried not to be overwhelmed at the sheer amount life I would have to figure out on my own.

Jordan pulled onto the highway and picked up speed. "Do you think it's going to be crazy this morning?"

"If the scene at Waldo's was any indication, definitely. They have to know that I go to school at the Academy. And paparazzi are basically grub worms. They'll do anything they can to get their next meal."

I said the words, but then realized how similar my family and the Alexanders were to the paparazzi, doing whatever it took to gain more money, more power, more of everything.

Part of me was thankful that I'd gotten away when I could, before I got too entrenched in the survival-of-the-fittest world of my father.

"You know," Jordan said, "we should have just had Kai heli-lift you to the school so you could just, like, rappel into first period."

I laughed, thankful for her sense of humor. I definitely needed it. "He'd probably just buy a tank for us to ride."

Laughing, she said, "Girl, he already has a tank. He just needs to bust it out of storage.

"You're kidding," I said.

With her lips pressed tightly together, she shook her head.

Laughing, I reached for the radio dial. "We should play pump-up music."

"Do you have a playlist?" she asked, reaching for a cord extending from the cassette player. "Do you have a playlist?"

"Of course, don't you?"

"Not unless you want me to start dancing right here."

"I don't know, mine's pretty hopping," I teased and plugged my phone into her dangling cord from the cassette player. Soon, light-hearted, fast-paced pump-up music was playing in the car. I turned the music loud and closed my eyes, trying to focus on the lyrics and the beats instead of the nightmare that would surely find me at school.

As if sensing my change in mood, Jordan stayed quiet, just sitting beside me and being there like a true friend. Part of me was glad she and Ginger were only going to UCLA next year so we could still see each other. I didn't know what I would do without Rory and Callie when they were away at college in the fall. It wouldn't feel right not having all of us together.

"We're almost there," Jordan warned, slowing the car.

I blinked my eyes open and saw the chaos that had already begun at school. Headmaster Bradford must have threatened the news crews, because they were lined up along the street in front of our school, not in the parking lot or in front of the building like I'd expected. There were three police cars in the school parking lot, though, flashing lights and keeping the crowd of reporters at bay.

"I thought reporters were allowed on public property," Jordan said.

I shook my head, remembering something from journalism class. "It's a private school. They can't get on the grounds."

"Ah," she said. "You ready for this or do you want me to make another loop?"

"Go ahead." If I learned anything from this mess, the pain was going to come one way or another. It was best not to prolong it.

She nodded and slowly turned into the parking lot. One of the paparazzi saw me in Jordan's car and shouted so loudly I could hear them through the car window. Like a swarm of bees, they surrounded our car, and Jordan gunned it into the parking lot.

I screamed, worrying that she was going to run someone over, but they all jumped out of the way as if they'd practiced it before. Maybe they had.

"That was crazy!" I yelled.

"Girl, I've got you," she said, a spark in her eye.

"You're loving this, aren't you?"

With a smirk, she shrugged, "I like to live on the edge."

I laughed but stopped as I saw a police officer coming toward us. He waved us toward the front, and when Jordan stopped, he asked for her keys. "I'll park for you."

She nodded stiffly and reached for her bags. Headmaster Bradford approached the car, along with our PE teacher and Mr. Davis.

I stepped out of the car, and the craziness fully reached my ears. From the street, reporters shouted questions at us.

"Are you staying with your friend?"

"Why aren't you staying with your father?"

"What were you doing with Roy Taylor's stepson?"

"Do you plan to make things right with Ryde?"

"Ignore it," Headmaster Bradford said, taking one of my elbows. Our gym teacher took my other side, while Mr. Davis walked with Jordan.

"Keep your head down," Headmaster Bradford ordered.

I followed his directions and walked quickly with them into the school.

Once we were inside the doors, everyone in the hallway was staring at us. But at least they were smart enough not to try anything with the head-master around. Headmaster Bradford raised his voice and said, "Back to business, students." Then he turned to Jordan and me. "Jordan, you may go to your first-hour class. Zara, come with me."

The stern way he said the last part made my throat tighten. An impossible, terrifying thought came to my mind. Had my father retracted his tuition payments? Was I still a student at Emerson Academy?

Headmaster Bradford walked beside me to his office, staring down everyone who gaped at us—or rather, me.

Thank god we had a dress code, because I couldn't stand the thought of seeing everyone wearing those shirts staring back at me. Then again, Merritt and her crew practically ruled the world. I wouldn't put it past her to have the dress code changed.

We walked into Headmaster Bradford's office, and I took it in. Mrs. Bardot sat in one of the two leather seats facing an ornate wooden desk. There were art pieces on the olive-green walls, along with multiple diplomas.

He moved behind his desk, sat down, and folded his hands together. "Sit, Zara."

I stared between him and Mrs. Bardot, terrified of what was to come next. Was this the last I'd see of the Academy, the only school I'd known since kindergarten?

"Sit," he said again, more forcefully this time.

Though each movement felt like my muscles were made of stone, I forced myself to sit in the chair, but my words came easily. "I'm out, aren't I?"

"Out?" For the first time in my life, I saw Headmaster Bradford look confused.

"My dad canceled my tuition payments. I need to leave."

He cleared his throat and tried to hide the displeasure that was obvious on his face. "We have a no-refund policy at Emerson Academy, and I refuse to threaten a student's educational future based on a familial disagreement."

Relief like I never felt before flooded through me, and I sagged in my chair. I had no idea how much finishing school really mattered to me until the opportunity had almost been taken away.

"However," Headmaster Bradford continued, "we are not keen to handling things of this nature. You are being put on academic probation, and we expect you to keep your grades high and behave as an Emerson lady should in the seven weeks left until graduation. Can you do that?"

I nodded quickly. "Trust me, none of this was in my plans."

"The riding on the back of some boy's motorcycle part?"

I opened my mouth to respond, but Mrs. Bardot jumped in.

"Of course it wasn't." She gave Headmaster Bradford a look like he'd been too hard on me, then turned back to face me. Her wormy apple earrings were like a slap in the face to Headmaster Bradford's tailored suit and imposing office.

She gave me a sympathetic smile, which seemed honest enough, and then said, "Zara, please let me know if there is anything I can do to help during this time. We've all been watching the news, and of course we are not sure how much is true, but if you need a place to stay, help filling out college applications, if that's in your plan, or anything else, please let me know."

My first instinct was to say no. I didn't like relying on people, and I certainly didn't like placing my trust in people who wore rotten fruit as accessories on purpose. But at this point, I needed to get a plan together and fast.

"Let me think about it," I said.

She smiled like she'd already won. Maybe she

had. "Let's meet in my office today after school. It will be a great way to avoid some of the press. I'll see you then."

As Headmaster Bradford excused me from his office, I knew the torment was far from done.

EVEN THOUGH THE first bell had rung, there were a few students left in the hallway. All of them stared at me. If the world's most serious hall monitor, Pixie Adler, hadn't been there, I bet it would have been worse than it was.

She stood from her chair at the end of the corridor and waved her arms toward the classrooms. "Go on, folks, nothing to see." But even she cast a sideways glance at me, like my mere existence made her job that much harder.

Headmaster Bradford had asked me to keep a low profile, and I wanted nothing more than to do exactly that. Unfortunately, there was something else I needed to handle before I could get to flying under the radar.

As soon as first period was over, I went to Merritt's locker and waited. She came down the hallway with Tinsley and Poppy, strutting in her heels that were well above dress code regulation height.

Her eyes lasered in on me, and her glare narrowed to ash-inducing levels. She had a vendetta, and it wasn't hard to see who it was against. The people around me who had been staring and pointing this entire time now saw what I was looking at—who I was looking at—and a low murmur broke out.

Whispers of "fight" and "drama" rang throughout the crowd, but I ignored them and kept my eyes on Merritt.

Finally, she stood only feet away from me, and students circled us.

"What do you want, harlot—I mean, Zara?" she asked.

I rolled my eyes. "That was weak, even for you, Merritt."

"Well, try this on for plus-size," she jeered. "We had our home disinfected after you were there. Didn't want dirty slut all over our seats."

A gasp rang out around us, and even my jaw went slack. Merritt wasn't one to be hostile like that in public. Ever since getting in hot water over the cupcake situation when she had the whole school throw cupcakes at Rory, she usually played it safe. Made her insults so subtle that if a teacher overheard them, they wouldn't get her in trouble.

Her steely gaze stayed on me, daring me to say something, to even *try* to fight back. But she didn't know who she was going up against. I'd lost everything that mattered to me. It was one thing for her to decimate my life—it was another yet to bring Ronan into it.

"Look," I began, "I know this marriage was important to your family—"

Her eyes turned wild, desperate, and she cut me off. "It was important to my brother because he *loved* you."

The skill with which she said it made me laugh. "That's hardly true. If anything, he's in love with Ambrose."

Poppy's eyebrows rose. "Ryde's gay?"

"No, no, no." I shook my head again. We were getting way off track here. "I just wanted to let you know, Merritt, that it wasn't okay to go to the press. A lot of people have been hurt because of you."

"I could say the same for you."

The bell rang for second period. And we all

looked around like we were suddenly being snapped out of a trance.

Mrs. Bardot came down the hall, saying, "Get to class, everyone," in a sing-song voice, as if she somehow missed the tension hanging over the halls like the graduation countdown banners.

The people around us reluctantly departed until it was just Merritt and me standing there.

"Why did the marriage matter so much to you anyway? Your family's loaded."

She snorted bitterly. "Talk to my dad and his bad investments about that."

Mrs. Bardot approached us. "Girls, do you have a class to get to?"

I didn't respond to her. Not yet. Instead, I kept my eyes on Merritt.

She didn't shy away from me, but her eyes seemed too moist. What was going on? Finally, she nodded and said, "Yes, it hurt our family, and it wasn't me who shared the news. And"—she lowered her voice—"Ryde was in breach of the NDA they signed by telling you. I didn't even know about it until that night."

My mouth fell open. Partly at Merritt's display of vulnerability. She had never let her perfect façade fall. Not when she "apologized" to Rory in front of the whole school, not even when Beckett broke up with her. But now? She looked so defeated, and I swore I saw dark circles under her eyes.

"Please," she said, "don't tell anyone about the...finances," she whispered. "If it gets out, it will *ruin* us."

I was still reeling from her ask. I felt for her; I did. But if she hadn't told the press, who had? My dad? That didn't make sense. It made him look just as bad as me. Was this just another ploy to try and force me into an arranged marriage that I didn't want? The thought made me sick to my stomach.

I didn't have time to think about that though, because Mrs. Bardot was putting her arm around my shoulders and saying, "What if I walk you to class?"

"I can do it on my own," I said, feeling each and every word. I held my chin high and continued to my locker, where I got the books I needed for each class until the end of the day. Even though my backpack felt like a ton of bricks, avoiding excess time in the hallways seemed like an important survival skill right now. And the day had only just begun.

The teachers had obviously been prepped for

the day. Despite the awkward looks and comments I got in the hallways, the classrooms were all business. They kept us busy throughout the hour and never once left the classroom. Eating lunch in the cafeteria was out of the question, so I booked it to the AV room after fourth hour

Walking into the room full of dusty shelves of VHS tapes and Mr. Davis sitting at his computer in the corner felt as much like home as anything else had lately.

Rory and Callie were already sitting at the table, and they'd somehow gotten another table set beside our original so the guys could fit with us.

"How was today?" Rory asked. "I heard about the face-off with Merritt."

Callie cringed. "What happened?"

I shook my head, set my heavy backpack on the ground, and dropped onto a chair. "It was a weirdest thing ever. Merritt basically accused me of sleeping around and then proceeded to tell me that she did not break the news to the press. All of that before asking me not to tell anyone about her family's financial situation."

A sardonic laugh sounded from behind me, and I looked over my shoulder to see Jordan carrying her tray in. "Merritt asking you for help? Now? That's rich."

Kai followed a few steps behind her and sat at the table next to me.

The irony of my argument with Merritt didn't escape me. "It was a weird though," I said. "It was like she was defeated or something. I didn't want to, but I felt kind of sorry for her, at her situation." I knew what it felt like to have your parents keep secrets and fall short of who you thought they were.

The door opened again, and Ginger came in next with Ray. She set her tray alongslide Callie's. "What did I miss?"

Rory shrugged. "Merritt asked Zara for help and down is now up."

Ginger began opening the wrapper with her silverware inside. "Tell me more."

Within a few minutes, all of my best friends and their boyfriends (or friend in Callie's case) were around the table, talking, sharing food with me, and somehow, laughing.

Some people believed in soulmate, singular. I didn't. These people around the table, they were my soulmates, and I couldn't imagine my life without them. I needed them now more than ever.

## THIRTY-NINE

LUNCH with the girls was exactly what I needed. Unfortunately, after lunch, there came classes. And one of those was current events. As I walked down the hallway, it seemed to be getting longer and longer, and each step I took I had to suck in more oxygen to keep from feeling dizzy.

I'd read all the online articles, but I could only imagine the headlines that would show up in the *Everyday Emerson*. This story had it all. Business, Entertainment, Sports. I wouldn't be surprised if there were stories in each section.

An arm slipped through mine, and I turned to see Rory walking beside me. Her eyes were straight ahead, but she was whispering to me. "You can do this. I'm going to make sure no one talks about what happened. We'll be okay."

With each word she spoke, I could feel myself calming ever so slightly. How she knew exactly what I needed to hear, I had no idea. I just knew I was more thankful than ever to have her as a friend.

We had to separate to walk through the door, but she stuck close behind me and sat beside me in class. Mr. Sullivan acted as if it was just any other day, passing out copies of the *Everyday Emerson.*

My copy landed in front of me on the desk. A photo of Ryde and me stared back at me from the cover, right next to a photo of what was clearly Ronan and me arguing in front of Waldo's. A third photo showed Chester escorting me to his car and fighting off the paparazzi with his cane.

The headline said in big, bold letters, *The Heart-throb Meets His Heartbreaker.*

"They couldn't do any better than that?" Rory muttered, clearly seeing the same headline I was.

Mr. Sullivan loudly dropped the remaining stack of newspapers on his desk and then placed his fingertips on top of them, scaring everyone in the room. A hush fell over the students, almost audible in its silence.

"Listen up," he said harshly. "I don't know what your other teachers have said, but I'm putting it out on the table. Zara was involved in a news incident. I am not interested in hearing about it in this class. If I hear even a whisper related to Ryde Alexander, you will be sent to Headmaster Bradford's office for a week of in-school suspension. Is that understood?"

My cheeks burned, and I gazed at my desk while the rest of the students stayed silent.

Mr. Sullivan's voice boomed throughout the room. "Am I understood?"

The class muttered their assent.

How humiliating. It was one thing to hear the whispers, and it was another altogether to practically feel the thoughts echoing in their minds. I could only imagine what they would hold in and then spew after class was over.

But at least, for now, I was safe.

"Now," he said, "partner up on a news topic, and let's share the daily news."

Rory scooted her desk closer to mine, and I did the same, our chairs scraping over the tile floor along with everyone else's. We put our heads down, immediately flipping past the first page of the newspaper...and the second, where the lead story was continued. In the entertainment section, we read the headline, *Alexander Movies at an All-time High*. In the business section, *Bhatta Productions Falls in the Stock Market*. And in athletics, *Roy Taylor to Speak on Stepson, Bhatta's Love Interest, Tuesday*.

Just the sight of Roy Taylor's name frustrated me and made me think of Ronan. What was he doing right now? Was he missing me as much as I missed him? I wanted to text him, to ask if we could go on a walk or ride on his motorcycle up the coast or just sit in Seaton Bakery together and enjoy coffee. He was always my favorite escape.

But I couldn't, and that realization made missing him even worse, because I couldn't even cling to the hope of forgiveness. Ronan wasn't the kind of guy who played around with text messages and dates. He knew where his true north was, and it wasn't pointing to me.

"What about this one?" Rory asked. "We covered DP last time."

My blood pressure surged at the mention of Ronan's group. Now that I knew the leader and the people in it, it was all so much more desperate that they didn't get caught. I followed her finger to the newspaper story. *Officer Expects to Bust Elusive Group Within the Month*.

"Let's cover it," I said immediately, flipping to

the story in my own paper and poring over it as fast as I could.

*Emerson PD has been hard at work, cracking down on loitering, vandalism, and other crime that harms our community and its value. A long-standing rivalry has existed between Emerson PD and Dulce Periculum, an elusive group with its legends dating back to the early 1900s.*

*"It's time for the feud to come to an end and for our city to be safe," said Sheriff Allen in a briefing with the media.*

*According to his statement, his team has staffed multiple detectives, installed additional surveillance throughout the city, and begun patrolling spots suspected for DP stunts.*

*While the group has kept a low profile, they are suspected to be made up of five to ten individuals in their teens or early twenties.*

*"Throughout the years, they've been pinned with vandalizing public property, tearing up buildings, and diluting the integrity of our great city," Sherriff Allen said. "It is time to stop letting hooligans run the city and start letting the city run them."*

*While Sherriff Allen kept the source of his confidence hidden, he says he anticipates capturing the group within the month, upon which point they will be tried for previous misdemeanors and expected to halt all future stunting.*

*If you have information on DP, contact the Emerson Police Department.*

. . .

A sense of dread settled in my stomach. Ronan had said DP never vandalized anything, but there were years and years of charges stacking up against them, and I would hate to see him suffer the consequences for the police department's lack of suspects. I hoped he was being careful.

I had to find a way to see Ronan and warn him about the police. To keep him from getting in trouble for things he didn't do.

"Rory," I whispered, "hold up your paper?"

A curious look in her eyes, she obliged, and I reached into my backpack for my phone. I fired off a quick text to Ronan.

Zara: The cops are looking for DP. Be careful.

Rory's eyes were full of emotion as she took me in, but I tried to focus on the report we had to write. I couldn't face the fact that my only link to the guy I'd given my virginity to was now a text message I wasn't even sure he'd read.

My phone vibrated, and my heart leapt. Had Ronan seen my message? Had he replied?

*Message failed to send.*

I tried again and receiving the same notification.

I wiped at my eyes and blinked back tears. Rory rubbed my back, but that just made it worse.

"I'm sorry," I whispered and fled to the bathroom. The reality of my situation hit harder than ever. All the hope I'd been holding on to was gone.

I sat in a stall in the empty room and cried and cried. Only when my sobs subsided did I hear a sniff come from the next stall over.

My heart froze. Someone was in here. "Who's there?" I cautiously called.

A little sigh came first, then Merritt's voice. "I guess we're both having a hard day, huh?"

I snorted. "We agree on something?"

She laughed softly, then quieted. "I'm sorry about everything that happened."

I was silent for a long moment, then said, "Me too."

## FORTY

JORDAN HAD a Future Medical Professionals meeting after school, so I didn't really have an excuse not to go to Mrs. Bardot's office for our meeting. I dreaded it, but the whole day had been hard. How could this be any worse?

As I sat on the bench outside her office and waited by her closed door, all I could do was look at my phone and my failed text message to Ronan, wishing it would go through. That text bubbles would appear on the screen. I frowned. Wishing for things that weren't going to happen didn't do anyone any good.

Since Mrs. Bardot still hadn't come out yet, I decided to pace the empty halls. I hitched my backpack over my shoulder and walked to the other end of the school before turning around and walking back. On one end, I could hear the kids on the track team doing workouts in the gym, on another, music coming from the music room. All these people had lives, goals, things they were working toward. I hoped this meeting would help me find the same.

As I drew closer to Mrs. Bardot's office, I could hear her bird, Ralphie, chirping away. She was cooing something to him. "Sweet Ralphie boy. Want a treat? It's a good thing you're not a parrot, or that would make being a school counselor really difficult." She chuckled at her own joke. "It wasn't me; it was the bird!"

I cringed and knocked on the open door. As I walked in, Mrs. Bardot quickly straightened and stepped away from the bird, as if she didn't want to get caught. Just the gesture brought a smile to my face.

"Looks like you're feeling a little better," she said.

"A little." I turned to Ralphie. "How are you, sweet bird?"

"Brilliant as ever," Mrs. Bardot answered. "Now, let's get to you."

Resigned, I dropped my backpack by one of

the open chairs and sat across from her. "What do you want to talk about?"

"Well, first of all, I think we should talk about you. I know you said you wanted to work for your father's company. Is that still on the table?"

I glared at her. "Did the news headlines make it look like it's still on the table?"

She frowned. "So it's time for plan B."

"Yeah," I said, "I guess."

"Which is what?" She poised her pen over a blank sheet of paper and waited. Just the fact that I had nothing to add to her blank page frustrated me.

Finally, I said, "If I had a plan B, I wouldn't be here."

"There has to be something," she pressed. "What would you have wanted to do if your father hadn't planned on you joining the family business?"

"I don't play what-if games. Asking that question only leads to disappointment and sleeping in your friends guest bedroom and only having two bags of stuff to call your own." My voice cracked. "It means missing your dad. Even if he did something really bad."

Her eyes softened, and she set the pen down. "I have a few aptitude tests if you want to try one."

"Do you think it will help?"

She shrugged. "It's not a bad place to start if you have a little time."

"I have until the end of Jordan's FMP meeting, so I might as well."

She got out one of the school's laptops and pulled up an online test. While I waited, I looked around her office, taking in the diplomas on the wall from Ivy League colleges and her cross-stitched decorations. This woman really was a bundle of contradictions.

When the page loaded, I was faced with a series of true or false questions. Asking whether or not I liked working outside, whether I preferred to work alone or in a group—on and on until I reached the very end. The second I hit submit, my answer appeared on the screen.

*Leadership.*

They said that I would be great working with others, leading teams, and utilizing my problem-solving capabilities with others. I frowned at the screen.

"What did it say?" Mrs. Bardot asked.

I spun the screen to face her, and her eyes moved left and right as she read. "This is great," she said. "There's so much potential here."

That was the problem. When you have limitless

options, choosing one of them means saying no to everything else. And what if I chose unwisely? I didn't have a great track record of decision-making skills.

She shut the laptop screen slowly and clasped her hands. "Zara, I'm not speaking as your guidance counselor. I'm speaking as an adult who's made her own fair share of hard decisions. Any choice you make is the right one for you because you'll make it work no matter what."

My chest constricted at the idea. Was Mrs. Bardot right? I felt like I had already made so many mistakes. But what if they weren't really mistakes? What if they were just the right decisions for me at the time? I hadn't wanted to tell Ronan about my relationship with Ryde because I still hadn't known what it meant or how to get out of it.

There were better ways to handle things, sure, but now they were lessons, not errors. I could only fix the things I could and learn from the rest, and I planned to do just that.

## FORTY-ONE

I USED Jordan's phone to send Ronan a message on the way home.

*It's Zara. Can we talk?*

He didn't respond. Not after five minutes, not after ten, not after Jordan and I walked inside, finished our homework.

"What's up?" Jordan asked, putting her books back in her backpack. "I mean, aside from everything else… You've been quiet."

I shook my head. "I want to make things right with Ronan, but how can I do that if I can't even get him on the phone?

She pressed her lips together and look down thoughtfully. "Can't you just go see him?"

"I don't think it would be a good idea to show

up at his apartment unannounced." I sat back in the chair and ran my hands over my hair. "He's not the kind of guy you sneak up on, you know?"

She nodded, fiddling with the zipper of her bag. "Do you think he just needs more time?"

My eyes stung, and I tried to wipe the tears away. I would give Ronan anything he wanted—time, space, anything—if it meant he would give me another chance.

Jordan rubbed my back. "It's okay."

But it wasn't. "I feel terrible. He thinks I cheated on him, and the cops are looking for him, and his stepdad is talking about him at a press conference tomorrow, and I feel like it's all my fault." I sucked in a deep breath to catch up after all I'd just said.

Jordan lifted my chin and made me look at her. "You didn't know it was all going to go like this. You were being forced into a relationship you didn't choose. The Alexanders and your father should be cleaning up this mess, but you have such a good heart that you're trying to fix it. They're the ones who should be dealing with this. The fact that you're trying so hard just proves how much you care about Ronan."

"But they're not doing anything," I said, "and

you know Roy's just going to get up there and talk about what a disappointing vagrant his stepson is, how he's not in college, how he has tattoos, basically say he's worthless. And there's not going to be anyone there to tell the press otherwise. Ronan's name will be everywhere in the news, and none of it's going to be right."

Jordan straightened from her slumped position on the table. "Unless..."

"Unless what?" I demanded. If there was a way out of this, I was desperate to hear it.

Her eyes widened like I was being slow on the uptake. "Why don't you speak for him? You seem to know Ronan better than anyone else, and the media would go crazy about actually hearing from you."

Her idea could work, and that thrilled me. The news was practically begging to speak with me about Ronan. What if I told them all the true things? All the kind things? And what if I took the spotlight from Roy Taylor? The idea of stealing his fifteen minutes of fame was a pleasant one.

I nodded, liking the idea more and more with each second that passed. "I can get a cab after school, and I should be able to make it to the stadium in time to—"

"Whoa, whoa, whoa." Jordan put her hand on

my shoulder and stared at me. "When are you going to realize that we're here for you? I am taking you to the stadium, and there is no way the girls will let us go without them."

She was right. My friends had proven that they were here for me, and I was more than grateful. I'd happily have their support instead of facing a horde of reporters on my own. Still, it would be a lot. "Are you sure?" I asked.

Nodding enthusiastically, she got her phone and began typing out a message. "Wait until they hear about this."

The girls were not the only ones who wanted to go. That was how Rory, Jordan, Callie, Ginger, Beckett, Kai, Carson, and Ray ended up in a stretch limo on the way to Badger Stadium.

I couldn't believe that everyone was here with me. They all had different advice, from Ray, who told me to just give Roy Taylor the finger, to Kai, who'd had plenty of experience speaking with the press because of his game *Rush+*. Still, nothing could have prepared me for the horde of people outside the stadium.

Instead of setting up inside, they had a podium covered in Badger memorabilia with a massive speaker system set up outside. The crowd over-flowed from the sidewalk into the blocked off street. Our driver had to park nearly half a mile away.

I chewed on the inside of my cheek, taking in all the people.

Ginger squeezed my shoulder. "You can do this." She lifted her phone. "And I'm filming so even if they don't listen, you can get your word in."

My rapidly beating heart settled, if only a bit. I nodded and took a deep breath. I could do this.

I had to.

The limo driver opened the door, and we stepped into the chaos. There were fences leading us to the open area in front of the stage. It was packed to the brim with at least a hundred people, and we sidled along the back with the rest of the reporters.

I lowered the hat Jordan had given me to keep my identity on the down low, but my time would come soon to speak up. To step forward.

I couldn't help but look around for Ronan, even though I knew he wouldn't be here. Instead, my eyes landed on the sorry excuse for a human being walking onto the stage. Roy Taylor's smug grin and crooked nose made me want to punch him square in the face.

"Is that his stepdad?" Ginger whispered next to me.

I nodded, because even though I wasn't much of a sports fan, I would recognize that worthless face anywhere. "He makes me sick," I muttered.

"Me too, and I've never even met him," she said.

But then I saw something I hadn't expected. A slender woman walking behind him with dark, curly hair and soulful brown eyes.

Ronan's mom.

It had to be. Was she really standing beside that man right now? How betrayed must Ronan have felt when night after night he experienced new bruises, new burns, and she'd done nothing? And now she stood by Roy still while Ronan lived in a squalid apartment with four other boys, no help from anyone? It made me hate her just as much. Maybe more.

They sat in a couple of open seats in a row of chairs behind the podium. Another man in the procession behind them went to the line of microphones and introduced the press conference, reminded everyone why they were here. The fact that they even had a voice to speak about Ronan was despicable.

He introduced Roy Taylor and took one of the empty seats.

I watched as the man I despised stood to his full, massive height and walk confidently to the microphone. The pure size of him made me dislike him even more. Imagining him towering over a wiry teenager like Ronan, using his weight to abuse and intimidate.

He raised his hands, and the audience settled as if he held some magic power. He leaned forward and spoke into the numerous microphones on the podium. "Hello, everyone."

The people around me muttered greetings back, but I could only shake my head and try to keep the acid in my stomach from spilling out. I wanted to stand and shout, throw eggs or something as disgusting at Roy, but I knew now was not my time.

He cleared his throat and said, "We are here to discuss the actions of my stepson and one Zara Bhatta. I will be taking questions, but first I'd like to make a statement."

I braced myself for the vitriol about to spew

from his mouth. The words that followed did not disappoint.

"As many of you know, I had the pleasure of marrying this beautiful woman eleven years ago. I met her after a nasty divorce, and if I'm being honest, I didn't quite believe in love. She showed me just how real love could be.

"When we married, she brought a son with her. Ronan. His father was an addict, completely useless. Even though she escaped the abusive situation, damage had already been done to her son. We struggled for years with behaviors, therapy, special programs, and if you can't tell, none of it seemed to work. He grew progressively more defiant, more violent, and eventually so withdrawn, he left the house altogether rather than follow a few simple rules.

I glared harder at him than I could ever imagine, but still he continued.

"The actions of a delinquent teenage 'bad boy' are no representation of the Brentwood Badgers and the leadership of the team. Now, I'll accept a few questions."

The rush of questions rang throughout the space, but I stood to my full height, whipping off my cap and glasses, waving my hand high in the air.

Whispers spread around me growing to full-blown pandemonium, at first asking if I was Zara Bhatta and then shouting questions at me about why I was there.

All attention had turned on me, but my gaze stayed on the garbage standing at the front of the crowd. His eyes were narrowed as he spoke into the microphone. "Questions for me?"

My friends began chanting, "Bring up Zara! Bring up Zara!"

The entire crowd broke into the same chant, copying their cries.

With a poorly masked look of frustration, Roy Taylor said, "Would the rollicking teenage girl like to come up to the mic?"

"You're sick!" Jordan shouted.

I loved her more than ever.

I held my head high as I walked to the front of the crowd, ignoring the questions being shouted at me along the way. Like Roy, I had a statement to make, and this one true.

The entire crowd fell silent as I stepped up to the microphones. I could feel Roy and his evil aura on the stage, even though he now stood feet away. Despite my discomfort, I needed to speak up, needed to tell them who Ronan really was.

I took a deep breath and focused on my friends, my rocks. "In my culture, arranged marriage is a standard practice. Ever since I was a little girl, it was understood that my parents would be selecting the man I was to marry. For years, I dreamed of the kind of man they would choose.

"When my mom passed away, I'd hoped that my dad would pick a man who was kind, generous, brave, inspiring, and free of impositions. Instead, he introduced me to Ryde Alexander."

A small, uncomfortable laugh rippled through the crowd.

"While Ryde is a talented actor and many girls have fallen for him, he is not the kind of person I had dreamed of spending my life with. We attempted to date, to grow our relationship, and over time, it became increasingly evident that he was not the man for me. And then I met someone."

My eyes watered at the memory of Ronan leaning against his motorcycle, offering me a ride and instead handing me a lifeline.

"He came to me in a moment of distress, and even though he could have left me alone to deal with my problems, he gave me a ride. He showed me a new way of living. He exemplified how much bravery it took to step away from tyranny disguised in good intentions." I turned my gaze Roy Taylor. "Abuse disguised as a loving stepparent."

It wasn't my story to tell about what Roy had done to Ronan, so I didn't detail it, but I would make sure they knew who Ronan really was.

"Ronan showed me that the most precious things in the world can't be bought with money or social connections. That to help someone, you don't need to donate a million-dollar burn unit; you only need to lend your heart. And he showed me that to love, you need to be fully yourself.

"Unfortunately, I was not fully myself with him. I did not tell him about my father's wishes for my life, nor my own desires to break away from them. And so it looked like I lied. Like I cheated. But the only person I cheated was myself.

"Although I do not regret calling off my engagement with Ryde or my feelings for Ronan, I regret not being brave enough to share all of who I was with Ronan. I can only hope that as time progresses, he will find it in his kind and selfless heart to forgive me. And that you may find it in your hearts to look beyond the guise of money and polish"—I turned toward Roy Taylor and stared at him with all the hatred I felt—"and into the truth."

For a moment, the crowd looked at me stunned,

and then the applause erupted from my friends, toward the back. They stood and cheered. I had shown them who Ronan was, but more importantly, I'd shown myself who I really was. And I was the kind of girl who fought for the ones I loved.

## FORTY-TWO

BECKETT AND RAY came to the front of the stage and acted as impromptu bodyguards as I made my way to the back. A crush of reporters attempted to come closer, always looking for more information, even though I'd already said everything that mattered. They walked me to the back of the crowd, the spot where the limo had dropped us off, while the same guy from the start of the press conference tried to call everyone back to order.

Their noise echoed off the surrounding buildings, assaulting my ears. Finally, Ray and Beckett got me back to my friends, and Ginger and Jordan immediately put their arms around me. Callie and Rory surrounded us, patting me on the back, hugging me, telling me how amazing I'd been.

"I didn't do anything special," I said. "I just told the truth."

Rory shook her head. "Can't you see? You gave Ronan the voice he never had."

My heart swelled at the thought of him. I just hoped he knew how much he deserved every single word.

We continued walking toward the end of the barricaded street, a few reporters following us, but most swarming Roy for his response.

From a few feet behind us, a rough voice shouted, "Beckett?"

We all turned to see his father walking toward us. His eyes took us in, looking completely bewildered before turning back to Beckett. "What are you doing here?"

Beckett put his hand on my shoulder. "I had to support a friend."

His father's jaw seemed tight. "A little heads-up might have been nice."

Beckett's Adam's apple bobbed. "I'm—"

His dad shook his head. "Not now. Are you kids okay? Do you need help getting out of here?"

Kai spoke up. "The limo's almost here."

Mr. Langley nodded. "Do that. I'll get a couple officers to watch you."

He disappeared back into the crowd and returned with a couple of men in police uniforms. After telling them to watch us, Mr. Langley looked at Beckett and said, "I've got to get back in there." With a disappointed look, he turned back and walked away.

Beckett's jaw twitched before leading us toward the limo.

"I'm so sorry," I said. I knew how hard it was to be on bad terms with your dad.

"Don't apologize." He glanced over his shoulder again. "My dad will understand. You said what you needed to."

The guilt slowly eased. Not every parent was like my dad, turning their back on their child for a surprise or a betrayal.

"Let's get going," one of the two officers said, looking over his shoulder toward the crowd. "Don't want anyone getting ideas to follow us."

As he suggested, we picked up speed toward the spot where the limo had dropped us off. For a moment, I wondered what we must have looked like —a gaggle of Academy students hightailing it away from the stadium.

"This is it," Kai said, looking at an app on his phone. "He should be here in two."

The cops turned, facing the reporters who were now accosting Roy Taylor. Even from here I could hear their shouts, asking him about his relationship with Ronan, how he'd adjusted to having a son. The stutters I heard through the microphone brought me an eerie sense of joy.

My friends stood together discussing what had happened. There was an excited feeling within our group, but I still had an edge of worry. Would Ronan see what I had said? Would it make a difference?

Though I thought it was impossible, something distracted me. I heard the cops say "DP," and my attention immediately shifted.

"We got intel where they'd be tonight," one said low. "Can't believe I got put on the call."

My stomach clenched. They were going to find Ronan and his friends?

The other lifted his chin. "You'll be a god if you catch them."

The first one chuckled. "Yeah, but what's Chief gonna do without the white whale?"

The limo pulled up, and my friends began climbing in. Beckett glanced back at me. "Coming, Zara?"

I nodded jerkily and let him help me inside. It

was nice to be protected—but who would protect Ronan and his friends from the police? It sounded like the cops had a good chance of catching DP tonight, and I worried that they wouldn't be prepared. How would a criminal record look when they were applying for jobs or trying to support themselves? None of them exactly had anyone in their corner, and they didn't need anything going against them.

"Jordan," I said across the limo. "Can I use your phone?"

She nodded, handing it to me. "He hasn't texted back yet."

I tried to ignore the sting of those words as I typed in his number and hit call. It only rang once and went to voicemail.

Rory looked between us, confused. "Who are you calling?"

"Ronan," I answered, "but his phone must be off."

Beckett shook his head. "No, it's on. He blocked Jordan's number."

Every head swiveled toward him.

"What do you mean?" I asked.

"And how do you know?" Carson added.

Beckett leaned back in his seat and shook his

head. "After I broke up with a certain someone, she tried to call me so many times I had to take matters into my own hands. She was *ticked* when she found out I'd blocked her number. Apparently there's a way to tell. If they cancel the call, it should ring twice. If the phone is dead, then it should go to voicemail. One ring is a definite block."

I'd thought my heart couldn't hurt any more over him, but blocking Jordan's number just proved what I'd suspected. There would be no second chances. Not with Ronan. But that meant there'd be no way to tell him about the bust.

Then a memory struck me. Our friend group had known where DP would be once before. We'd watched them stunt outside of the local movie theater. And then Beckett had taken Rory to watch them another time...

I turned to Beckett, taking him in. "You know something we don't." My eyes narrowed, anger flaring within me.

He raised his eyebrows. "What are you talking about?"

Rory even shifted her shoulders, like she could protect him from my obvious anger. But she couldn't shield him from admitting the truth. "What are you talking about?" she asked, clearly on edge.

. . .

I still stared Beckett down. "How did you know that the DP stunt was taking place that night, at that time, outside the theater?"

His eyes darted away from mine. He was caught.

"And why was your dad there today?" I demanded.

Beckett let out a frustrated sigh and hung his head before looking back at me. The entire limo was silent, when only moments before we'd all been buzzing with adrenaline.

Finally, he said, "My dad's been making deals with Roy Taylor ever since he bought the team, negotiating players' contracts. After my mom left, I would have to tag along sometimes, and if we were at Roy's house, I would see Ronan."

My chest tightened, thinking of Beckett seeing Ronan, knowing him, in the middle of his pain. "You're friends with him?"

He gave a noncommittal shrug. "Not really. We were never close or anything, but we still talk from time to time."

Rory's mouth hung open. "You knew Ronan and you never mentioned anything all this time?"

Beckett shifted his gaze between Rory and me. "He's not exactly the kind of guy who wants his business being spread around."

Anger fired over Rory's face. "My best friend has been devastated for days, and you're telling me we could have done something about it? How could you keep that from me?"

The betrayal underneath her rage was clear, and I felt it too, if not as acutely.

"Tell me where he'll be tonight," I said. "The cops are going to bust them. I heard them talking at the stadium."

The corner of Beckett's mouth tugged down.

An even more horrified thought crossed my mind. "Were you the one who gave them away?"

His eyebrows furrowed, and he quickly shook his head. "What? No. Never."

"Someone did," I said tightly, "and unless you can get Ronan to tell you where he's going to be, he and a bunch of boys our age are going to be slapped with crimes they didn't commit."

Beckett's frown grew even deeper. "It's too late."

Rory's voice was dangerously low. "Is it too late, or are you just going to keep another secret?"

"I was going to take you there tonight," he said,

completely defeated. "They're going out to Seaton Pier. They have a prank planned too."

I hurried up to the window separating us from the driver and knocked on it frantically. As it slid open, I shouted, "Take us to Seaton Pier! *Now!*"

The driver jerked toward me, surprised at my vehemence. I didn't need his shock. I needed his action.

"The faster you get there, the bigger the tip!" I cried. I didn't care that I only had a couple hundred dollars to my name. I would give it all to make sure Ronan didn't give up everything he had too.

## FORTY-THREE

CALLIE LOOKED WORRIED as I scooted back to my seat in the limo. "What are you going to do?"

I shook my head, trying to think fast. What was I going to do? I had to figure out something, and fast. Was I just going to yell at Ronan as he ran along the boardwalk? Or should I try to distract the police? There wasn't a lot I could come up with right now.

"Kai," I said, "you wouldn't happen to have spray paint in the car, would you? Eggs?"

His eyebrows drew together. "That's not exactly something I carry around in my limo."

My chest tightened, and I turned to the limo driver again, knocking on the window. The car jerked as he turned down a street, but the window came down. "I'm driving as fast as I can."

"Good," I sputtered. "I need something that's going to leave a mark. Paint? Oil? Do you have any?"

As he kept one hand on the wheel and his eyes on the road, he reached over and pulled open the glove compartment. Out came at thick black marker. "That's the best I got."

It would have to do.

Ignoring my friends' questions, I looked straight at Beckett. "Where are they starting?"

"He only told me when the big trick would be," he rushed out.

I groaned loudly, feeling frustrated with Ronan for the first time. Why did they feel like they had to show off so much?

Before the question even worked its way through my mind, I knew it was not. Ronan wasn't the kind of guy who just "got by." He showed just how strong he was by *living* despite what had been done to him or said about him.

My mind worked over solutions. If the cops were catching them at the pier, we had to make sure DP didn't get there. "We have to try and stop them before they get cornered at the pier."

Jordan nodded and went to the window the driver had left open. "Stop us over by the old needle factory." She turned back to us, but spoke to me directly. "That would be a good place to start."

"Where next?" Ray asked, all power and purpose.

Kai looked to Jordan. "The end of the boardwalk?"

She nodded. "And then maybe just the streets leading up to the pier?"

"Yes," I said, feeling better to at least have a plan.

She gave the order to the driver, and she and Kai were the first to get out.

Ginger and Ray got dropped by the end of the boardwalk. Rory offered to stop at the marina, farther down from the pier to see if they were hiding in any of the boats. She glared at Beckett. "You better get out with me and help fix this."

He swallowed, nodded. "Of course."

The limo driver dropped them off there. Then it was just Callie, Carson, and me in the limo.

"Let's go to Schumer Street," I said to the driver, then spoke to Callie and Carson. "You guys can stop them if they pass you."

Callie nodded. "But what about you? Will you be okay on your own?"

Carson agreed. "I can go with you if I need, then Callie can stay with the car?"

I shook my head. "I'll be fine on my own." I had to be.

The car went down the main road and stopped a few blocks out.

Carson hopped out and took Callie's hand to help her down. He flung the door shut, and the limo sped off. I hadn't seen any police cars yet, but I asked the driver to slow down so he wouldn't draw any suspicion before the time was right.

He dropped me off by the boardwalk to the pier, and I got out of the limo holding the fat marker in my hands. It felt inadequate, small compared to the big weight hanging over my head. How could I protect someone I didn't know was coming from a threat I couldn't yet see?

My eyes darted around the pier, not seeing anyone except for an old fisherman, his line dangling over the railing. There was a couple farther down the beach, sitting on a blanket. It looked like they were having a picnic. It made me think of the first night Ronan had taken me here. When we'd sat together on the sand and he asked me what kind of adventure I would have if I could.

Now I knew the answer.

I was doing things I never imagined possible, facing challenges I hadn't anticipated, and still it didn't feel complete without him.

I wiped away saltwater of my own and started over to the ocean. There was a boat floating in the distance. The Coast Guard. The guy up front stood behind a massive gun, and acid rose in my throat. I'd been worried about Ronan getting caught; I'd never thought about him being hurt.

All I could hear was the sound of the waves and the rush of my pulse through my ears. It was like the time my father, Beth, and I had been in Florida on a business trip when a hurricane struck the shore. We hadn't expected it to come so soon, but our plane couldn't leave, so we were forced to stay in the hotel. Outside our window, palm trees practically snapped under the weight of the gales, and rain smattered against the windows like angry bullets. But I hadn't expected for the silence to come. For a moment, the wind had stalled, the wreckage lay out, clear through the windows.

I had asked my father if it was over, and he'd told me that the worst was yet to come. Right now, I felt like I was in the eye of the hurricane, by myself, with nowhere to go for shelter. Nowhere to shelter my loved ones.

I didn't even know if I was really in the right place or if Beckett had diverted us to protect Ronan's privacy. Beckett had kept the secret for too long. Maybe it wasn't really out of duty to Ronan, but out of a responsibility to someone else? I hoped Beckett was as honest as he seemed to be before today, but my father had shown me I couldn't trust anyone.

Now I knew I could only count on myself, and my friends—the family I chose.

A police car slowly drove up to the pier parking lot, and I watched the officer inside, sitting, staring. If I hadn't been on guard, I wouldn't have thought anything of it. Just another cop patrolling the area, looking out for drugs and troublemakers.

Knowing what I did, I followed his gaze to an unmarked police car about a half mile down the road. The police were going to surround DP, so they wouldn't have a next chance to escape.

Blood rushed through my ears even stronger than before. The worst part of the storm was coming. Was I ready for this?

My gaze swung wildly around, looking for

anywhere DP could be coming from, hoping I might see Ginger and Ray farther down the pier with a group of friends in black, flying under the radar. But it was just the two of them.

I glanced at an old fishing house near the boardwalk where they used to sell bait and tackle. Was DP hiding in there? Or maybe they were at the boats, the docks farther down?

Suddenly, I heard yelling in the distance and immediately did the only thing I knew how to do. I bent over the dock with a marker and begin writing in big letters while shouting, "DULCE PERICU-LUM! AUDENTES FORTUNA IUVAT!"

I prayed their phrase was right. That I might have some luck, because this was as bold as it got.

The police car door flung open, and a man in uniform ran toward me, shouting, "Stop right now, young lady!"

My hand moved furiously over the boardwalk. Keep writing, that was all I needed to do to distract them.

I heard other sirens blaring, other car doors opening, another man shouting at me to stop.

I just kept yelling, over and over again: *Fortune favors the bold. Fortune favors the bold.*

The full weight of a body crushed me to the

ground, holding me against the rough planks and then snapping handcuffs around my wrists. As the two officers hauled me to my feet, the last thing I saw of the pier was the big black lettering saying *AUDENTES FORTUNA IUVAT*.

FORTY-FOUR

THE OFFICERS MARCHED me to the police vehicle as they began reciting my Miranda Rights. "Anything you say or do can be used against you in a court of law…"

"Good," I said, strength I didn't know I possessed finding my voice. "It's been me all along. I am *Dulce Periculum*. Anyone else who has been affiliated with the group has done so because of my threats to them."

The officer at my right gave me a narrow gaze before shoving me into the car. I sat in the back seat for the most uncomfortable ride of my life as he drove across town. My heart raced, and despite the pain of cold metal cutting into my wrists, I couldn't help but smile. I'd drawn them away from Ronan. He and his friends were safe.

The officer parked behind the police station and walked me inside. I'd never been on this end of the law, on the end that was being forced and jostled and threatened as I faced the consequences of my actions. It made my heart race and my blood boil, and I'd never felt more alive.

Was this what DP was searching for? The adrenaline of life lived on the edge? How had I missed it all while living so comfortably I might not have lived at all?

The cop led me into a holding cell filled with other women of all shapes and sizes. He undid my handcuffs and shoved me in before clanking the gate shut. I stumbled and steadied myself before turning and watching him walk to the desk where another guy in uniform sat leisurely with his feet on the weathered wood.

He lifted his chin at me. "This is her? Doesn't look like she could jump in the air, much less do a flip."

If I wasn't behind bars, I would have thrown fists. Instead, I gave him the finger and a few choice words. America's finest, making fat jokes about teenage girls? It didn't get much lower than that.

The officer who'd brought me in chuckled, and the one at the desk one spat on the floor toward me.

I was disgusted.

"Don't worry," he snorted, "we'll call your parents. It's probably past your bedtime."

I thought I couldn't be angrier than I already was, but rage fired through my veins. Did they really talk to people like this?

I mean, I knew I was a criminal and all, but the fat jokes were a little much for an organization that literally had a reputation for liking donuts. The guy who brought me in walked out, clearly unfazed by the whole evening. I glared at his back, at the wreckage he wanted to cause a group of teenagers just living their lives.

Someone cackled behind me—an older lady with scraggly gray hair—and a sense of dread immediately went through me. I looked away, but that didn't stop her from laughing. In fact, she just laughed more.

"You got a lot of fight left in you," she said in a smoker's voice. "I like ones like that."

The way she said it made my skin crawl. I stood as close to the bars as I could get, hoping they would get ahold of someone to come and get me soon. But then my heart sank. Who would get me?

My father? They wouldn't even know to call Jordan's mom or someone who actually cared about me.

"Don't I get a phone call?" I asked.

The officer just laughed.

I slumped against the bars, still not making eye contact with the crazy lady. At least I could hope my diversion was enough to distract some of the officers. Plus, I confessed to the crimes DP had "committed." They didn't need more evidence than that, did they?

I leaned my head back against the cold metal bars. I felt like a colossal failure. I'd gotten Ronan into this publicity mess, and I felt like I'd made the world's most feeble attempt at getting him out of it. Talking into a microphone? Writing on the dock with what basically equated to a Magic Marker? Weak.

Not only had I done so little, but this would surely land me a one-way ticket to expulsion. I could only imagine the heyday Birdie would have with my psychological state and blatant disregard for my future. Clearly not all the decisions I made would be the right ones.

Time seemed to pass slowly, especially since I could feel the eyes of the other women on me.

Someone tried to talk to me, but I kept my face straight ahead. I didn't know these people, and I definitely didn't trust them. My own father had basically sold me into marriage, and he wasn't a criminal.

Familiar shouting reached my ears, and my eyes widened.

"GET MY DAUGHTER OUT OF HERE RIGHT NOW... NO, SHE WILL NOT BE SPEAKING TO YOU WITHOUT AN ATTORNEY."

My dad was here?

The officer spoke dulcetly in response, but clearly it didn't work because my father yelled, "DO YOU KNOW WHO I AM? I COULD BURY YOU WITH MY POCKET CHANGE!"

"Oh damn," a woman across the cell muttered.

They burst into the room, the officer right behind my dad, and I saw anger and worry in his eyes. "Zara!" he cried, rushing to me. "Get her out of here," he said in a deadly voice. "Unlock this, *now*."

The cop took his sweet time putting his key in the lock and twisting it so it made a heavy clicking sound.

Dad shot the gate open and held me in his arms

tighter than I ever remembered him holding me. He ran his hands through my hair. "Zara, thank God you're okay."

I reflexively hugged him back. *This* was my dad. The man I'd cried with and grieved with after my mother died. But then, as I stepped out of the cell, all of the feelings of betrayal came right back.

I stepped away from him distrustfully. "What are you doing here?"

The old lady cackled from the cell and said, "You tell him, sweetheart."

I glanced over my shoulder at her and marched out of the police station. He followed behind me, quietly for once. When we got outside and into the open spring air, I whirled on him. "What are you doing here?" I asked again.

He slowly licked his lips, a sign that he was thinking of something. But there was no way to just explain away his behavior—his utter absence and then utter presence.

"What did you expect me to do when they told me my daughter was in jail?" he finally said.

I rolled my eyes. "I don't know, maybe turn your back on me like you did when I didn't accept your arranged marriage to further your career?"

His eyes shined in the streetlights. I almost

thought I was mistaken, because this man didn't cry. The only time I've ever seen him cry was the day my mother died, and then after that, it was back to business. The business of his production company, the business of being a father but not a caregiver. But right now, his eyes were red, and he whispered, "You were right. Your mother would be ashamed of me."

"Why did you do it?" I asked. I had to. His actions just didn't make sense. The father who raised me never would have signed a deal with the Alexanders like that. I think that's what hurt the most.

He looked around us, like he was worried someone might overhear, but when he realized there was no one outside the police station, not at this hour, he whispered, "I'm losing the house, Zara."

My eyes flew open. "What?" There was no way I had heard him right. How did this align with him paying the Alexanders for Ryde to marry me?

He hung his head, hardly able to meet my eyes. "The business has struggled the last two years, we took some risks we didn't need to, and we passed on some things that would have been sure money. I was ashamed, and I hated the thought of you not having everything you deserved in life."

This still didn't seem right. "If we're running out of money, how did you have the money left to write them a check?"

"I took out a loan against the business. It was the only thing I could think to do."

My mouth was slack, taking in everything he said. He was ready to give everything he had left so I could live with Ryde and rely on his money to give me the finer things in love. The problem was, he had it all *wrong*.

"Don't you get it?" I asked, frustrated. "All my life, we'd had plenty of designer clothes, people to help us around the house, cook us meals, but what I've missed out on in all of this is my *dad*."

I thought of Jordan and her mom and all the love that filled their house. I would trade everything, all my possessions, for my dad to love me the way Jordan's mom loved her. The way Mom used to love me. That love was more valuable than anything else in the world.

Dad swallowed and met my eyes. "But you deserve so much more, Zara."

I shook my head. "I deserve nothing less."

"Can you ever forgive me?" he asked, taking my

hands. "I promise, I'll do what it takes to learn, really learn, how to be the dad you deserve."

I wanted that more than anything, I did, but something still held me back. "Why did you go to the press about the engagement? The last few days have been miserable."

His lips formed a thin line. "I didn't. Ryde's parents did. They thought they could blackmail us into following through with it." He seemed to sag. "I guess people will do a lot they shouldn't when they're worried about their security. Even hurt their children."

"You tried to cancel my tuition," I accused.

"I couldn't come to apologize to you without being sure you had a place to live. The settlement I was planning to pay the Alexanders only covered a few months of the mortgage at our house."

My mouth opened and closed. He needed my tuition to keep the house? "Is it that bad?"

Slowly, he nodded and ran his hands over his thinning hair. Instead of the big, strong man I'd always seen in my dad, he seemed small to me. Helpless.

No matter how much anger I had, no matter how much he had hurt me, I realized that I needed him more. I reached out to him and hugged him, and he sighed into my shoulder. "I'm so sorry, Zara."

"I am too," I breathed. This was a horrible situation, and we both had lost our way. But I hoped we could find the right path, together, as a family.

FORTY-FIVE

ON THE WAY HOME, Dad asked me about *Dulce Periculum*. About Ronan. I told him about the night I'd left the party with Ronan, how kind he'd been and how much different he was from Ryde. When I was done, Dad said, "I'd like to meet him."

My eyes stung as I looked out the window. Lights from the cars passing by blurred in my vision. "I don't think that's going to happen."

Dad reached across the console and squeezed my hand for a moment. "If there's one thing I learned from your mother, it's that love tends to find its way."

I hoped he was right.

When we got inside, he went to his office to make calls with his lawyer, and I went up to my room to plug in my phone and call my friends. There were about fifty texts from them, and I quickly thumbed through them to see what had happened with Ronan. A text from Jordan made my entire night.

Jordan: HE GOT AWAY.

I pumped my fist in the air and grinned at the screen, thankful my plan had worked. I dialed a group call, and each of my friends' faces quickly popped on the screen.

"What happened?" Jordan asked first. "Ginger said the cops hauled you away!"

"They did." Ginger squinted on the screen. "Are you in your room?

Callie asked, "Did you get in trouble?"

"Are you okay?" Rory asked.

I held up my fingers, ticking off each of my answers. "The police caught me and took me into the station. Where my father came and got me."

Each of them looked equally surprised, and Jordan even gasped.

"He apologized and he said that the business isn't doing well. He's about to lose the house."

Jordan's mouth fell open. "So that's why he wanted you to marry a rich guy…"

"Yeah," I said, the weight of it all falling on me.

"So are you staying at my house tonight?" she asked.

I looked over the top of my phone screen at my room. It wasn't the sanctuary it had once been, but it was well past midnight. "I think I'll stay here. It's late."

She nodded. "You're welcome anytime."

"Thank you. You have no idea how much that means to me."

She lifted up the corner of her mouth in a smile. "So tell us what happened after the police got you. Has Ronan called you?"

I shook my head. Unfortunately, his was not one of the names I had seen on my screen.

Rory smiled at me and said, "My mom saw you on the news. She said that you were amazing."

I grinned back. "I can't believe we did that." But it had been so much easier than I had thought, speaking to a bunch of people under pressure. Maybe public speaking could be in my future. But I didn't want to talk about me. "Did you guys all make it back okay? Was someone able to tell Ronan?"

"None of us saw him," Rory answered. "Or I

mean, we did; we just couldn't talk to him. They were base jumping from the needle factory, but when we heard your shouting and the police sirens, they stopped and turned around."

A huge sigh of relief escaped me. It had worked. My feeble attempt at helping them had succeeded. I don't know whether they would get caught tomorrow or months from now. But at least I had helped them today.

## FORTY-SIX

WHEN I WOKE up in the morning, Dad asked if I would stay home from school. We had a lot to figure out.

I agreed, because even though there were only several weeks left in the school year, everything seemed to be up in the air. We sat at the dinner table, eating cereal and milk, talking about everything. For the first time, I felt like he spoke to me as an adult and not as one of his employees or someone he needed to shelter. I found out that he had been paying his employees' paychecks before putting anything toward the mortgage, and we either had to find a way to make money for back payments or find a new place to live.

The business would be okay at least until the

Alexander film released this summer and he could make some of his investments back, but we would eventually have to downsize our own life.

"So what do you think we should do?" he asked. "I can file for an emergency loan to cover the mortgage payments."

I shook my head. "No. Let's find somewhere else." I thought of the last place that felt like home to me and smiled. "Actually, there are these cute townhouses…"

By the end of the day, he had called a realtor and signed a lease on a three-bedroom townhouse just a few rows down from Jordan's.

After signing papers, we walked into the empty place, and I could see my father's shoulders sagging. I put a hand on one and said, "We made the right decision."

He covered my hand with his and shook his head. "How did I have a daughter who is so wise?"

With a smile, I shrugged. "Maybe I got it from Mom."

Laughing, he said, "You definitely did." His face turned somber again. "We have a lot of work to do."

"We do," I agreed.

And we got busy. For the rest of the week, we

marked everything that we wanted to keep in our house and arranged for Beth to sell the rest of it. Telling her that we would have to let her go once the estate was taken care of was the hardest part of all. She hugged me tight, and I cried into her shoulder.

Patting my back, she said, "Don't you cry for me, sweetie. It's been the greatest blessing of all watching you become the woman you were meant to be."

I wondered how I was even close to who I was meant to be, but as our apartment came together over the next week, I realized that I was ready to step into my new phase of life. Even if it came with a lot of boxes and baggage.

Jordan and her mom were lifesavers through it all. While my dad worked long hours at night to help the business catch up, they spent time with me and even made a few videos for her mom's YouTube channel about how to clean and organize a new apartment.

All of my friends came over Friday night after school to help us unpack. Even their boyfriends and Carson came by. They helped me arrange my room so all of my furniture that I had kept was set up just like I liked it. When we were done, they went downstairs to see how they could help my dad, and the girls and I spread out in my new, smaller space.

"What do you think?" Callie asked.

I smiled at the room, at the sheer white curtains over the window facing the community's common grounds, a bright yellow blanket slung over the only chair in my room, in my closet that was practically overflowing with clothes. "It's home."

Ginger grinned at me. "It is pretty nice, but I'm definitely going to miss the hot tub."

I managed to laugh. "You and me both." This move wasn't without losses. I had also gained my dad, and that was the most important thing.

Rory looked down at the floor, picking at a fleck of paint left on her finger.

I frowned. "Are you and Beckett okay, Rory?"

Her lips tugged down in the corner. "Honestly, I'm still a little mad at him. I can't believe he knew Ronan and didn't say anything to me."

I hugged a pillow to my chest, trying to shove down the guilt I felt. "I'm really sorry. I didn't mean to come between you guys."

Quickly, she shook her head. "That's not your fault. And honestly, it was our first fight since we've been a couple. It gave me a chance to see how we would handle it."

"And?" Ginger asked.

Rory shrugged. "We talked it out. I understand why he wanted to keep Ronan's privacy. But I also told him that if something is affecting my best friend, he better tell me.

I smiled at her. At all of them. "I'm so lucky to have you guys."

Callie tilted her head, grinning. "I agree. You guys made my senior year so much fun."

"I can't believe we only have a few weeks left," I said.

"And," Rory added, "only a week until your birthday."

I ran my hands over my face. "Don't remind me."

"What?" Ginger teased. "You're finally going to be able to buy lottery tickets and you don't want to be reminded?"

Laughing, I said, "No, it's just I don't really have a plan." All the years before, Dad threw big blowout parties for me where he invited all of his friends and I pretended like I wouldn't rather be doing something a teenager would enjoy. This year, though, we had nothing. I'd be surprised if Dad even remembered it with how hard he'd been working.

"That's fine," Callie said, "because we've got you covered."

My eyebrows drew together. "What do you mean?"

She gave the other three a conspiring look. "Let's just say eighteen's going to be epic for you."

With a smile, I said, "Low key is just fine. I think I've had about enough 'epic' to last me a lifetime."

As long as I had my dad and my friends, I knew everything would be okay.

FORTY-SEVEN

WHEN I WOKE the morning of my eighteenth birthday, Dad was already at a meeting to sign the final papers on the sale of our old home. Giving my keys to him the night before so he could pass them on to the new owner felt like a loss all its own. The place we'd called home for years was now a place we couldn't return to, but there was also freedom in knowing we were letting go of old patterns, old priorities.

For whatever reason, I felt different. Maybe it was the fact that I was finally an adult. Or that I was in such a different space—physically and emotionally.

As I went to the hall bathroom to get ready for the day, I checked my phone, scrolling through message after message. I leaned against the sink, reading each one.

Rory: Happy birthday, Zara! I can't tell you how happy I am to have you as a friend, and I can't wait to give you your present!

Jordan: HBD! Secretly wishing you still lived with me so I could have filled your room with balloons or something this morning. Love you, girl.

Ginger: Have you bought any lottery tickets yet today??? Hope you find a winner! ;) But seriously, I stinking love you. I never would have been able to find my happily ever after without you telling me I deserved one. I hope you know how amazing you are and that you will ALWAYS deserve the best — today and every day of the year!

Callie: Happy birthday!! I can't believe the school year is almost over and that we only became friends this year. I almost wish we could go back to freshman year and do it all over again so I could have you by my side. I love having you as a friend. If there's anything you need at all today, let me know! Love celebrating you!

Tears spilled over my cheeks as I read each message, one after another, filled with so much love and hope. These girls were my people, my soulmates, and they saw me through the mess, even when I couldn't see it myself. My mom would have loved them—I could only imagine the slumber parties we would have had with Mom making special tea and plenty of pastries to pig out on.

It had been years since I'd been to Mom's grave, but after getting ready, I went to the store and got flowers and drove to Emerson Cemetery. The tree-lined drive brought back painful memories, but I kept driving and parked at the space closest to her grave.

Dad had bought a massive headstone for her shaped like a pair of angels, because Mom was one. He used to introduce her as his best half. The thought made me smile as I walked closer to the place where she lay to rest.

Next to her name on the stone was Dad's name with his birth year, a dash, and an open space. A reminder that life didn't last forever—but love did.

I rested the flowers next to the multiple bouquets that surrounded her grave and pressed my hand over my mouth. Dad still brought flowers here —still made sure she was adorned like the queen she was. It made forgiving him that much easier.

I sat cross-legged on the ground and fumbled with my fingers in my lap, already holding back tears. I turned my eyes up toward the clear blue sky, at the few clouds that wisped through the air.

"I miss you," I breathed.

No answer came. But that didn't stop me from remembering. From imagining.

Mom had said I was born on the most perfect spring day. She said the heavens were ready to welcome her baby girl and that she could see the sun shining through the window of the hospital room as she had me.

That had been eighteen years ago today.

Would she have done it all over if she had known what she'd be saying goodbye to? What we'd have to mourn?

I reached forward and touched the carved letters of her name. *Amara*.

In my mind, I saw the memory, felt her pushing her frail fingers through my hair. "You know my name means eternal? That means no matter what happens to me, whether I'm living on earth or in heaven or reincarnated as a cup of tea, I'll be with you. Every day for the rest of time I'll be with you."

I closed my eyes and tears slipped down my cheeks. My mom had been with me—she'd given me friends when I'd needed them most. She gave me an adventure in Ronan when I thought I would have none. And today she gave me a beautiful spring day.

I felt the sun's rays warm my skin and imagined her feeling the same eighteen years ago. And in that moment, I knew she was right. She was with me, and my heart was with her.

## FORTY-EIGHT

DAD and I sat at our new table for a late lunch. At our old house, we'd always had so much space, but at the four-person table, I could practically reach across the glass top and touch him.

He took a bite of the curry chicken and rice he'd cooked and set his spoon back in the bowl as he chewed it over. "Your mother made this way better."

I smiled, thinking of her homemade meals. "She was a good cook, wasn't she?" Dad had always told her that we could have a chef cook for us, but she insisted. To her, food was love, and if she was making it, then she knew exactly how well we were cared for.

"The best," he agreed, eating quietly for a moment. "What did you do this morning? Did you meet up with some friends?"

I kept my eyes on the table, at my feet I could see through the glass. "I went to see her. At the cemetery."

I looked up in time to see his hand freeze midway from his bowl to his mouth. He slowly lowered it to his bowl. "You went to see her at the cemetery," he repeated, as if the only words he could conjure were the ones he'd just heard.

"I just kept thinking that she gave birth to me on this day—that we were as close as we'd ever been when I was inside her and..." My throat got tight, and I blinked quickly. "I don't want to forget her."

He reached across the table and rubbed my shoulder. I was still trying to get used to this new dad—the one who was emotionally available, who listened to hear instead of reply. "I'm sorry we don't talk about her more," he said.

I wanted to say it was okay, but it really wasn't. I missed my mom, and while he'd thrown himself into the business, I'd had nothing left. Beth had been basically a stranger then. My friends at school didn't understand what I was going through. Fifth graders were hardly a font of empathy.  And even the people who were sorry stopped being as sorry as time went on. To them, it was old news, leaving me to mourn alone. There had been little reminders everywhere. The fact that no one braided my hair after showers so it would be wavy the next day. The missing scent of spice tea when I got home from school. The prepped meals that populated our fridge instead of fresh ingredients carefully selected from the store.

"I miss her," I finally said.

"Me too," Dad said softly. "She loved you so much."

I nodded, my throat feeling tight. "She loved you too. Do you remember the way you guys used to kiss in the kitchen when you thought I wasn't looking?"

He chuckled. "When you have a little one running around and a business to run, there's not much time to sneak a kiss."

"You didn't need to sneak," I said. "I always wanted a marriage like yours."

His eyes were soft. "And I think that's why I need to let you choose."

We hadn't brought up the topic of arranged

marriage, since the wound was still so fresh, but I was surprised he was speaking so openly about it now. "You mean... a love marriage? But you've always talked about arranging a marriage for me."

He took another bite and shook his head. "Life was different in India twenty years ago. We are somewhere new, around new people, new challenges. You're clearly up to the task."

My eyes widened. "So I get to decide? No questions asked?"

"When you want to get married, *if* you want to get married, I will support you."

Relief washed over my entire body, making me feel lighter than I had in months, and tears poured down my cheeks. I didn't have anyone in mind to marry, and maybe I wouldn't ever get married, but I loved that if I ever got another chance with Ronan, I wouldn't have to worry about what my father would think. Who I might betray in the process of following my heart.

"That's a pretty good eighteenth birthday gift," I said, wiping my eyes.

He grinned. "I actually have another one."

My eyebrows rose, and I glanced around the house not seeing anything wrapped or new. "What is it?"

He glanced at the clock. "Give me about ten more seconds."

As if on cue, a knock sounded on the door.

He tilted his head toward the entryway, and I got up to answer it.

I thought maybe he had invited my friends over for a midday birthday celebration, but when I checked the peephole, I didn't recognize the woman who stood at the door. She was thin, with wildly curly hair and big glasses. She seemed familiar, but I knew I didn't know her.

I swung the door open to see who she was.

"Zara?" she asked. She extended her dainty hand. "Pleased to meet you."

Awkwardly, I took her hand back. She was my present? How?

Dad was standing behind me. "Nattie, nice to see you."

That name was definitely familiar. "Nattie Jones? You wrote…"

"*When We Were Free*," she said. "May I come inside?"

I realized how rude I was being, making her stand in the doorway. "Come in," I said, stepping out of the way.

She walked inside and said, "It smells delicious."

I smiled. It wasn't, but I wasn't about to tell my dad that. "It's my mother's curry recipe. Would you like some?"

"Absolutely," she said, her eyes shining. She was one of those people you felt an instant connection to without ever having shared a word. It made me curious to know her better. To understand her story.

While she and my dad greeted each other, I went to the cabinet for a bowl and made her a dish, along with a cup of creamy chai tea. I knew she would need it to go with the spice. Plus, I wanted to feel like my mom was here, and she never would have let a guest sit down without a cup of tea.

When I reached the table, Nattie was sitting down in the empty seat between my father and me, her purse hanging over the back of her chair.

Her eyes lit up even brighter when she saw the bowl. "I love Indian food."

"Well," I said, "you're in the right place."

With a smile, she took a bite, and while she chewed, I gave Dad a look. What was a #1 *New York Times* bestselling author doing here? In our house?

She caught sight of us and the silent conversation we were having and wiped her mouth with a paper napkin. "Oh, I'm sorry. I'm being so rude." She looked at Dad. "Have you told her yet?"

He shook his head. "I thought I would let you do the honor."

She smiled at him, and then turned her full-wattage grin on me. "Zara, your father and I have been talking about the adaptation of my novel, and he told me about his teen lessons with you. And how much he had learned after they stopped. He might have told me a little bit about your arranged marriage—and how it fell through—as well."

My cheeks pinked as I imagined what she must have made of it all. But her smile only seemed to grow. My agent and I have decided that Bhatta Productions can produce the movie, but only with you as the executive producer."

My jaw dropped open, and I was sure she could see bits of chewed up food inside, but I was too shocked to worry about it. "Executive producer?" I asked.

She nodded. "I saw what you did on the news, standing up to the owner of the Brentwood Badgers. That was huge. And not only that, but you told that boy's story beautifully, with all your heart. I trust you to keep the film true to the heart of the story. Are you up for the task?"

Eagerly, I nodded. Just like Ronan, I was so ready to make my own mark in the industry and to help tell people's stories, as truly as I possibly could.

"Great," she said and added, "I'll see you in the studio the week after graduation."

FORTY-NINE

AFTER WE ATE the rest of lunch together, I brought Dad and Nattie to Seaton Bakery. Gayle welcomed us with open arms, and within minutes, she and Nattie were deep in conversation. It felt like showing Dad and Nattie a piece of my heart, and I loved how they embraced it.

While we ate through the array of cupcakes Gayle set out for my birthday spread, I got a text.

*Jordan: Meet us at the Emerson north trailhead at 8.*

Seeing the address, my heart clenched. They probably didn't realize that that was where Ronan and I had shared so much of our time together. But I was curious too. Why weren't we going to Spikes for a night at the club or someone's house to celebrate? Even going to the movies could have been fun. Why a deserted trail?

I tucked my phone back into my purse and enjoyed the rest of the afternoon with Dad and Nattie. She was easy to get along with, and I was really looking forward to working with her. I needed to start reading her book now so I could become more familiar with it. Now that I had my freedom, it wouldn't be so painful to read about characters having their own.

After we got home, I excused myself to get ready for the party with my friends. I wasn't sure what to wear, so I just put on a pair of distressed jeans, a black T-shirt, and sandals that were comfortable enough to walk in. My friends weren't exactly the athletic type like Ronan.

After touching up my makeup, I went downstairs to find Dad at the table, a book open in front of him. He had his notepad out and scribbled on the yellow paper.

"What are you reading?" I asked a little apprehensively.

Abashedly, he held up the book *The Connected Parent* by Karyn Purvis and Lisa Qualls. I couldn't help but smile and melt a little at the same time. Dad was trying, and that meant the world to me.

"Happy reading," I said and walked out of the house.

It struck me that Jordan and I should have carpooled.

Zara: Wanna ride together?

Within seconds I had a reply.

Jordan: Already here. See you soon. :)

What did they have up their sleeves? I got into my car and looked over the for-sale sign in the back glass. Downsizing meant more reasonably, and I was okay with that. If Kai Rush could drive a dented-up Honda, I could give up my Rolls-Royce.

The closer I got to the trails, the more my chest tightened. The last time I'd pulled into the parking lot, I'd been greeted with Ronan's lean frame propped against his motorcycle. He'd taken my hand and showed me one of the most hidden parts of himself.

Today was supposed to be a day for celebration, but a crushing weight settled over me knowing Ronan wouldn't be there to celebrate with me. That I may never talk to him again.

A small part of me had hoped that he would see the press conference, that he would know I had tried to protect him from the police, and that he would forgive me. With each day that passed, that hope was fading. I hardly had any left to hold on to. But maybe Ronan wasn't meant to be in my future. If losing my mom had taught me anything, it was that we weren't promised tomorrow, no matter the circumstances.

As I pulled up to the trailhead, I saw all of my friends' cars parked around the small parking lot. There was hardly room for me there, but I wedged in between Ray's muddy pickup and Kai's Honda and turned off my car.

They weren't in their vehicles, and as I looked around, I didn't see or hear any of them. Where were they? I checked my phone and saw that Rory had texted me.

Rory: We're a little farther up the trail! Come check out your party.

Feeling one part sad and one part excited, I put my phone back in my purse. Maybe this was good. I would be making new memories here, and then it wouldn't always be haunted with what I had lost with Ronan. But then again, I didn't think he left the kind of memory you could erase.

I continued down the trail, keeping my eyes and ears perked for my friends. They must have walked a little farther in, and I was glad I'd worn my

Birkenstocks, which were comfier for walking than a pair of flip-flops or dressier sandals.

I stopped at the spot where I first learned Ronan was a member of *Dulce Periculum*. Shuddered at the memory of peeling back his mask and kissing his perfect lips. I closed my eyes, savoring the memory of him being so close to me, and then other memories pushed their way in. Of him and me on a beach—of me giving everything I had to him.

I opened my eyes, blinking quickly, not wanting to ruin my makeup or break down in tears right before my party.

"Hey," a soft voice said, and for a moment, I thought I might have imagined it. Feeling crazy to even hope, I turned, and my breath caught in my chest.

Ronan stood several feet away, dressed in dark jeans and a loose-fitting T-shirt. His hair was longer, curling around his ears. And his eyes... they captivated me just as much as they always had. He was every bit as perfect as I remembered him, and it literally made my chest ache.

"Happy birthday," he said.

I still couldn't breathe, much less talk. What was he doing here? Had this been an accident?

"I saw you on TV," he said as if he were relating the weather.

I blinked, but it felt like my eyelids were slamming shut and I was forcing them open.  I was scared to move, terrified I would spook him away.

"What you said about me..." He shook his head. "No one has ever said that about me."

My breath was ragged. I wanted to apologize for overstepping my bounds, but I couldn't find the words. Not the right ones anyway.

"I wasn't going to watch it, but Drex made me." His jaw tightened, and I waited for the anger that was about to spill out from those perfect lips, to tell me to get out of his life, for good this time. But those words didn't come. Instead, his jaw quivered as he took me in, all of me. It was like he was seeing me all over again, but for the first time. "And you took the fall for all of us. You kept us safe."

Moisture filled my eyes, and I spoke over the lump forming in my throat. "I just didn't want you guys to be hurt. I care about you. Even if..." My voice cracked. "Even if you don't care about me."

Slowly, he stepped forward, as if he were afraid of shattering what was left of the walls holding me together. His hand reached out, and he brushed his thumb over my cheek. I practically disintegrated into his hand. My body had missed him, his touch, more than my mind even comprehended.

I had to speak, had to do something to make sure this wasn't goodbye for good. "I know you're mad at me for not telling you about Ryde, but I promise you, if you could give me another chance, I'll never keep a secret again."

He shook his head quickly, and my heart fell. It was senseless of me to hope for a second chance when I had so colossally ruined the first. I look down and nodded. "You're right. I shouldn't have even asked."

His fingers lifted my chin, and his dark eyes captivated mine. "Don't you *ever* apologize to me again. You made a mistake, but I did too. I found gold in you, but I let the tarnish of the world keep me away. *Amore et melle et felle es fecundissimus.*"

I panned my memory, trying to figure out what those words meant, but I couldn't remember a one.

"Love is rich with honey and venom," he answered my unspoken question. He cupped my cheeks with both of his hands, so close now I could feel his breath on my skin. Smell the freshness of his gum. It intoxicated me, but not as much as his next words. "I would get stung a million times before I would ever give up something so sweet."

I held my breath, scared to even dream of what this meant. "You told me we were over?"

His eyes softened, and he tilted his head so we were eye level. "No one ever said I was smart."

The meaning struck me fully, but so did fear. "But what if I mess up again? What if I do something else wrong? I don't think I can take you leaving again."

He shook his head. "I'm going to mess up, and you are too, but I'm here for you. For us. I'm not leaving if you're not."

"You're not?"

"No." He was resolute. "If I've learned anything, it's that there are some things worth getting burned for."

The strength in his words, the message behind them, caught me right in the heart. Tears leaked from my eyes, happiness at what he was saying and sadness at his past. "What does this mean for us?"

"It means we're doing the biggest *Dulce Periculum* stunt of all."

"And what would that be?" I asked.

"Falling in love."

A light only Ronan possessed shined in his eyes, and I drank it all in, getting lost in the sunlight. I leaned in close and pressed my lips against his, tasting everything that was uniquely Ronan.

His hands caressed my face, the back of my neck, tangling in my wavy hair and then moving down my body. He had missed me too; I could feel it in his touch and in the way he savored each moment. I recognized the feeling in myself.

"I love you," he said against my lips, and I barely broke the kiss long enough to whisper it back.

I had meant what I said in front of the cameras. Ronan was everything I had dreamed of having in a guy, but now he was right here in front of me, making my reality even better.

The sun had begun fading when Ronan pulled back and linked his fingers through mine. It made me think of my mom saying the sun was shining through the window as she had me. Maybe this was the birth of something new—something incredible.

"We're going to be late for your party," Ronan said.

My eyes flew open, and a cuss word slipped past my parted lips. "I completely forgot. My friends are going to be so mad at me!"

He chuckled low, in a way that told me he knew something I didn't.

"Why are you laughing?" I demanded. "You're going to be the stranger meeting them for the first time and taking the blame for making me late!"

"What if I told you I was part of the birthday present?" He waggled his eyebrows, lighter and more carefree than I'd seen him. I liked the look on him, and it made me feel like maybe we were getting back to where we'd been before—but better.

"If that were the case, I would say best present ever."

He smiled wide and then placed that smile against mine. I loved it when we were so happy, we couldn't kiss without grinning against each other.

"Come on," he whispered, inches from my face. "You're not going to want to miss this."

FIFTY

AS I FOLLOWED Ronan down the trail, my hand linked with his, I asked, "Why have a party? How could it get any better than this?"

His smile absolutely consumed me. It was warm, light, perfect. "I hope you say that every day we're together."

With my heart soaring and a permanent grin on my face, we continued down the path. Soon, I could hear the voices of my friends and a few others coming through the trees. Ronan led me off the beaten path and through a copse of sycamore trees.

The voices grew louder, along with music, until we reached an open expanse of grassy pasture. In the opening, there was a giant inflatable mat, and as

I watched, I could see a guy leap from a stand inside a tree and fall, what had to be thirty feet through the air, until he landed on his side and the mat swallowed him.

A strangled scream escaped my mouth, but Ronan laughed beside me. "Surprise."

At hearing my scream, my friends seemed to notice our arrival, as did all of Ronan's roommates.

"Happy birthday!" they cried in a mismatched chorus.

My heart was still beating fast, thinking that Ronan's friend had just died, but as the friend rolled out of the inflatable, I began to breathe easier. "I almost had a heart attack! I thought the point of the party was to celebrate, not kill the birthday girl!"

My friends laughed, and the girls surrounded me, their boyfriends close behind. Rory wrapped an arm around my shoulder. "You're a hardened criminal now. You can take it."

I rolled my eyes and put my free arm around her waist. Ronan still had his hand in mine.

"What do you think?" Rory asked and lowered her voice. "Beckett made up for his mistake, didn't he?"

I laughed, squeezing Ronan's hand. "He more than made up for it."

"Introduce us!" Jordan cried from the other side of Rory. She looked over Ronan. "He's cute."

I almost didn't believe it, but I could have sworn Ronan's cheeks turned pink.

He lifted a hand and smiled shyly. "I'm Ronan, the idiot who almost let Zara get away."

That earned a laugh from almost everyone.

Ginger lifted an eyebrow though. "How do we know you're not going to hurt our girl again?"

The entire group seemed to fall silent, even Brock, who was now walking over to us like he hadn't just fallen thirty feet through the air.

Ronan looked each of them in the eyes, and I think we both understood that this wasn't just him and me. It was him and me and us. My friends were here for me, and they weren't going to let me go through something so awful again.

"I don't make the same mistake twice," he said evenly, and the serious way he said it seemed to be enough for everyone. Ray slapped him on the back and passed him a red cup, and then handed one to me as well.

"Good luck, man," Ray said. "These girls are crazy."

I rolled my eyes and sniffed at the liquid in my cup. "What is this?"

"Sangria," Carson said sheepishly. "My sister gave me the recipe."

I laughed. "It's not exactly my twenty-first birthday."

He winked and drew an X over his heart. "We can keep a secret."

Callie smiled up at him adoringly, and suddenly it didn't feel so frustrating to see them in love but not admitting it, because I knew love made its own way. This guy standing beside me, it wasn't just some flame or some intense level of attraction because of his looks or his money, but something that was built on a foundation stronger. I loved his soul, and I could tell that he adored mine too. That wasn't something that could be rushed or planned.

"Time for presents," Ginger said. "I can't wait for you to see mine and Ray's."

Ronan leaned over and whispered to me, "Twenty bucks she just signed his name on it."

I chuckled but grinned at the present Ginger was carrying toward me from the stack of presents surrounding the base of a tall cypress tree.

Immediately, I ripped the tissue paper away

and pulled out a T-shirt. As the pink cotton came into view, I glared at her. "You did not."

Laughing, she said, "Look at it."

I pulled it open, expecting for her to have given me a **_THAT B*TCH_** shirt, but instead I saw a photo of me with the text **_THAT BAD*SS_**.

My mouth fell open in a half-shocked, half-amused expression. "You made this for me?"

She nodded, and then I looked at Ray. "You were in on it?"

"My mom may or may not have a Cricut that we used to make it."

Shaking my head, I reached out to Ginger and hugged her and patted Ray's arm with my hand. "I love it," I said, putting it on over my black T-shirt. I was never taking this thing off.

"Me next!" Rory said. She went and got a bag, and out of it, she retrieved a beautiful canvas painting of Ronan and me. It was so stunning, and so special knowing it had come from her. "Thank you," I said, my eyes watering.

"It's amazing," Ronan added softly.

Rory fell silent, obviously embarrassed.

"There is something in there from me," Beckett said.

I put my hand farther in the bag and pulled out a framed photo of the vandalism I had done at the pier.

"They sanded it off," he admitted, "but not before I got a picture."

I smiled at the messy writing and looked over at Ronan. His eyes were still on the photo, soft, shining. I gave it to him to hold while the others gave me my gifts. Callie and Carson had gotten me a dozen sugar cookies designed to match the shirt Ginger and Ray had gotten me. Jordan and Kai went above and beyond, presenting me a custom-made sarong. I felt the ornate fabric in my hands. "It looks just like the one my mom used to wear."

They smiled at each other, and then Jordan said, "Actually, your dad showed us a picture and we gave it to the designer."

My eyes watered. It really was like my mom was there, like her love had found me through all of these incredible people. And now, my group of friends were growing. Even the guys from Ronan's apartment had brought little gifts of their own, from small treats to handwritten cards. They were all precious.

When all the gifts were gone from the tree, my

heart sank a little. Ronan hadn't gotten me a gift. I tried not to be sad, considering just the fact that he was here was enough, but he must have caught me with a down expression because he lifted my chin with a crooked finger and nodded toward the inflated mat. "That's your present from me."

The blood drained from my face and ran cold through my fingertips. "What?" I stammered.

"Your initiation," he said.

"Into what?"

It seemed like everyone was listening intently to hear what he would have to say. And finally, he said two words: "*Dulce Periculum.*"

"The first female member," Drex added.

Brock shook his head. "DP's an urban legend. Definitely not real."

Which, of course, ensued in laughing and bickering. Ronan shook his head and led me away from the arguing, toward the rope ladder they had hanging from the tree.

"I am not climbing that thing," I said, folding my arms over my chest.

He quirked an eyebrow and gave me a challenging smirk. "Oh really? Miss *Audentes Fortuna Iuvat's* afraid?"

I was already feeling frustrated by the challenge and wanting to claim it just to put his smirk in its place. "Really," I said. "I have nothing to prove."

He shrugged. "That's too bad, because I was really looking forward to climbing up the ladder behind you."

My mouth fell open, and my stomach heated, thinking about the innuendo behind his words. "Is that so?"

He lifted his eyebrows, a smile on his lips.

I couldn't believe I was about to do this, but I had done a lot of things I hadn't thought I was capable of. I'd fallen in love, left everything I knew behind, moved out of the house I'd lived in with my mom for so long. This was just one more step in the incredible journey called life.

The ladder swung as I held on to each rung, and slowly but surely, I made it to the platform someone had built atop a tree. From up here, my friends seemed so small. My stomach seemed to sway with the wind, and my legs shook as fear flooded me. "This is so high," I said. "How do you do it?"

Ronan shrugged, completely unfazed. "To enjoy the fall, you have to jump."

My friends cheered us on from below, but my

eyes were on Ronan. He took my hand, and said, "Ready to fall with me?"

Smiling, I looked over the platform and jumped. As I flew through the air with the love of my life beside me, I couldn't help but think I already had.

FIFTY-ONE

NEARLY A HUNDRED STUDENTS clad in caps and gowns milled around us, reveling in the end of the graduation ceremony. I could hardly believe that I was standing here, officially done with high school, saying goodbye to Emerson Academy.

All the classmates around me had been passing like ships in the night for the last four years. We'd been on the same journey, sailing the same waters, but my friends had been more like anchors. Anytime I had been lost this last year, they were with me, guiding me, holding me steady.

I looked for them and saw Ginger's bright red hair first. She stood by Ray, holding his hand. So close to each other in those baggy black gowns, it almost looked like they were wearing one big black garbage sack.

I chuckled at the image, but felt a disappointed ache in my stomach. Ronan had to work today, and even though he was coming to the graduation party later, I still felt a little lonely now. It was too bad my last name was so far apart from the rest of my friends. Since my last name started with B, I had been in the front row with hardly a clue of what was going on behind me.

I scanned the rest of the school's lawn, looking for my other friends.  Callie and Carson had found each other and were already laughing about something. They always had one inside joke or another. And I was pretty sure they were the only two people in the world who didn't realize they were in love with each other.

I hoped to find Jordan, but when I caught sight of her, she and Kai stood together as well, posing for a selfie on her phone. Rory and Beckett were practically surrounded by the rest of the football players and the cheerleaders. Even though school was over, the quarterback still got all the popularity.

Someone bumped into me, and I looked over and saw Merritt. "Sorry," I said.

She shook her head and continued walking, her

heels sinking into the grass. She had a sour expression on, and I wondered what she must be so upset about on graduation day. But then again, when high school was the best time of your life, that basically meant nothing else would measure up.

I sighed and readjusted my mortarboard. My hair was getting sweaty, so I looked for a nearby tree to find some shade and wait while my friends finished with their boyfriends. I'd realized a lot lately how much I appreciated my solitude. Sometimes it was nice just to have time to think. And take in everything. I was having a hard time comprehending it all today.

I leaned against the trunk of the tree, feeling the rough bark against my back, and closed my eyes to take a slow, steadying breath. In only a week, I would be working with a major author and my father to bring a highly anticipated book adaptation to life. It felt like a lot of pressure, but I was so excited to get started. The fact that Ronan got to be on the writing team as an intern made it even better.

"Hi there." The voice sounded so close to my ear, and I jumped away.

Immediately, Ronan started chuckling from where he hung upside down from a branch of the tree. His hair swung loosely around his head in curls, and he looked way too pleased with himself.

I smacked his hard stomach, laughing myself. He brought so much joy to my life. "What on earth are you doing here?" I asked. "I thought you had to work."

He reached out to hold the branch and let his feet down to the ground. I didn't think I'd ever get tired of watching the nimble way his body moved.

"I got someone to cover my shift," he said. "I couldn't miss your big day."

I smiled and tugged on his black T-shirt, pulling him close. His unique smell, like cologne and sunshine and leather, lifted my spirits. "I'm so happy you're here," I said against his chest.

He held my hair against my back and squeezed me even tighter. "You were so beautiful walking across the stage. And I definitely saw your dad cry."

"You sat next to him?"

"Oh yeah, Papa Bhatta loves me."

"It is so weird that you call him that."

He laughed as he pulled back and shrugged. "Papa Bhatta doesn't seem to mind."

I rolled my eyes.

"Zara!" Ginger called. "We have to get a picture." She waved me over to where the other girls were standing along the fringes of our graduating class.

I gave Ronan an apologetic look. "Be back soon."

"That's okay," he yelled at my back. "I'll go hang with the rest of the reject boyfriends."

I laughed and shook my head as I joined the girls.

Callie smiled between me and the spot where Ronan had been. "I'm so happy Ronan made it."

"Me too." I couldn't help the cheesy smile that filled my face.

"Okay." Ginger pointed her phone at me. "Tell us how you feel to be officially done with high school!"

My smile stayed just as wide. "It feels amazing." But then my happiness wavered. "I'm going to miss you guys like crazy. What am I going to do without AV room lunches every day?"

Frowning, Ginger put her phone down. "We have the whole summer. Right?"

"Exactly," Rory said.

"And we'll hang out every chance we get," Jordan agreed.

"Except for when you guys are all hanging out

with your boyfriends," Callie said, giving us a teasing smile.

We all gave her a look.

"What?" she asked defensively.

The four of us looked at each other. "You've got it?" I asked.

"I'll tell her," Jordan said, then put a hand on Callie's shoulder. "You and Carson are clearly meant to be."

"But I like Oliver," she argued.

Ginger rolled her eyes and held up one hand. "Oliver, philosophy major who loves playing video games, or"—she held out her other hand—"Carson, hot football player going to college on a swim scholarship to study engineering. Kind of having trouble seeing the competition here."

With a dismissive shake of her head, Callie said, "We're just friends. Just like you girls and me." She put her arms around Jordan and Ginger's shoulders and looked at Rory and me. "And I think it's time to celebrate the fact that we all made it through the Academy in one piece."

Rory nodded. "That's true. I survived an entire cupcake avalanche, Ginger nearly died, Jordan almost killed Kai, Callie is in deep denial about her feelings, and Zara was practically a media sensation. It's been a rough year."

I glanced over my shoulder at Ronan, where he stood with the guys, laughing. He didn't fit in, not with them in their graduation gowns, and not with all the rich siblings back from college to see their family members graduate. But somehow, he and I —we worked.

"It hasn't been too bad," I said. "I think it's all been worth it."

We smiled at each other, taking in this moment, taking in the end. Because we were moving on, or getting ready to at least. None of us knew what tomorrow or the next week or the start of college would bring, but I knew one thing: I was free to choose.

The hum of a tattoo gun sounded, and I turned away, trying hard to focus on the rest of Kai's expansive basement instead of the sharp needle plunging into Zara's skin and leaving a mark that would be there forever.

Her sharp gasp sent my stomach squirming.

I turned toward Carson and said, "Why is she doing this? Doesn't she know it will be there forever?"

He smirked. "That's kind of the point." He took a sip from his cup and glanced over at the tattoo setup in Kai's media room. "Don't look now, but I'm pretty sure they're drawing a penis on her arm."

I slapped his shoulder, laughing. Carson always had a way of making the dumbest jokes that could turn a moment from terrible to funny in a fraction of a second.

"Still," I said, "a tattoo? I know it's not something embarrassing, but it's just so…"

"Permanent," he finished for me.

I nodded. "What if she doesn't like it in five years?"

He shrugged. "What if she does?"

"But what if she doesn't?" I pressed.

"I think some things are meant to last."

I looked up at him, at his sea-green eyes, which seemed to be so deep in thought. "What do you mean?"

He took another sip and swallowed, sending his Adam's apple bobbing. Then he met my gaze and held it. "I have a feeling that Zara and Ronan are more like an eternal flame than a quick strike of lightning."

I tended to agree. The way that they looked at each other, all that they were willing to give up for each other, it was like nothing I had ever seen before. My parents had been married my entire life, and they had such a quiet, content love that the kind of passion Zara and Ronan shared seemed so far off limits.

But that's what I wanted for myself. I'd been the

good girl for so long, never taking risks, always walking the narrow path that everyone expected me to. I had one summer left before college, before marching band took up all my time, along with my studies.

Oohs and aahs sounded behind us, and I turned to see the tattoo gun thankfully sitting on a side table by the chaise lounge where Zara was sitting.

She held a mirror in front of her while the tattoo artist had a mirror behind her so she could take in the black ink along the back of her arm. The Latin words stood out in scrolling cursive. *Audentes fortuna iuvat.*

I smiled at the phrase. It had been true for her. She has taken so many risks, changed in so many ways the last few months, and she seemed happier than ever. Free and less restrained.

"My turn," Ronan said, and a morbid curiosity drew me forward. He had so many tattoos already. What else could he add to his skin that would be new or different?

He gave directions to his friend holding the tattoo gun, but I couldn't quite make out what he said.

I stepped closer, and Carson said behind me,

"Have you taken your anti-nausea medicine? I don't want you barfing all over them."

I swatted at him and watched as the tattoo artist placed the needle against Ronan's skin, near one of the tattoos on his elbow.

As I looked closer, I realized that the person was adding a letter around what looked like a compass splaying from the epicenter of his elbow. The tattoo was done within seconds.

"What is that?" I asked.

He held his arm out for everyone to examine. Where the north should have been on the compass, there was now a heart.

He looked at Zara as he said, "Love will always lead me in the right direction. *You* are my true north."

My heart melted, but I turned away as they kissed. It seemed like such an intimate moment. I realized how deeply I wanted a love like that for myself. And I knew this summer was my time to make it happen.

Thank you so much for reading Zara's story! Want to stick with Zara and Ronan a little longer? Check out **Hardened Hearts**, a FREE bonus scene written from Ronan's perspective. You'll get to see him discover Zara's note on the boardwalk!

Use this QR code to get the free bonus story!

Continue reading in the Curvy Girl Club with Callie and Carson's story, **Curvy Girls Can't Date Best Friends**. You'll love their sweet, angsty romance, written from *both* of their perspectives!

Use this code to discover Callie and Carson's story!

## The Curvy Girl Club

Curvy Girls Can't Date Quarterbacks

Curvy Girls Can't Date Billionaires

Curvy Girls Can't Date Cowboys

Curvy Girls Can't Date Bad Boys

Curvy Girls Can't Date Best Friends

Curvy Girls Can't Date Bullies

Curvy Girls Can't Dance

Curvy Girls Can't Date Soldiers

Curvy Girls Can't Date Princes

## The Texas High Series

Chasing Skye: Book One

Becoming Skye: Book Two

Loving Skye: Book Three

Anika Writes Her Soldier

Abi and the Boy Next Door: Book One

Abi and the Boy Who Lied: Book Two

Abi and the Boy She Loves: Book Three

## The Pen Pal Romance Series

Dear Adam

Fabio Vs. the Friend Zone

Sincerely Cinderella

## The Sweet Water High Series: A Multi-Author Collaboration

Road Trip with the Enemy: A Sweet Standalone Romance

## YA Contemporary Romance Anthology

The Art of Taking Chances

## Nonfiction

Raising the West

Can I tell you a secret? Zara was the character I was looking forward to writing the most. Sometimes I would get to daydreaming about her and her strong personality and the kind of guy it would take to steal her heart.

One of the most powerful forces in the world is a woman who knows her worth, and Zara knew hers. She knew she deserved to have her own voice, that she deserved support from her family, and that she deserved a man who loved her just as she was. And when a woman knows her worth, she won't settle for less than, which is exactly what Ryde Alexander was.

Imagine, being presented with that kind of future: a marriage to a famous movie star with a nearly limitless supply of money and notoriety. The luxurious kind of life you would lead would be incredible, but Zara was willing to give that up for the true gold: not love, not comfort, but *freedom.*

In life, we're presented with choices every day. What should we eat? Where should we go on a date? How should I wear my hair? And then we have the harder choices: where should I live? Who should I marry? What career should I choose? The issue is that *every single one* of these choices are based on self-worth.

What to eat? If you care deeply for yourself, you may choose a healthy diet full of rich foods that will fuel your body and brain? Feeling like crap about yourself? Hello ice cream sundae. (A trademark move of mine.)

What to wear? Do you want to wear something that makes you feel good about yourself or do you hide beneath layers and layers that cover up both the good and what you perceive to be bad?

Who do you love? Someone who repeatedly degrades you and focuses on your flaws or someone who cherishes you just as you are?

This year for me has been a journey in self-worth, discovering who I am and what I deserve as a human and as a child of God. I've learned so much about what I'm willing to accept and how many times I've settled for less. If you're like me and have overlooked yourself time and time again, I encourage you to take a second look.

Once you believe the best of yourself, you'll be amazed how many things change. Some people in your life may resist the changes they see in your, because making yourself small only give them room to grow big. Keep fighting anyway. You are *fearfully and wonderfully made* and deserving of all the good things this world has to offer.

ACKNOWLEDGMENTS

In the writing of this book, I've discovered so much about *true* friends. Those people who wouldn't dream of betraying you or turning you away. Cling to those people. Mine come in the form of friends and family. My husband, my children, my siblings, and parents. My husband's grandparents. My writing friends, especially Sally Henson. I love you all more than you know and couldn't do this without your support.

To the wonderful people at my local Panera—you may never read this but thank you for creating an escape for me to write. I cherish it more than you know.

My dear readers subscribed to my list and are members of Kelsie Stelting: Readers Club, you are the light of my writing life. I can't tell you how much joy you've brought me even on darker days. I love being able to create for you.

My editor, Tricia Harden, has nailed yet another story. Each time I dive into her edits, I'm reminded of how precious she is. Her kind and careful work with my stories is nothing short of magic.

My narrator, Joyce Oben, has been such a gem in the process of writing this series. She reads each book and provides such wonderful insight, I can't wait to hear what she says next, much less how she'll bring the characters to life.

Lastly, to you, the person reading this story, you are absolutely wonderful and cherished. Thank you for taking this journey with me.

GLOSSARY



*Latin Phrases*

**Ad Meliora:** School motto meaning "toward better things."
**Audentes fortuna iuvat:** Motto of *Dulce Periculum* meaning "Fortune favors the bold."
**Dulce Periculum:** means "danger is sweet" - local secret club that performs stunts
**Multum in Parvo:** means "much in little"

*Locations*

**Town Name:** Emerson
**Location:** Halfway between Los Angeles and San Francisco

**Surrounding towns:** Brentwood, Seaton, Heywood

**Emerson Academy:** Private school Rory and Beckett attend

**Brentwood Academy:** Rival private school

**Walden Island:** Tourism island off the coast, only accessible by helicopter or ferry


*MAIN HANGOUTS*


**Emerson Elementary Library:** Where Rory tutors Anna, open to students K-7

**Emerson Field:** Massive park in the center of Emerson

**Emerson Memorial:** Local hospital

**Emerson Shoppes:** Shopping mall

**Emerson Trails:** Hiking trails in Emerson, near Emerson Field

**Halfway Café:** Expensive dining option in Emerson, frequented by celebrities

**La La Pictures:** Movie theater in Emerson

**Ripe:** Major health food store serving the tri-city area

**Roasted:** Popular coffee shop in Emerson

JJ Cleaning: Cleaning service owned by Jordan's mom

**Seaton Bakery:** Delicious dining and drink option in Seaton where Beckett works

**Seaton Beach:** Beach near Seaton – rougher than the beach near Brentwood

**Seaton Pier:** Fishing pier near Seaton

**Spike's:** Local 18-and-under club

**Waldo's Diner:** local diner, especially popular after sporting events

*APPS*

**Rush+:** Game app designed by Kai Rush and his father

**Sermo**: chat app used by private school students

*IMPORTANT ENTITIES*

**Bhatta Productions:** Production company owned by Zara's father

**Brentwood Badgers:** Professional football team

**Heywood Market:** Big ranch/distributor where everyone can purchase their meat locally

**Invisible Mountains:** Local major nonprofit - Callie's dad is the CEO

# ABOUT THE AUTHOR

Kelsie Stelting is a body positive romance author who writes love stories with strong characters, deep feelings, and happy endings.

She currently lives in Colorado. You can often find her writing, spending time with family, and soaking up too much sun wherever she can find it.

**Visit www.kelsiestelting.com to get a free story and sign up for her readers' group!**

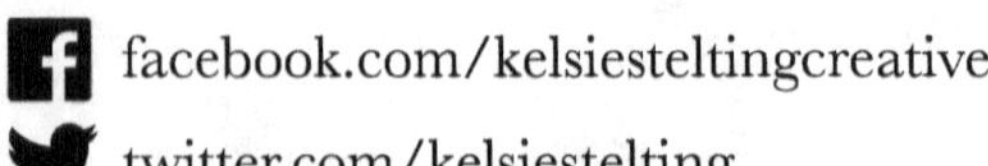 facebook.com/kelsiesteltingcreative

twitter.com/kelsiestelting

instagram.com/kelsiestelting